ABOVE THE ITALIAN WOODS

D. OSBORNE HUGHES

There are poems whose presence, never truly leave us, rhymes whispered by loved ones; the voices of distant generations, whom, having taken their journey before us, wait patiently for our return.

This is one such poem.

…to Nain and Taid, and all who held my life in trust

PROLOGUE

Who are you?

I pose the question, knowing the answer will be shallow or maybe even veiled from the truth. I often ask the same question of those I meet, but my enquiry is rarely spoken. I have learned through sad experience that most of us lock our true selves away and only show small facets of who we really are.

Communities are similar in many ways, hiding never to be told secrets, of sad, lonely and sometimes, dangerous individuals. We rarely catch more than a glimpse into the lives of those familiar to us, yet some, particularly in small communities, hide in the shadows, never to be seen. Shunning human contact, they avoid the judgemental gaze of those around them and we have no inkling of their presence, let alone, who they are or how their lives have been ordered.

If over the next few hours you follow me through one summer of my youth, you will discover one such life.

Where all our stories began, I cannot say, but I remember as clearly as yesterday, when I came to be a man and the course of my life changed forever; although the child within me still trembles at that thought. They say with greater age comes greater understanding, but that only partly explains, why, after almost forty five years, I still see those heady, carefree, salad days of my youth so clearly.

My childhood was like no other, at least that's how it felt in the innocence of my youth. Born the second of eight children to parents who gave us just enough, no more, no less; I was free to roam wherever my heart would take me. But at the end of each day, I always longed for home. It didn't matter where I had been or what I had done; no spilt milk or broken eggs, no grazed shin, no torn or dirty jeans would hinder my homeward path. Home was a place where all my troubles were soothed away by the love and care that waited for me there. Whether from siblings, friends, parents or grandparents, I was constantly surrounded by love, and with the sprawling woods of the Clwydian Mountains as my playground, I wanted for nothing.

As I have indicated, I was free; but I still had a stringent set of rules to live by. Maybe it was my unquestioning adherence to those rules, which gave me the sense of freedom that has brought me to where I stand here today.

On occasions I can still see the bright eyed child I once was, staring back from the mirror in the hall. If I listen carefully, I can still hear Carlo barking at the lazy sheep in the fields, the constant hum of the summer woods and the stream tumbling over its rocks. Breathing my life slowly in, I can still catch the faint smell of mothballs, hidden in faraway wardrobes and the intoxicating scent of wild garlic, growing by the stream or down by the River Alyn.

My life is good, but when it does hedge up my way, I climb to the mountains, and, slowly walking the familiar landscapes of my youth, I am renewed. As I wander the narrow lanes past the cottages and farms I once knew, I am inevitably drawn back to the Italian Woods and their little mountain stream.

In the memories of my youth, it was a magical place, a rhapsody in green tumbling off Moel-y-crio, The Mountain of Tears. Deep inside me, I am still in love with every sight and sound of its changing seasons, but one summer shines brighter than any other; all I have to do is close my eyes and I am there, walking between the trees in the intoxicating summerwoods.

Long before I knew you, my heart was set amid the maze of tangled pathways that lead along and up its babbling brook.

Local children still sneak past 'Ruby Brick' and carefully stepping, rock to rock, they follow the stream, where the trout hide or dart to and fro. Young hands (and hearts) still search for those secret watery chambers, where, cold and numb, they fish for trout with their hands.

We were once such children.

CHAPTER ONE

There had been some talk of us buying a house in the village, but our house in England sold the day it went on the market and time apparently made it impossible. So we had to stay at 'Llys Onen' until we could find a suitable place of our own.

Whilst I loved every moment of our visits there, some things never changed and on that first night, the sitting room floor was as hard and unforgiving as ever. In spite of having the floor as my bed, I was cosy and comfortable, snugly wrapped up in the love and care I felt whenever we came to stay. But at the beginning of that summer, my comfort was all the greater knowing our stay was indefinite.

My younger brothers, Gareth and Andy, had long since fallen asleep, but for some reason that nether world had eluded me as the familiar sounds and smell of my old home seeped back into my memories. I was home, every sight and every sound, every flavour of scent in my nostrils and every creek and groan of the old place told me, I was home, and in the darkness, I lay in my new down sleeping bag, surrounded by shadows of the past.

In one corner of the room stood an ebony-black piano, which was always polished like new. Lining its top were faded sepia photographs of distant generations; trapped, somewhere in time. Their familiar spirits conjured an eerie presence. During the day the piano was rarely silent. Carole, my older sister, would practice constantly and when Dad was home he played a repertoire of the only two tunes he learned, by heart, as a child; 'Once In A While' and 'You Belong to Me'.

Next to the old piano, and in front of the wide bay window, stood a large drop-leaf wooden table. It had a thick dark wooden top, supported by one robustly turned banister rising out of an equally sturdy base. Covered with a lace tablecloth – one Dad brought back from Tripoli after the war – its centre was always adorned with a large geranium plant in a terracotta pot, which in turn, stood in a dull, but intricately-patterned brass urn, another trophy of war. The lace draped windows were topped with simple stained-glass panels, which brought an auspicious reverence to the old sitting room. On bright summer days the sun would project their coloured reflections across the table, piano and walls.

Along the far wall, directly at my head, was an old wooden geist (blanket box) which contained neatly folded and laundered sheets and thick Welsh Woollen blankets. A hand carved panel on its side contained the inscription, 'D J. 1723'. whoever 'D' and 'J' were, there was no doubt in my mind that some remnant of their blood still flowed through my veins.

Although covered with a thick rug, reaching from one wall to the other, the dark almost black floorboards creaked as I rolled onto my side to face the dying fire. Above the mantle hung a round, intricately decorated mirror, which always reminded me of a psychedelic flower, similar to the design on the album-cover of one of the more obscure rock bands I listened to back then. It had different coloured petals, made of varying types of glass. Slightly convex, the mirror's distorted reflections were no-less psychedelic than the music from the album.

In the flickering light of the dying fire, I could just make out the mantelpiece where yet more photographs stood. At their centre was a large shell, which, if held to the ear, conjured the sound of countless rolling waves, endlessly advancing towards some tropical shore. There were various rock samples, including my favourite, a chunk of lead ore hewn from the bowels of the mountain. It was larger than my fist and as a child I could barely lift the dark crystal like metal. I once dropped it on the hearth, shattering one of the tiles and in the darkness I reached out, feeling for the sharp splinters of my clumsy fingers.

Listening in silence to the darkness, the rustle of the beach trees lining the crest of the steep fields opposite, reminded me of the woods and I longed to walk up their little stream. My eyes grew heavy watching the last remnants of the fire glowing in the hearth. It shared a chimney with the fire in parlour-bach and above the crack and spit of its simmering furnace; I could hear the drone of their muted conversation echoing through from the room next door. The conversation suddenly went silent, as though, instinctively she knew I was listening. The sound of footsteps was followed by the door to parlour-bach opening and then another moment of silence was stifled in the darkness.

I could almost hear her breathing in the hallway just outside our room. The handle twitched, then rattled slightly, but before the door opened, I knew Nain (Welsh for grandmother) would step into the room to check on us one last time, before, she too, retired for the night. And as if in answer to my silent prayer, Nain tiptoed into the darkness. Although silhouetted by the light in the hall, in my mind I could see every detail. Her long grey, almost white, hair was woven into a bun at the back of her head. In my imagination I could see the familiar catch light that sparked in her fading green eyes and her knowing smile that never failed to draw me in.

"Night Nain!" I half whispered, from somewhere amid the scattered shadows sleeping at her feet.

"Ni-night cariad!"

'Cariad' (sweetheart)…the word still fills me with an overwhelming sense of love and security. My grandmother was a woman of few words and she rarely spoke without full meaning or purpose, but the words 'David bach' and 'cariad' were never far from her lips. Everything she ever did or said, witnessed of her love, not just for me, but for all my brothers and sisters. She was not the type of grandmother who would constantly take you in her arms, hugging and kissing. On our visits, we would receive a kiss as we arrived and one when we left, with no other physical display of affection. Nain's love was demonstrated in thought and deed; everything she ever did witnessed of her love for us and the space that had grown between us was as secure as any grandmother's arms.

I know of no known likeness I could compare to her. We had moved away from the village when I was young, but had returned home to visit for extended summer holidays and the occasional wedding or funeral. When we arrived, no matter what time of the day or night, Nain was always waiting at the wrought iron gates in front of her little red-roofed, two bed-roomed bungalow ('Llys Onen'). Standing with her arms draped across the stile of the gate, she would rub her thumbs gently backwards and forwards over her forefingers. A broad, warm smile would spread across her face as we came into view and decamping from the 'old bus', she would kiss the top of our heads, whispering 'cariad' to each of us in turn.

As a child I used to watch her sitting, quietly, rubbing her thumbs backwards and forwards across her fore fingers, as if there was silk between them and I imagined she was testing the quality of life; making absolutely sure it was all it should be for her precious grandchildren to live inside it. She was an old, grey, robustly built woman; although, to me, everything about her was soft and cosy. But there was a, certain rigidity about her, an indefinable strength; she could seemingly walk forever, without ever tiring and I always struggled to keep pace with her.

I can never remember her being unkempt; everything about her was neatly ironed or tied into place. She always wore a blouse and a dark flannel skirt or dress, covered in front with a full-length, blue paisley-patterned apron to keep her clothes clean; she worked without ceasing.

Strangers couldn't see it, but Nain had a power and magic all of her own. Even my friend Hefyn recognised it, always referring to her as 'Nain Hughes', showing her the utmost reverence and respect.

I have seen photos of her when she was a young woman. She was beautiful; the type of young lady who wouldn't be short of male callers. But Nain didn't marry my grandfather until she was in her early forties, my mother being their only child. But wrapped up in the comfort of my own little world, I had no real appreciation of who she really was or how the web of her life had been spun.

Stepping into the room, carefully picking her way to the fire, Nain bent down. Picking up the poker she raked at the embers and then placed two large lumps of coal at its centre.

"There cariad!" She whispered, as the fire caught the inspiration of her touch.

A fire always burnt in the bungalow. The fire in parlour-bach was a huge ornately tiled cooking range, with large oven doors to one side of it, and although Nain had long since bought a more conventional oven; she would still cook using the open fire. Some years before, the third bedroom had been converted into a bathroom, but still every evening the old tin bath would be placed in front of the fire and filled with hot water so my younger brothers and sisters could bathe.

Whenever we came to stay, in the late afternoon, a fire would be lit in the sitting room, 'to keep the damp away!' Before putting on new clothes, Nain would take them in her hands; rubbing them between her fingers, putting them up to her face and nose, checking to make sure they weren't damp. I loved it, cosy and comfortable, – there are those words again – wrapped up in Nain's snug and freshly laundered world, and as I lay there at the beginning of that summer, my bubbling expectations were almost too much for me and staring into the simmering fire my mind raced down hill, out of control.

To my surprise, Nain returned to pallor-bach and my mother's endless want for news. Lying awake on the floor, listening to the comforting hum of their conversation, I pulled the lip of my sleeping bag over my shoulders. I could clearly hear my mother's voice, but Nain spoke with a very strong accent. Some of what she was saying I could just make out, but most of it was just a smudge of words. The odd phrase would sound clearly in my ears, but the rest was a foreign language to me; maybe even literally.

Mums first language had been Welsh and although she hadn't really spoken it since a child, Nain would sometimes forget.

Listening to my mother's voice, I could see her careworn face in my mind. The weeks before our move had been hard on her. Mum and dad seemed to have been arguing more than usual; maybe too much. Dad's work revolved around the planning and construction of motorways and as a family we followed that work up and down the country, but this move had been different somehow. He had received a promotion and would be working at the companies head office in London. Staying there during the week, he would only be returning home at weekends. Apparently we couldn't afford to live in London or even close by. Why we had to move, I didn't fully understand, and I think there was more to it than just 'Dad's work', but in the innocence of youth, I could only feel the fervour and excitement of returning back to the refuge of Nain's secure world.

The drone of conversation from the room next door kept me from that 'nether world'. Turning over, I looked straight into the fire, the faint smell of its smoke lingering in my nostrils, but still brimming with anticipation, its warm glow failed to drag me off into the night.

Half dreaming, I thought of what the morning would bring, a new day, at a new school, but more than anything else, I was looking forward to seeing Hefyn.

Hefyn had been a friend as long as I could remember. Apparently, when his parents, Uncle John and Aunty Glynwen, first moved to the farm, Nain had helped them settle in. She had become a close friend to Hefyn's mother who was desperately homesick, having just got married. The farm they lived on had been Nain's family farm for generations, my grandmother having lived there herself as a child.

I had seen Hefyn every summer since we left the village and we'd had many adventures together. He was tall and thin with olive skin and a mop of jet-black hair, which he wore long, when his father let him; as was the fashion in those days. His dark eyes were always edged with a hint of mischief, but despite his wild ways, he was always dependable and there was an air of confidence whenever he was around. Constantly fooling around and joking, his humour was never cutting or malicious. Hefyn was always full of fun.

We had arranged for him to call for me in the morning and we would both catch up on fishing and the like as walking down to school. Apparently he was seeing a girl from the village and no doubt she would be the main topic of conversation.

It was the last week of term; why we had to go to a new school just for one week, I didn't know, but the news had been broken to us a few weeks earlier. We had finished the term at our old school – another reason not to go – but moving into a different school area meant we had another week left. No matter how much we protested, Dad gave no ground.

With so many things jumbled up inside my head, I tried to settle my thoughts. I wondered how the fishing would be down at the 'Ruby Brick' and I turned over on the hard floor to a dream of walking through the Italian Woods, catching trout from its crystal clear stream. But the floor of the sitting room was unforgiving and I turned again and again and then again back towards the fire with my shoulder beginning to ache.

The conversation had paused in the room next door or it had stopped altogether and I checked my thoughts to see if I'd fallen asleep. I was sure I hadn't. Listening to the night, my ears strained in the darkness and then I heard it for the first time; her name, on my mother's lips. It was only a whisper, but its sound echoed as clear as a bell, setting my heart racing downhill and out of control once more. Nain remained silent, but Mum went to say something more and with my heart beating the retreat, she whispered again.

Instantly her twisted face flashed in the darkness. With her eyes burning like coals, the gruesome spectre of all my childhood nightmares appeared as some terrifying ghostly apparition, haunting my mind.

"Old Gwennie!"

I didn't know why at that time, but even the mention of her name was like pouring poison into my ears.

There was a pervading silence in Palor Bach with Nain remaining quiet. I could hear Mum saying something more, but couldn't make out exactly what. Old Gwennie's name was mentioned again, but it was followed by a long pause. I opened my mouth, trying to control my breathing, so I could hear every word.

"Quiet now Pam(My mother)…!" And I knew that would be the end of the matter. The door to parlour-bach opened and a moment later Nain's bedroom door closed. A few minutes passed before Mum made her way to her room, with my sisters. It had taken her some time to settle, but eventually I imagined that I was the only one left awake, with the fire of Old Gwennie's eyes staring out at me amid the flames that suddenly seemed to leap from the hearth.

CHAPTER TWO

I stood outside 'The Head's' office, facing the apprehension and uncertainty of that long dreaded week; but it was the continued nightmare of 'Old Gwennie' that played on my senses, and in my mind I was still lying on the sitting room floor listening to the uncertain echoes that sounded through the chimney of my Grandmother's little bungalow.

I was sixteen and above such tattle, so I couldn't quite understand my own feelings as the hairs on the back of my neck bristled, with a sudden chill running through me. As a child, my only recollection of fear was 'Old Gwennie'. At the beginning of that summer, I had thought myself older, wiser, maybe, and I certainly knew not to listen to such prattle. I had never heard Nain speak of her and if Old Gwennie was mentioned in her presence, a frown would appear on her face and we knew to say no more. But, sitting here these years later, those uneasy feelings still chase through me.

I had never seen her, nor had Hefyn, but he had said she was a Witch, in fact 'the meanest, maddest, ugliest witch in the whole of North Wales'. I knew it was just the vivid mental conjuring's of a boy I had once witnessed running through the village, dressed in one of his mother's old frocks with lipstick smeared across his face, shouting, 'I'm a Denbigh Loonie'. But his wry smile and dark eyes were poor cover for the obvious apprehension he felt whenever he uttered her name. He would always whisper as if she were listening: As though, somehow, she was making notes that one day would be used as evidence to heap all her evils upon us. But in my heart I knew it was true and whether on 'The Shippon' steps or high in the hayloft; in Palor-Bach, out in the fields or on top of the mountains; no matter how quietly we whispered, I knew, somehow, and in no small way, she could hear us, and that thought torments me as much today as it did as a child.

Hefyn had told me that 'Tebbutt' had been kept off school in increasingly mysterious circumstances. When he returned, he had bruises and scabs on his arm, supposedly where Old Gwennie had grabbed him. Some of the scabs turned septic and he had to go to the doctor. Apparently the police were called, but they were seen running from her cottage. They came from Denbigh, 'Old Bill,' the village bobby, not daring to go near her house, having learned over the years of the evils that laid in wait for him there. How much of the tale was true, I had no way of knowing.

The stream through the Italian Woods, led past her old rundown cottage and we always scrambled down onto a large boulder, stepping rock to rock under the old metal bridge, keeping below the stream's banks to pass out of sight. Going under the bridge I could feel the evil radiating from her tatty tiny hovel. The rocks and stream there felt unbearably cold, and I would always try not to touch the inside of the bridge in case, somehow, her evil drained all the goodness from my body. Dark horrors seemed to radiate out, seeping into the ground and through the old rusty metalwork of the bridge. Although large trout swam in the many deep pools there, we would not stay and fish, eager to be rid of Old Gwennie's ever watchful eye. Sometimes that feeling of impending doom would come upon us and we would take the long way around, walking up past the old brickworks ('the 'Ruby Brick'), to join the stream up by the old Winding House.

One time, a group of lads, led by 'Tebbutt', stood on the quarry track, daring each other to knock on her door. They were too afraid and just stood shouting obscenities at her lonely little cottage. Not wishing to be included in such reckless behaviour, Hefyn and I started to make our way up stream. The group began picking up stones and a shower of rocks peppered the already cracked and broken slates on the roof.

We were level with Old Gwennie's when I heard the first window break. Looking back towards the group, I could see they were all running off, except for Tebbutt, who was picking up more pebbles from the bed of the stream. I heard the sound of breaking glass, and looking back, I saw Tebbutt running as fast as his chubby little legs could carry him. Hefyn and I decided it would probably be as well for us to do the same, and we didn't stop to catch our breath, until we reached the old winding house further upstream.

My mother once told me, when she was a girl, she had known Old Gwennie; met her even; in fact she had given my parents a hand sewn quilt as a wedding present. I remember that old patchwork quilt, thick and warm, dark and drab. Its cover was intricately sewn in strange patterns with dark greens, browns and blacks, but had I known its origins, I would never have slept beneath its stifling cover. Who knows what incantations had been woven into its web.

None of it made any sense, just like me standing outside 'The Head's office, but there I was! It should have been the beginning of an exciting summer holiday and yet Old Gwennie had haunted my every thought since hearing my mother utter her name the night before. I needed something else, a touch stone, to reach out to and calm my mind.

I forced my thoughts to trace our journey back home, the day before.

All our furniture had to be placed in storage with Dad catching the train to London and Mum driving the one hundred and twenty miles home, alone. I don't know why I use the word 'alone' because she had all of us with her, but it still seems appropriate. Although I didn't know it at the time, she was pregnant with my sister Helen. With all the packing, driving and looking after us, I can remember her tiredness showing.

There were six of us all-together and Mum made seven. Carole was the eldest then me; Andy and Gareth (daddy's little blue-eyed boy), followed by Katie and Anne. Oh and I shouldn't forget Smoky the cat.

Just before entering the village, I had looked across at Mum. Sitting in the front seat, I could see the strain in her eyes, but she still looked back at me and smiled. The rickety old VW caravanette (the old bus) chugged downhill; the hum of the engine and ticking of the tappets had been almost hypnotising, but entering the village, my senses seemed to come alive and I wound down the window. Feeling the cool late afternoon into evening air on my face, I took a deep breath, while looking around at the familiar sight of summer hedgerows, woods and mountains, forests and streams.

"Yes!" I said to myself, on smelling the pinewoods. With my concerns for my mother fading, I closed my eyes and imagined; mountains I had not yet climbed; woods I had not yet explored; streams I had not yet fished and trout I had not yet caught.

"Shut the window!" my sister Carole, grumbled from the back, as she looked up through her long thick black hair cascading down onto the pages of the book she was reading; usually something by 'Hardy'. Her curt words dragged me from my fantasies.

"Take a deep breath," I said.

"Smell the air…we're home!"

Everyone took a deep breath, but as I wound the window back up, I knew that not all my brothers and sisters shared my excitement. Some, like Carole, were leaving good friends behind. Although I wasn't short of friends, for some reason, I was looking to new horizons and adventures, and those adventures outweighed the loss of any friend; besides which, Hefyn, my one true childhood friend, lived on the farm at the top of the hill, just above Nain's'.

Looking out into the woods, which lined either side of the road, they seemed to sail endlessly by; firs so thick the ground beneath had never seen the light of day and I imagined places where men had never trod. 'Coed Du' (The black woods), where wolves and wild boar once roamed, shunning the paths where Druids and Witches once trod.

The summer hedgerows half hid the sign 'Rhydymwyn', the village where I was born and the place where my life is instantly restored.

I remember thinking, that despite my longing for home, I would be a lonely stranger. My Welsh wasn't brilliant and living in England for so long I had lost my accent. I knew enough Welsh to get myself into trouble, but certainly not enough to talk my way out of it again. As a family we knew a lot of the locals and were related to some of them, but that wouldn't stop those who didn't know us from treating us as outsiders. I had explored all of the surrounding woods; fished for trout in all the streams; climbed in most of the local quarries and on the cliffs in the woods; I had walked the surrounding mountains and probably knew paths and places a lot of the locals had never seen, but I would still be an outsider. That summer, I was determined, would be a magical time.

Rhydymwyn was my home, but more tangentially, it was where my family for as far back as I knew, or my grandmother could remember, called home. It is a jewel set in a secluded valley, surrounded by woods and forests and the Clwydian Mountains, with Moel Fammau at their centre, which I considered, my family's very own mountain.

The woods were filled with streams, which tumbled down to the river Alyn. In the summer, the river bed was usually dry, flowing underground through the numerous limestone caverns and caves, which honeycomb the surrounding area. The old lead mine had large open mineshafts hidden in the undergrowth, some of which had been covered over, but others lay, like huge mantraps, littering the landscape. Trees concealed caves and tunnels that led deep underground.

Turning from the main road the The Old Bus slowed, straining as it climbed up the steep hill towards my grandmother's. I looked across at my mother and she smiled back, with her familiar warm safe smile.

Eagerly watching, the bungalow came into view and there she was, just as I knew she would be; Nain, waiting at the front gate with her arms draped over its stile.

There are warm secure places that grow in the space that exist between those who foster special feelings, one for another. We fill those spaces with many different things: some with light, others with darkness; some with love, and there are those that contain hate. I believe all things have a space around them: rocks, trees, people, everything. The space between Nain and myself was full of love and care; it seemed to protect me wherever I was, no matter how far I wandered. It was as if her space reached out to mine and I continuously felt her presence in my life. My grandmother was, and always will be, part of the space that surrounds me; it is a place where she quietly watches over the life she gave so much for.

She once spoke to me of something; I refer to as, 'the power of generations'. She explained that she came from good people, who had taught her good things, and she always tried to live by what she had been taught. I could see and feel the power of those things in her life. As a child I felt that power growing in the space between us and I have also felt the unseen power of those generations who look on. They somehow watch over me and their presence is a constant feeling in my life.

Still standing outside 'The Head's' office, with my mind flitting from one day dream to another, a warm feeling came over me and it was as though my grandmothers strength was somehow being poured into me.

One thought quickly jumped to another and I remembered stories Nain had related to me. Memories from her past, adventures she had as a child and people she had known.

My grandfather, on the other hand, had told us far different tales. He would conjure stories of witches and giants and tell us of the strange wild animals that used to roam through the woods, and I fancied he could even remember wolves. One story in particular he related was of Nain's grandmother – very strange – meeting a she wolf in the woods. Nain tut-tutted continuously throughout his fanciful tale and rebuked him in welsh, but he continued nonetheless. Whether true or not, his stories had always stirred my imagination, but unlike my grandmother's stories, I always took his words 'with a pinch of salt'. I would doubt my own memories of what was said or done, long before I doubted a single word my grandmother ever uttered.

Taid (my grandfather) died when I was nine. He was a fine old gentleman who had a club foot and always walked with a limp as far back as I could remember. I still have two of the walking sticks he used whenever we walked along the 'Coach Road' or through the hazel woods. Taid shared the same power and magic as my grandmother. The old miners referred to him as 'Jack the lamp' because he trimmed the lamps as the night watchman at the lead mine. He had a full head of bright grey hair that had once been young and black. He always wore a pair of thick tortoiseshell-rimmed glasses through which his fading eyes caught every beat and moment of our lives. He never missed a thing and nothing could ever be hidden from him.

Memories of my grandfather were now thick in my head. It was he who first cut a stick of Hazel for me to string up into a bow and searched long and hard for straight shoots of Hazel for arrows. I can vividly recall him taking me out on 'bottom field' with his old shotgun to teach me the art of squeezing a trigger instead of pulling it. But the one enduring memory of him is of the time he took us down the old lead mine before it became derelict. Health and safety would have an epi-fit these days. We wore old miner's helmets with lamps on the front that dimly lit our way. Leading us along crooked corridors deep underground, where the lead had been mined since before Roman times, we finally came to a place where he warned us to be careful. Inching forward, he told us to stand quite still.

"What can you see then, cariad?" My eyes gradually grew accustomed to the dark, with my dim light struggling to pierce through the vast unlit space before me. Gradually a huge underground chamber opened to my view. Stalactites hung down in front of me; suspended like the giant pipes of some ancient organ in the vast underground cathedral of the mountain. A huge grotto eventually stretched out before my eyes, continuing far beyond the limitations of our meagre torches.

In the bottom of this monolithic labyrinth, was an enormous underground lake, whose waters were only partially visible to me. In the dim light, I was barely able to see its gentle ripples; silently lapping just below my feet. But echoes from its distant reaches sounded in my ears.

On hearing my gasps, Taid picked up a small stone and threw it out into the black void before us. I have never forgotten the sound it made as it broke the surface of the pool, and it echoed around the rocky chamber.

It was as though we were perched in the womb of the mother of mountains and it took my breath away as dark ripples spread out over the pools of my mind and a fantasy of bubbles spewed from the pebble as it traced a meandering path into the unfathomable depths of the earth.

"No one knows how deep it is!" My grandfather whispered, as he shepherded us back through the mine. But as Taid guided me back, my mind came to the sudden realisation that I was still outside 'The Head's' Office, wondering how long he would keep us there.

But, with no impending dangers looming, I allowed my memories to mull over Hefyn's last phone call; before the move. He had been a little coy, teasing me with descriptions of a new girl he had been seeing. He then proceeded to give me an, almost military, blow by blow briefing of their last campaign. Girls were never that matter-of-fact to me. They were always mixed up in a confusion of excitement and uncertainty.

Hefyn had said he had a surprise waiting. Apparently it was something at school. He would say no more, but his teasing was sufficient to keep my interest.

Bet School-House dragged me back to reality as a warm familiar smile spread out onto her face, but it wasn't enough to steady my waning confidence. Her white hair hung down to her shoulders in neat waves, glowing with her smile in the dim light of school's musty old corridor. The hall and corridor were lined with intricately carved, gothic-style wooden architrave and smelt like old churches.

Bet was my mother's cousin and I knew her as 'Aunt Bet', but referred to her in any conversation as 'Bet Schoolhouse'. Having greeted us at the school gates, she had led my brother Andy and me to the Head's office to make the necessary introductions; not that any needed making.

The door opened and my brother Andy and I were ushered in.

"One week left boys...no trouble now, mind my words...off to your classes then...take them to their classes Miss McLean!"

We were all related in one way or another; The Head was in fact Bet's uncle or cousin once removed or...well, you get the picture. But his words had shown, not one hint of recognition or kindness toward us. So much for relatives, even if he was one, we never saw from one year to the next.

'Weddings and funerals!' Nain would say, describing people who only pay attention to family affairs on such occasions.

Andy was taken to his class and introduced to his teacher for the week, as I was left to ponder outside the door.

I was the last, the last Celtic Warrior up to the battlements and my particular battlement was the last classroom at the end of a musty old corridor.

There was a nagging, sick, sinking feeling in the pit of my stomach and I struggled to hold on to the facade of my cool exterior. The nagging sickness grew and the warmth of Bet's hand on my shoulder did little to comfort me as I stood staring at the thin pane of glass in the door, but my eyes saw nothing beyond my own timid reflection. I was aware of 'My new class', sitting, chatting and messing around on the other side of the door's faint mirror, but it was my own reflection, on which my gaze was focused, and as I stared out from the mirrored door, I could see and sense my own apprehensions.

My long thick hair, which my sister Carole had cut into something of a feather cut – a bit like Rod Stewart's at the time – hung down past my shoulders. The mass of layered hair on top was, for once, reasonably neat and tidy; although my father would not have approved of its unkempt style and length. He never approved of long hair and it was a constant battle for me to keep it how I liked it; past my shoulders.

After the move, I thought I would be rid of the school tie and blazer, but there they were, marring the image. Hung at half mast, my tie was skewed to one side as it struggled to close the gap at the neck of my open shirt. Looking appropriately casual, I was pleased with what I saw. The summer's free and easy ways were calling to me, but why I was being forced through that door, I have never worked out; it seemed so pointless.

I stood back in my thoughts as my mind wandered through lazy summer woods. I was desperate to be anywhere but there, and even in my mind I was lying on a cool flat slab of rock with my arms dipped into the stream, hands searching for hidden trout.

Bet gently squeezed my shoulder and much to my disappointment I found I was still outside a classroom door, with dread rising inside me. Sensing my apprehension she placed her mouth close to my ear and whispered,

"You ready, David bach? Don't worry now…he's not as bad as all that cariad!"

Of course, I knew different; Mr Robertson's temper was notorious. He could fly into a rage for no apparent reason. Stories of his sadistic discipline had even reached England. Hefyn had told me of his having to kneel in a tray of dried peas; for no other reason than Mr Robertson's own heartless pleasure and I was about to be pushed into his classroom. If I could have got away, I think I would have run at that very moment, but Bet pulled at the handle of the door and gradually pushed it open. All idle chatter in the classroom ceased as I half stumbled before the fray.

CHAPTER THREE

Despite the rush of conflicting feelings inside me and with no small encouragement from Aunt Bet, I managed to walk into the classroom, with some semblance of order. I was aware of only two things; Mr Robertson sitting at his desk, in front of the black board, and a sea of faces looking at me, somewhere to my left.

The clatter of the door handle had woken Mr Robertson from the muted silence of his nights, whiskey induced stupor. Raising his eyes over the top of his half-cut study glasses, he called with a posh Scottish lilt.

"Can ye no keep quiet?" Even though, at that moment, you could have heard a pin drop.

Aunt Bet shepherded me towards Mr Robertson, but in walking the few paces across the room, I couldn't prevent my eyes from scanning to my left. You know how it is when you're first plunged into an alien environment. We can't prevent ourselves from sizing up and searching for any danger. It is some inbuilt primitive conditioning; we judge before we know, pigeonholing people, gauging the threat. It was only a fleeting glimpse, but in that moment an encyclopaedia of unconscious thought was processed through my mind. But as my eyes scrutinised my new classmates, I knew they would be doing the same. Everyone was looking up at the new boy and I felt uncomfortable, forced out onto the edge somehow. Despite my relationship to some of them and knowing others quite well; I was unnerved by their prying eyes.

There were three rows of desks, each lined from front to back. Hefyn was sitting about half way back in the row nearest the windows. He nodded at me and I nodded back; I think he could sense my unease, but I hoped he was the only one.

Tebbutt was sitting at the back; he was an awful bully back then, but for some reason he hadn't given me any trouble. I noticed some faint scars on his arm that he was picking at, and Hefyn's story about Old Gwennie came flooding back.

There were girls. There were always girls. As a lad I seemed to enjoy their company; they were far more interesting than the boys. I could never understand lads playing football in school, when there were girls there. It was an innocent attraction back then; I found them easier to talk to, to be around and then, of course, there were those other feelings.

I was just about to return my attention back to Mr Robertson, when a girl sat just across from Hefyn took my gaze. She had long dark hair, whose waves tumbled down over her shoulders to well below the level of the desk. Her skin was pale as moon-agate and her eyes were the purest shade of green I have ever seen. At that moment an uncertain sun blazed through the windows, instantly catching the wild waterfall of her hair, making it glow with all the lustre of fresh autumn chestnuts. Her soft silky complexion seemed to shine, as though she had been out in the night and caught the radiance of the moons milky glow.

She smiled up at me and I panicked; feeling caught out in some way. But no matter how startled I was, I couldn't take my eyes off her, like a rabbit caught in the searchlight of her smile. There were other girls in the room, beautiful girls, shapely, bubbly, bon vivant girls, but there was something about this girl's smile that drew me in; it had kindled a fire inside me and I struggled to quell the flames.

She sat next to a bubbly looking redhead, and their chatter had stalled slightly as they put me under the microscope. The redhead furtively whispered something in her ear and they laughed together. Then the first girl's head tilted back as she continued to laugh playfully. And as she did so her head dropped forward, our eyes meeting again. A familiar glint sparked in her smile as she looked straight into me, piercing my cool façade and I struggled to hold on. I must have lit up like a firework and felt my heart pounding beneath my chest as my throat instantly dried. Belly hooked, I was caught fast and half smiled back, but feeling awkward and knowing she could see the convolutions her smile had caused; I quickly looked back to Mr Robertson.

It wasn't a moment too soon. His ruddy complexion blazed with his impatience and the previous evening's last wee dram. His strawberry red nose glowed bright in the uncertain light of the classroom as he waited for my undivided attention. I could almost sense his instability and swallowed hard as he stared back at me. Two wisps of hair, which should have been neatly combed into place over the top of his bald head, were hanging down, teasing across his face. He looked a puny, insignificant excuse for a teacher, but I could feel the heat of the simmering volcano that lay beneath his sickly smile and I knew I would have to treat him with the utmost respect during my short stay in his class. Brushing his hand over his face, his thin, slender, pianist-fingers caught the wisps of hair and dragged them back on top of his head.

Bet made the necessary introductions and went to leave. Mr Robertson minced around her with his sickly smile chiselled onto his face. Fawning over her, wringing his hands, like Sweeny Todd weighing up his next victim.

"Thank you, Miss McLean!" The words slithered from his mouth, but unimpressed, she left without any acknowledgement of his constant spooning.

There were no such pleasantries for me; without saying a word, he shook his head as if he disapproved of me in some way and then marshalled me to my seat.

I couldn't believe my luck when he led me to sit immediately in front of the girl with the soft warm smile and long dark hair. The morning break seemed an eternity away. I wanted to turn, to talk; I wanted to look and listen. In that first quietly fleeting moment something had happened to me. I wasn't sure what, but it felt good, and warm, and I hoped, on all hope, that she wasn't the girl Hefyn had been seeing. I couldn't wait and checking to see if Mr Robertson was watching, I turned around, but her attention was elsewhere. I longed for more and I could already feel her space encroaching on mine. I quickly looked again. She looked straight into me and her green eyes grew wide as she smiled.

Mr Robertson finally introduced me to the class and we settled down to a double period of maths.

'Just my luck…double maths!' Although it was the last week of term and at least half the class would not be attending school, of any kind, following the summer; Mr Robertson was there to make sure we worked till the final bell. The kids in the class gradually stopped staring at the new boy. Tebbutt nodded at me and I nodded back.

The classroom was large with high ceilings, and tall studio windows lined the far wall – although, I remember, it seemed quite dim at the time. It was decorated with the same gothic architraving as the corridor. The windows looked out to the woods above The River Alyn and beyond them, the mountains.

There were large clouds moving across the sky, covering a grey hazy sun and the first few specks of rain glanced off the windows as a storm poured in over the woods and off the mountains. I thought of the summer, hoping the weather would be good.

I had planned to go on for A-levels the following year, Art, Tech Drawing and hopefully English if I passed the O level?...all my fingers were crossed. Beyond Art, there was only Poetry. It was a strange path I had trod, because I struggled so much with English; spelling mostly, but my punctuation and grammar were also very poor. I maintain I was 'lessdyxic', or is that Dyslexic; for some reason, English Literature held a similar passion for me as Art; I loved the play between words, their meanings, their cause and their eventual triumph over ignorance.

Algebra hours later, the bell went. Mr Robertson left the classroom after informing us it was a 'wet break' and we would all have to remain inside. That meant I could spend time getting to know my new classmates and I hoped one in particular. As he left the room, everyone started to talk and the drone and the chatter of my new classmates filled the air.

A ball of screwed up paper went flying past my head. I looked across at Tebbutt, who was grinning like a grass-snake. I nodded towards him, as I turned towards the girl who had taken all my thoughts, since I entered the classroom. Smiling up at me, as though she had been waiting patiently for my attention, I almost fell off my chair as she said,

"Hello David" as if we were old friends. On seeing my surprise her head tilted back as she laughed playfully and then a soft warm smile poured into the space between us as our eyes met once more.

"Hefyn's told me all about you!" she said, as awkwardness eased and I untied my tongue sufficiently to ask her name.

"Anne Jones," Looking down slightly she slowly raised her deep green eyes back to mine.

"I live on the farm above The Italian Woods!" She said 'Above the Italian Woods, knowing I would understand where she meant. I knew the farm quiet well, or at least I had passed it when fishing in the woods, but I had only ever seen or known of an old farmer and his wife who lived there. They had kept a big old sow in the Bottom Field. It was ferocious and better than any guard dog.

Conversation was uneasy at first and we casually danced around things, but I soon started to ask more. That's what I wanted, more; I wanted to know more about Anne Jones from the farm above The Italian Woods. The uneasiness slowly vanished and as we danced in our conversations we found we had a lot in common; music, art, poetry, including my favourites: Tennyson's The Lady of Shallot, Yeats, Elliot and Rossetti. She was even well versed in the modern, more contemporary poets, some of whom I hadn't heard of and only occasionally would I be able to mention a poem or poet that she hadn't read or heard of before.

We talked of art, the Pre-Raphaelites, whose paintings had stirred both our passions and minds. Anne favoured the romance and tragedy of Millais and Rossetti while I was drawn more to the intrinsic beauty and narratives in John William Waterhouse's work. We spoke of their paintings 'Autumn Leaves', 'April love', 'The Light of the World', 'Ophelia' and 'The Lady of Shallot'. Again, there it was, I thought, 'The Lady of shallot', and I imagined her as a tragedy, floating…

'Down the river's dim expanse

Lying robed in snowy white

That loosely flew to left and right.'

The poem whispered in my head.

But as I sit here looking back at it all, you were perhaps most like Miranda from Waterhouse's depiction of Shakespeare's The Tempest, with your full beauty hidden from me at that time (In Waterhouse's painting, 'The Tempest', Miranda's beauty is tantalisingly turned from the viewer, but still overwhelmingly obvious).

My questions faded slightly and I listened. Her voice was soft and warm, but there was something more; there was a certain understanding in the way she spoke; a calm inevitability.

Anne told me that often, as walking through the woods, she would take time to sit by the stream. Sometimes she would just meditate and other times she would sketch the stream as it tumbled over rocks in little cascades and waterfalls.

Anne was mature for her age and it showed. So it surprised me slightly when she mentioned fishing. Most of the lads in the village would fish for trout in the small brooks and rivers in the valley. No one ever fished with a rod; it was all done by hand. To me there was nothing greater on a hot summer's day, than to lay face down on a large cool rock, hands draped in the water, searching for the trout that wallow in the rock's underbelly. The cool damp surface of the giant limestone slabs would seep through, with the heat of the day on your back and the uncertain touch of a trout in your hand. I had never yet met a girl who could fish with they're hands and I wondered about her and who she really was.

For a mountain farmer's daughter, she didn't have the usual deep North-Walian accent most of my new classmates possessed. A lot of the class spoke Welsh at home and only spoke English at school. My curiosity got the better of me, so apologising for being rude, I asked her about it. But the explanation she gave seemed too incredible for words. Up until the previous year, she too had lived in England; her father having moved there to manage a large farm in the Midlands. But with the death of her grandfather, they had returned home to the family farm. To think, the year before, she too had been the lonely stranger returning home, just as I had been the previous evening. It seemed we had far more than just music, poetry and art in common. Anne had lived on a farm a little over ten miles from where I lived, and we had never knowingly met.

I still find it hard to grasp exactly what I felt, but there was, most certainly, a recognition between us. Anne had an obvious beauty, nothing glitzy or glamorous, but something that shone in her eyes and filled the warmth of her smile. I still can't find the words, but there was something more, something I couldn't quite place or grasp. I am tempted to use the word power, but that would imply dominance of some kind, which isn't at all what Anne Jones was about.

Someone called her from the far side of the classroom; it was the bubbly redhead. Her bushy hair did little to hide a mischievous grin that seemed to be constantly painted on her face. A milky-way of freckles was strewn across the bridge of her nose, spreading out onto her cheeks and there was always a knowing glint in her eyes. A group of girls was gathered around her and she beckoned Anne over.

My head began to pound as a voice inside cried out.

'No, stay…please, stay…let's talk…tell me of your life…your loves… your dreams!'

But I could only watch as she walked away; my eyes following every movement. She was slim, not skinny, and she moved with a certain grace and ease. My eyes tracked the shift of her body beneath her school uniform, watching the tilt of her hips, her legs and the sway of her hair. Again I found myself wanting to know more and I felt crushed as she walked away.

Tebbutt interrupted my gaze, glaring at me as someone touched me on my shoulder, making me jump. It was Hefyn.

"Well…what d'you think?" He said with a grin on his face.

"What's wrong with Tebbutt?" I asked, totally missing his meaning; the surprise he had spoken of on the phone.

"He's madly in love with Anne, but she refuses to talk to him." Hefyn laughed.

I could see Tebbutt glaring at me again. The last thing I needed on my first day was an enemy like Tebbutt.

"He thinks you're a threat!" Hefyn whispered, leaning in towards me.

"I wonder who gave him that idea." I scoffed and Hefyn grinned.

He went on to tell me that Tebbutt had jumped on Anne one evening on her way home from school, frustrated at her spurning his over boisterous and bullying courting rituals. Anne had been walking back through the woods where Tebbutt was waiting for her, having bunked off school. Apparently she directed a swift knee to his groin and having escaped his clutches, she hadn't stopped running until reaching the safety of her farm.

"Good girl!" I said to myself; although Hefyn would have heard it plain enough.

I glanced across at her and our eyes met, with a soft warm smile sparking in the catch-light of her eyes. Hefyn began to laugh and I half joined in, until Tebbutt stepped into my view, glaring at me once more.

"Ignore him!" Hefyn said as I turned away. Tebbutt didn't concern me as much as the trouble I would be in dealing with him. I would usually walk away from trouble; nothing ever seemed that important, but if trouble came, I was quite strong and if my strength failed, I could run like the wind. 'No shame in it', I thought once, while running from three lads, who were all much bigger than me.

The morning continued with geography and English. Mr Robertson had a voice that could put bees to sleep.

I checked the windows.

'Still raining!'

I looked up at the mountain, Moel Fammau, with low cloud draped over its summit.

Nain had once told me how all her family as far back as she could remember were born, worked, lived and died, all under the watchful eye of our mountain. She had once referred to it as the Mother Mountain. It had a small mound on top, which in days gone by would have been a beacon. Dominating the landscape, it could be seen from every hill and rise in the area. The mountain looked like a giant breast with the mound on top shaped like a nipple, which I imagined had never rested or tired from suckling countless generations of my family.

One class merged into another, but an eternity passed before dinner break, when Hefyn showed me the ropes in the canteen.

"I'll show you the ropes!" He said with a grin on his face and as he walked into the canteen come gym, he pointed to the ropes tied against the far wall; then he walked off leaving me to fend for myself.

When I had got my food, I walked over to where Anne was sitting next to the bubbly redhead, 'Megan'. They were sitting with Hefyn on a long wooden bench at the furthest dinner table; tucked away in one corner. I was eager to resume my quest for more and Anne motioned for me to join them. Not wishing to be presumptuous, I sat the other side of Megan, next to Hefyn. I didn't want to get between Anne and her friend, but Megan immediately got up and climbed in between Hefyn and me, physically pushing me back towards Anne. It was then the penny dropped. Megan was the girl Hefyn had been seeing. I had been so consumed with my thoughts of Anne; I hadn't made that simple connection. They had been going steady for a couple of months. She was a fun loving girl and I didn't fully realise at the time, but her wry smile and red hair could not be separated from her fiery personality. Hefyn and Megan seemed to be a perfect match.

With the rain steadily drifting down through the valley, we returned to the classroom. Science was the first lesson in the afternoon and while we were at lunch someone had placed all the chemistry glassware on Mr Robertson's table. We would no doubt be cleaning it and putting it away ready for the next term. With half an hour before the end of break, Hefyn and I half sat, half leaning on a desk at the front of the classroom, with the girls leaning against the front wall, facing us. Catching up on changes in the village, we made plans for the summer, with Anne and Megan included.

The classroom was becoming quite noisy and Tebbutt ran in front of us chasing another lad into the corner where he thumped him in the back. Quickly running off, the lad was left moaning and holding his back. Propped up in the corner was a long metal pole, which would have been used to open the top windows to air the room. The lad must have fallen against it, making it stand upright, because as he walked away it started to fall in front of us, towards the desk full of glassware. Hefyn and I reacted in unison, jumping forward, catching the poll just in time.

"You Two!"

A voice bellowed from the doorway.

"Fighting with that pole…and with all this glass on the table!" Mr Robertson had entered the classroom hearing all the commotion, but despite our protests of innocence and the girl's petitions, we were sent to The Head.

I was outraged, six of the best on my first day and for something I hadn't even done. The head kept his cane supple. Someone told me later that he rubbed Vaseline into it, to make it more flexible, and I believed every word of it.

"How's your mother David bach?" The Head asked as he bent me over his desk.

"You must tell her to come and visit us now!" I heard his cane singing through the air. 'So much for blood is thicker than water.' For the rest of the afternoon, Hefyn and I stood outside his office adjusting our school trousers to keep them from rubbing where his cane had stung into our flesh.

"Stand still boys!" he shouted through the open door, but Hefyn could only smirk.

My luck with teachers had worn thin at my last school. They had banned kissing or should I say, snogging. I think they were concerned that it was getting a bit out of hand, although I never indulged in such practices myself; well not much. Anyway the week before we moved, I had been in the main playing field with Carole and her friend Yvette. When the bell went they both kissed me; Carole on the cheek and Yvette right on the lips, just to tease. Walking off towards the new block they didn't see Mr Attwood collar me.

"Kissing!" He shouted.

Standing right in front of me, bellowing at me, spittle spraying out onto my face.

"You know it's banned!"

No matter how much I tried to tell him it was my sister, I still got six of the best.

Mind you, a kiss from Yvette was worth a lot more. She was gorgeous and always wore tight fitting, faded Levis and T-shirts that hugged her curvaceous figure. My favourite was a black rolling stones T-shirt which had their logo on it; big red lips with a large tongue protruding at their centre. She was divine and continually teased me. I remember watching her once walking up the street. Yvette had the most tantalising figure I had ever seen. A peck on the lips was nothing; she once gave me a full snog.

"Oh come on then!"

She had said once when Mum and Dad were out.

"I'll show you what it's all about!"

I was overwhelmed, with her lips and tongue blazing into me. I had never been kissed like that before and I felt as though I would burst at any moment.

The rest of the week passed without event as we drifted from one lesson to the next. Anne and I were spending more and more time together, she seemed to like me, but I was uncertain as to how much. We spoke endlessly of wants and dreams and our conversations had grown increasingly intimate as time went by. During one dinner hour I had asked her about other lads or boyfriends, with very little response. She just smiled as I asked the questions, gently probing the space between us.

"Anyone special at the moment?" I asked.

She continued to smile looking down at the grass where we were sitting.

"Anyone you're…." Anne looked up at me, causing me to pause, leaving my questions floating in the breeze off the mountain. Then she very tritely said

"Maybe!"

'Maybe what?' I had thought, struggling to make sense of her meaning amid the confusion that reigned inside me, and then wham; like a blow to the head.

"If you ask me out, I'll say no!" The look on her face said, 'You better believe me!'

Talking around things, she told me of her Uncle who had proposed to her Aunty by saying;

"Do you want your children by me?"

She laughed her laugh as I pondered the crass absurdity of the question. I didn't understand what she was saying at the time. She obviously felt something for me, but nothing was certain; it never was. I only hoped I was the 'maybe'.

There was only one answer to my problem, 'Carole!' Older sisters had to be useful for something! And all these years later, she's still the one I turn to when trying to understand the workings of the fairer sex. I was pleasantly surprised to find that Carole was light years ahead of me in matters of the heart. I told her everything; each detail, down to the last word. Carole thought, Anne was more mature than other girls her age; something I had spoon fed her, but that was the only clue I had given away.

"She probably doesn't want the usual playground romance… both of you walking around like Siamese twins…maybe she is looking for something more than a quick snog behind the bike-sheds…maybe she's looking for a friend more than a puppy following her around trying to look big!"

Thank goodness for big sisters.

No homework for the holidays, but classrooms had to be tidied, with everything put in its place for the following term. Countless civilizations were built and passed away as we waited for the final bell that signalled our freedom for the summer.

Its knell was still ringing in my ears as we tumbled out of school with all our cares behind us.

Tebbutt was waiting at the school gates and I virtually fell into his arms as he grabbed hold of my tie. Dragging at it, pulling me up close, his face was bright red with his anger boiling beneath it. I had been talking to Anne unaware of his presence until it was too late. Pressing his face into mine, I could feel his hot stale breath on my cheeks. Spittle from his lips sprayed out as he spat his words into my face, his teeth grinding together as he spoke.

"Stay…… away….. From Anne!"

His fist was clenched tight against my jaw and as I looked down I could clearly see the scars on his arm as his muscles tightened their grip around my tie. A wicked thought quickly ran through my mind and I prayed Hefyn's story was true.

"You bin talking to my friend, Old Gwennie?" I whispered.

He knew Nain Hughes was my Grandmother and her reputation of being the oldest member of the community, I think, had played on his mind. I could see in that moment, him mulling over the thought or possibility of whether my words were true or not. Staring straight into him, with not one speck of fear, I think convinced him, and my supposed revelation stabbed into him, punching at his gut, inducing the desired effect.

With the colour instantly draining from his face; he turned white as a ghost, almost before I had finished. Tebbutt was a big chubby lad; a bully, but all strength seemed to drain from him.

Quickly seizing the moment, I turned away and walked over to Anne with a broad grin etched onto my face. Although Anne asked what I had said, I just walked past her continuing up the road, knowing they would follow.

"Wait up!" Hefyn called, and the girls ran after me; struggling to keep up.

I learned later that Tebbutt happened across Old Gwennie in the woods. He had been so terrified, that he turned and ran straight into a fallen tree and its broken branches were responsible for the scars on his arm. In a weaker moment he had trusted one of Megan's friends with the truth, but it wasn't the story he told his parents, or the police.

We walked up, passed Llys Onen, to the farm gates. Megan lived on the farm beyond Hefyn's and he continued up the hill, as he had done every evening that week. I turned to Anne and offered to walk her to the bottom of Parry's Lane. Anne smiled in appreciation and we started to pick our way down the overgrown muddy track that led by the side of Hefyn's farm towards the Ruby Brick. Her father always picked her up on the main Denbigh Road, or Bottom Road, as it was known. He had been worried, having heard about her experience with Tebbutt in the woods.

I had walked Anne to the end of the lane every evening, but had not dared to hold her hand. Talking as we walked the space between us became more inviting, with Anne walking ever closer. My heart beat a symphony inside my chest and I struggled to contain it. We reached the far end of the lane and I found I was holding her hand.

That's not entirely true. My mother always says I have a selective memory, choosing to remember things just as I would wish them, and not necessarily as they were; but the truth is generally mixed up somewhere inside what I say.

The facts of the matter are probably more like this; we did talk as we walked, but I couldn't concentrate on what Anne was saying, my heart was too busy racing my mind and both seemed to be running out of control. Desperate thoughts entered my head; a culmination of all my waking dreams since first seeing Anne in the uncertain light of that musty old schoolroom.

'Go on…take hold of her hand!'

The argument was compelling and echoed in my mind,

'But don't make it too obvious!'

My heart then accelerated, leaping and bounding down the hillside, causing paralysis in all my major limbs. So instead of taking her hand, I chose to walk a little closer. Feeling my arm brushing against hers, Anne eventually took hold of my hand and then looking at me, she smiled.

Standing at the bottom of Parry Lane, holding Anne's hand, Carole's words echoed in my ears. She was right, I had followed Anne around like a puppy, but I didn't want to be anywhere other than, at her side.

Anne's father hadn't arrived; he had been five or ten minutes late almost every evening that week. So we stood between the overgrown hedge on Bottom Road and the first bush on the corner of Parry's Lane.

"Time and place is everything!" Carole had said. School was in the past, so time was on my side and as for the place, anywhere close to Anne would be the right place. So I turned towards her. It was now or never. Our eyes met. Letting go of her hand, I eased my hand into the small of her back and gently pulled her towards me. Each movement seemed to ease into the next as we slowly leaned towards each other. Our eyes gradually closed as our lips met. I remember how soft and warm her lips were and as I pulled away my whole body was numb. Anne's eyes opened momentarily and wrapping her arms around me we sank back into each other.

Our kisses were soft and gentle at first and my lips trembled at the touch of hers. I could taste her, like the morning dew and I could smell the faint scent of the woods in her hair on my face. We seemed to kiss forever. I wanted the moment to go on and on, but eventually our kisses exhausted themselves and we stood for a while just looking at each other.

Being so engrossed, we didn't notice her father's Land Rover pulling up beside us, until the two black-and-white collies started to bark at the stranger man-handling their Anne. I watched as she drove off into the distance and I could see her smiling as she looked back through the rear window. As the Land Rover disappeared out of sight, I looked across the road, towards Old Gwennie's cottage, which was half hidden in the treeline.

"Whoever you are, Old Gwennie…I thank you!"

I half whispered to myself.

Unwittingly, her name had just saved me from Tebbutt. Turning, I started back up Parry Lane with my heart still pounding.

"Damn it!" I said out loud.

I had forgotten to ask Anne when we could see each other again.

CHAPTER FOUR

Sometime before five, with the slow grey light of dawn seeping into the sky, I crept out of the back door. There was a chill in the air. Quietly closing the door behind me, I ran up the hill. In the dim light, I picked my way down Parry Lane tracing the path Anne and I had walked the evening before. Looking over the road, I could see the valley with its little stream shrouded in mist. It floated free from the fields in thin veils as it drifted over hedgerows and between the trees. I could hear Carlo barking at the cattle as they sauntered into the milking parlour and in my mind I could see Hefyn, with his boots on; ducking under, and in and out of the cows as he chained them into place with Uncle John pouring cattle cake into the cows feeding bowls.

Quickly scurrying across Bottom Road, I followed the line of the stream up towards the woods until I was almost level with Old Gwennie's. Jumping onto the large boulder in the centre of the stream, I watched the morning mists float by. Carefully stepping from rock to rock under the bridge, I passed Old Gwennie's, without incident. Picking up speed, my eyes scanned ahead as my confidence grew.

Hurrying my pace, I was soon hopping and jumping along and up the tumbling brook.

The old winding house came into view, standing like some ancient derelict temple; a memorial to the miners who gave their lives working the lead. I thought of the mine shaft hidden behind it and imagined their ghosts clawing up its steep walls, trying to climb out of their damp, dark tomb.

I could hear a song thrush off in the thick brush to my left. Soon its endless singing would wake the weary woods. Deeper under the trees, the lazy sun still hadn't found the shadows of the night. The smell of wild garlic was thick in the air with the morning dew wetting my jeans as well as my heart. The tune of the streams wild waters filled my ears as the woods rose up on either side.

I sprang from the bank to a rock, rock to rock and then back to the bank again. Climbing the stone staircase, I could see, half in my imagination, the shadows of trout darting to and fro; dashing into the hollows under the rocks. I continued up past the 'old brick tunnel' with mist looming over Ruby Pool, buried beneath a halo of misty sunlight. With my feet on solid ground, the overgrown path was almost indistinct as I ran past the Fallen Wall. Pausing at the place where I caught my first trout, I then continued up towards the Wooden Dam, under the Rabbit Warrens and along High-banks, climbing forever up and on, my confidence growing with the morning's light.

Not yet in sight, the sounds of sheep dogs barking and the clatter and chime of milk churns echoing through the woods, spurred me on. My legs and feet worked faster and faster as my eyes searched the shadows beneath the trees. With my senses heightened, I could hear noises on every side. A fleeting shadow tore past startling me, a tawny owl on its way home after the night shift.

I could hear something off in the woods to my left. Its sounds seemed to be keeping pace with me, faster and faster, I stepped from one rock to another. There it was again, off to the left, footsteps that seemed to track my every move, twigs cracked and I could hear the rustle of holly leaves under the trees. Whatever it was it easily kept up with me. Stopping, I turned to look, but as I strained my ears and eyes, I could hear and see nothing. 'Just my imagination,' I thought, but I lengthened my stride and quickened my pace, just in case.

Up and out of the stream with its gentle flow behind me, I vaulted the low stonewall by the big old Beech Tree at the bottom of the field. Running along its edges, the morning dew soaked in as the following footsteps faded in the woods. The farm buildings with their warm lights and the sounds of the cattle on the cobbles beckoned me closer. An atmosphere of uncertainty surrounded me as my eyes quickly scanned my unfamiliar surroundings.

'Where is she?'

I had thought of nothing, but Anne all night and her deep green eyes had stared back from the fireplace of my dreams. I just had to see her, even if she was dressed in dirty wellies and her old scruffs to help her father with the milking.

Standing at the corner of the barn, I hesitated, listening to Anne's father shouting and cursing, in Welsh, at the cows. Stepping around the far corner of the milking-parlour, with milk splashing from a churn she was struggling to carry, was the focus of all my dreams. I half waved; went to say something, but then remembering her father in the Shippon, I closed my mouth without uttering a word. But Anne had seen me in the shadows. Startled, she almost dropped the churn. Taking a deep breath, she looked me straight in the eye and then seemed to compose herself.

"Have I finished Dad?" She shouted back into the Shippon.

"Yes, yes cariad!" his voice echoed out.

"I'll pick some mushrooms for breakfast!" she called as we turned towards the field, pursued by the dogs that herded me neatly through the gate. Anne looked at me and smiled.

"Don't do that again!" She said, thumping me in the chest, almost winding me. "You frit me to death"

Anne gently petted my chest, where her blow had struck, and we walked into the field. Back at the bottom end of the field we walked towards the Old Beech where

I remembered seeing some horse mushrooms. Taking Taid's old penknife out, I cut away several with their stalks intact. We carefully checked them for grubs. I could feel the warmth of her hands as our fingers touched, turning the mushrooms over and passing them back and forth. Anne dropped one and I bent down to retrieve it, constantly looking up at her. She smiled as my hand lingered in hers, placing the mushroom back with the others. I had never associated those other feelings with checking mushrooms for grubs, but I had never before been around Anne Jones from the farm above the Italian Woods.

The sun was creeping above the trees, bleeding into thin wispy clouds, slowly burning the mist from the fields. Sitting under the tree on the low dry stonewall, I looked out into the woods.

"What evil lurks beneath the trees?" I said remembering the noises I had heard. "What do you mean? …I love the woods" I was trapped, so I described the noises I thought I'd heard when running up the stream. Anne seemed to take everything I said seriously and told me they had lost some lambs in the spring. Her father had found their remains; it hadn't been much, mainly blood. He had thought it was most probably a stray dog; he hadn't seen anything, but constantly kept his shotgun to hand on his nightly checks.

We sat awhile on the wall, holding hands, the mushrooms resting at our side. On the other side of the wall there was a rotten tree stump and on one side, I could see the torn golden-shawl of Chanterelle mushrooms. It was something I hadn't seen since mushrooming with my grandfather years before. Jumping from the wall, I was soon picking some of the golden-yellow horn-shaped fungi. Returning to my perch, one of the dogs started to growl as I eased myself down.

"Quiet!" Anne snapped.

"He's my friend…be good now" she half shouted.

"I'll be good!" I whimpered with a timid puppy dog look on my face and I jumped down from the wall holding Anne's gaze.

"Not you!" She said, as I moved up to where she was sitting.

Holding the Chanterelle Mushrooms up between us, we both tentatively leaned forward smelling their pungent scent of apricots. Placing them with the others, I stared at Anne as the orange glow of a big bright early morning sun found her pale skin; highlighting her long dark hair, just as it had done that first morning in the classroom.

"Can you eat them?" I was lost, but half nodded, thinking only of her, as my lips longed for hers.

One of the dogs was snouting and pawing at my leg, so I crouched down to spend some time stroking and petting the dogs and after a few minutes of sniffing, licking, panting and nuzzling; the type of minute's only dogs understand, I was finally accepted.

Time passed as we continued to build that special place in the space between us. Words gave way to smiles and long moment's just looking. Things were easy between us; natural even and we began to kiss. We kissed again and again. I could feel her legs either side of me as she sat on the wall with me leaning in towards her. We kissed long and slow with our tongues, each teasing the other, exploring feelings that wildly raced through us. The taste of Anne's lips was overwhelming and I lazed like a bee drunk on summer nectar.

A low growl from the dogs forced us apart. Through a gap in the fence, on the other side of the tree, they stared out into the woods, snarling and drooling, the fur on their backs bristling and standing tall. My eyes searched past fern and tree, into the dark shadows beneath the pines as I strained to see.

Anne's father called to the dogs from the top of the field, but they were transfixed, on guard, as if their lives, and ours, depended on it. Both Anne and I were unable to move or respond, with our eyes fixed firmly on an uncertain shadow deeper in the woods. Realising there was something wrong, Anne's father came running with the shotgun in his hand. Fumbling in his pocket for two cartridges, he dropped one and dipped into his pocket again, discarding the one that had fallen to the ground, as he continued towards us. By the time he came to a halt at our side the gun was loaded and he brought it up to aim.

We all stood like stone statues, with her father breathing heavily from his frantic sprint. Only our eyes moved, scanning the trees and undergrowth. I could still hear rustling a little way off in the woods; it stopped, then nothing. We waited for what seemed like hours, not daring to take our eyes from the thick undergrowth.

After a while we tentatively relaxed, with Anne's father checking me over and with an apparent look of distain on his face he turned to Anne.

"Thought I'd told you about talking to strangers!" They looked at each other and both tilted their heads back as they laughed. Anne and her father looked nothing like each other, except for their eyes; they both had piercing deep green eyes. He was tall and thin, dressed in green overalls with a dishevelled mop of greying dark hair thinning at the front. But in certain mannerisms, Anne and her father were identical; the way they laughed was one of them. There was an easy way between them and Anne seemed more than relaxed at the prospect of introducing me to him. The love they shared was obvious and seemed more natural than anything I had witnessed with any of my other friends; if that makes any sense.

"Don't tease Dad!" Anne said, pushing at her father's shoulder.

"Sweet on my daughter are you?" With a broad smile spread across her face and leaving me to fend for myself, Anne stooped to pick up the mushrooms and feeling a little safer we all walked up the field with Anne making the necessary introductions.

On reaching the Shippon, I turned to go, making my apologies.

"I'll be late for breakfast!" I said, thinking of Nain, who would already be raking at the fire and preparing food for my sleepy brothers and sisters.

"Hang on a moment David bach!" 'David bach'; the words were naturally spoken and instantly put me at ease.

"I've got to go down to the village before breakfast myself, and you're welcome to a lift…Anne too!"

Anne smiled at me and took hold of my hand as we walked across the yard towards the Land Rover with the dogs barking as clambering into the rear. Her father disappeared into farmhouse for a few moments then returned to where Anne and I sat waiting.

The Land Rover was an old 'two seater', a bit like those 'Pickups' that the Yanks are so fond of. The front seat was a bench seat with plenty of room for all three of us and I was happy to cuddle in close to Anne. Every part of the old jeep seemed to rattle with patches of rust infesting almost every panel. The noise of the old tappets, and the whinny and wiring of the engine made a strange percussion.

The dogs stood in the back with their snouts in the air. They barked at every car or person we passed, tantalised and teased by the scent of a thousand sheep trails in the fields on either side.

I sat where Anne had sat the night before, with Anne leaning against me. We held hands on the seat between us, just out of sight of her father, who constantly chatted just above the noise of the engine. Apparently they were all going to be at The Fechlas (Hefyn's farm) later that day, so Anne and I would be able see each other there.

Pulling up abruptly outside Nain's, Anne handed me half the mushrooms, with a warm smile on her face.

"Dad doesn't like the looks of some of them!" They both tilted their heads back laughing again, as Anne moved across to the window. Winding the window down, she hooked her fingers over the door frame. Her deep green eyes beckoned me closer, but her father dipped the clutch and the Land Rover slowly started to roll down the hill. Again, she looked back as they drove off and I could see her smiling as the dogs barked their goodbyes.

As I turned towards Nain and breakfast, I imagined Anne at her father's side, smiling; with her hand cupped under his arm as he drove down the steep hill towards the village.

My legs seemed to strain slightly as I walked down the steep drive. I broke into a jog as I cornered the far-end of Nain's small bungalow, but I paused before turning into the back yard. I looked across at the small vegetable plot, Nain struggled to keep, and in my mind; I could see my grandfather bent over his fork, raking at the soft rich earth with his fingers, searching for that last elusive spud.

Walking into the backyard, Nain was standing, waiting on the doorstep, just as I knew she would be. The kitchen door was open and the smell of breakfast drifted out into the morning.

Climbing the small flight of concrete steps our eyes met. I held out my hands to show her the Chanterelle mushrooms. Nain's eyes seemed to mist over for a moment as she took hold of my head, kissing me on the hair. Chanterelle mushrooms were my grandfather's favourite and I felt a sliver of grief enter the space between us.

"How was Anne then?" Nain asked.

Not waiting for a response, she continued.

"Ooh, no trout then cariad?"

She smiled and then looked up slightly as she went to laugh.

How on earth did she know where I had been?

CHAPTER FIVE

Hefyn opened the gate. Carlo, his dog, clawed at the ground and sprinted along and up the hedge line of Pen-y-cae (top Field). The sheep were already running to the centre of the field, with their heads in the air, looking back at Carlo. Tucking his stick under his arm, Hefyn placed his fingers to his mouth. Rolling his tongue back, he gave a shrill long whistle. Carlo immediately stopped. There followed a succession of short whistles, staggered whistles, long whistles and Carlo instantly reacted to each of them, lying down, standing motionless with a front paw off the ground, or moving one way, then the other.

I watched as Carlo and Hefyn guided the sheep slowly, but surely towards the pens. Opening the gate, I stood to one side of the entrance allowing Carlo to do his work as the sheep were carefully encouraged into the first pen. His work done, Carlo half lay at Hefyn's feet and looked up at him with his head against Hefyn's leg. Bending down, Hefyn patted and praised Carlo in Welsh as I closed the gate.

With the pen full it was easy to catch the sheep, then, taking their front legs, we walked them into the next pen. Rolling them over, we set to work, clipping and cleaning their tails of all the filth they'd gathered since the spring. Once finished we released them back into the field. The young lambs, cleaned and released, would wait by the pens, bleating for their mothers.

The fewer sheep in the pen the harder it was to catch them. I was struggling to get hold of an old ewe, when someone pushed at my side with their arm barging me out of the way and I hit the floor with a bump. A flash of bright red hair caught my eye, it was Megan. Stepping forward, she caught the ewe with ease and rolled it onto its back. I could see the whole of its underbelly with its swollen udders full of milk. Megan took hold of a teat and squeezed. A thin jet of warm milk hit me square in the face, splashing in one of my eyes. Walking the ewe into the next pen she looked back at me grinning. I wiped my face as Anne laughed from the next pen.

Standing just to one side of the fencepost, she looked sideways through the gaps in the fence to where I was sitting in the mud. Wearing a figure-hugging black T-shirt and faded Levis; she smiled across at me. It lit something inside me and I tentatively smiled back. It was the first time I had seen her dressed that way, without any other influence; no school uniform to wear or cattle to milk. She was beautiful.

On that first day at school I was wrong about her. She was slim with a good figure, but she was powerfully built, her body delicately toned; sculpted by an active life. I got up and walked over to her. Leaning forward, careful not to touch her with my grubby hands, I kissed her, once, on the lips.

"You look amazing!" I whispered, stepping back to admire her, letting my eyes take in everything, the waterfall of her long hair, her soft lines and the shape of her body beneath the 'T' shirt, the glow of her pale cheeks and the warm glint in the catch light of her eyes. She flushed a little and was embarrassed at the attention I gave her in front of the others. It was the first time we had shown any affection towards one another in public.

Looking me up and down Anne's eyes eventually rested on my dirty hands.

"You're not so bad yourself." Her head tilted back and she laughed her laugh.

Megan walked over to where Hefyn stood, leaning against the other side of the pen and pulling at his arm, she said,

"Why can't you be like that with me?"

Then calling across the pen to us, she shouted,

"Come on you two, we can't go until we get this finished!" She pointed towards the last few sheep in the pen.

"It must be love!" Hefyn said, winking at Megan, turning up the volume for Anne and myself to hear. Megan grinned, again poking fun.

"Go where?" I asked, desperate to know what they had planned.

All the others had phones at home and had already organised the day. At Nain's' we had no such luxury, so I was invariably left in the dark.

Anne looked me straight in the eye.

"I'm going to teach you how fish!"

Her voice was soft and low, edged with a serious tone, but I saw the slightest glimmer of a grin appear on her face.

"Good" I said,

"Bring it on."

I looked deep into her green eyes and she smiled her smile; soft and warm like the morning sun and I was a lazy bee once more.

"My father saw Old Gwennie yesterday, in the Post Office!"

Megan said, bringing an instant chill to the pens. We all looked across at her, she had our full, and undivided attention as she continued.

"He said, 'Maggie' had been flying about outside, squawking and making a hell-of-a-din!"

Maggie was a scraggy old magpie, which apparently followed Old Gwennie around. It was almost tame with only one eye and half a scruffy tail. She was always around the village, begging, teasing cats and stealing anything that wasn't nailed down. She took a fancy to all things shiny. Nain once told us that Maggie had flown in through the open kitchen window and stolen one of her prized 'apostle' teaspoons. Whenever she heard the wretched bird, she would curse 'Hen Walch' in Welsh. I didn't know what it meant, but I knew the bird was evil.

"You're joking!" Hefyn said, not quite knowing whether to believe her or not, her freckles hiding any mischievous intent.

"No; really…old Will B' dropped a pound note as he left the shop and as he chased it up the street 'Maggie' swooped down stealing it from under his nose!"

Anne laughed.

Will B was known for being extremely careful with his money.

"I'm surprised his money saw the light of day long enough for Maggie to get her beak on it!" Anne chuckled as she spoke.

"Apparently, he went back into the Post Office, red-faced and with steam coming from his ears. He shouted at Gwennie.

"Your damn bird's got my money."

Everything went quiet in the Post Office; no one dare say anything. Old Gwennie gave him a look that instantly froze his blood and Will B suddenly woke to the awful realisation of what he was doing. He ran out of the Post Office as fast as his little old legs would carry him!"

Megan could string out a pretty good yarn. She gave a wry grin and we all began to laugh. The thought of Will B running, at all, somehow, tickled our senses. He must have been ninety if a day and he always shuffled slowly around the village with his walking frame out in front of him. According to Nain, as a boy Will was one of three Will's in his class. The first was known as Will 'A', 'Old Will', being Will 'B' and the last, Will 'C'.

We finished the sheep then washed and cleaned ourselves down, and before long we were walking down Bottom Field, towards the Ruby Brick and the Italian Woods. With the sun out, the day was already hot and we wandered off into the afternoon, still laughing and joking.

Anne and Megan were carrying small rucksacks and I wondered what on earth girls found to fill the myriad of bags they always seemed to have with them.

CHAPTER SIX

Chattering like magpies we crossed the road and walked over the bridge towards Old Gwennie's. Slowly, we made our away under the Iron Bridge, stepping from rock to rock, keeping low, being careful not to make a sound; passing Old Gwennie's cottage without incident.

Sunlight streamed down through the trees, with the hum of summer woods all around us. Rooks cried and circled high above their nests. The water in the stream tumbled over its rocks, bubbling into pools as it flowed from the mountain. The thick intoxicating, pungent smell of wild garlic filled my lungs, suffocating my senses as we walked through the dense beds of its white flowers. Occasionally the scent of freshly cut summer fields drifted through the trees in the haze of the sun's amiable rays.

A song thrush began to sing from somewhere above a thicket of holly and I strained to catch a glimpse of it. I couldn't see it, but I paused for a moment. Its shrill song reminded me of Taid. It was the first songbird he had introduced me to and over the years I had grown to love its call, with those quiet memories it woke inside me.

Anne jumped down from the bank onto a large smooth rock, waking me from my memories. Laying belly down, she moved towards its edge. With her arms draped over the side, her hair tumbled free, with its ends touching, and then drowning, in the stream's cool waters. Scooping her hair back with her right hand, she dipped her left arm into the crystal clear water. Running her hand carefully underneath the large boulder, she searched for the chambers hidden beneath it. They were the streams secret hideaway places where the trout wallowed, waiting patiently for the touch of her hand. A smile appeared on her face and her arm stopped moving momentarily.

Laying there for about a minute, the muscles in her arm tensed as she worked her hand further under the rock. There was no compulsion or violence in what she did, the trout willingly submitting to the touch of her fingers as she carefully stroked her hand along its underbelly.

If you fished properly the trout would submit themselves to you, lying on a flat hand as you took them from the water. They lay mesmerised by your touch, just long enough for you to flick them onto the bank.

I can remember when I was very young, watching two lads fishing down by the 'Canda' with a bucket. They had dammed up a pool with stones, then proceeded to chase a poor little brown trout relentlessly around the pool; scooping with the bucket, stamping on the water and thrashing about so much that eventually the trout, exhausted and suffocating, surrendered to the fray. Anyone who doesn't know how to catch a fish properly, with some dignity and respect, does not deserve to catch it at all.

Slowly Anne brought her arm out of the water. A large brightly coloured rainbow trout lay across her flat palm. Mesmerised and gulping for its last breath, she lowered it back into the water. The trout seemed to wake from its trance and slowly swam to the bottom of the pool. Coming to its senses, it quickly fled, with clouds of silt rising through the water as it vanished into the streams secret places once more.

Anne climbed back up the bank to a rapturous applause; her lesson for the day was over. I smiled at her in genuine admiration and in that moment I caught a glimpse of the power I knew she possessed. I had sensed it on that first day, but did not fully understand what I felt and I wondered what it was about her that entranced me. She was certainly beautiful, but there were other beautiful girls. There was something more about Anne, something that drew me in, some elusive feeling or thought or power. There's that word again; power. It's not quite right, but it's pretty damn close.

Power conjures an image of domination or force, but that's not at all what Anne was about. After all these years the nearest comparison I have found is the one I thought at that moment, as I watched her catching then releasing the trout. The thought had flashed into my mind, a thought I dare not utter out loud. Somehow, Anne contained the same power and magic my grandmother had. Nothing was ever forced; everything seemed to move neatly into place, quietly falling into line around her, submitting itself, utterly and completely, to her will.

I have never dared to tell you of the comparison I had drawn between you and my Grandmother, but I know you will now understand the compliment it bestows on you.

We walked deeper into the Woods and the old winding house came into view. Hefyn picked up a large rock from the bed of the stream and we scrambled up around the side of the crumbling old building, where the open mineshaft lay. Large timbers had been placed over its mouth years before and were rotten, with huge gaps between them.

According to 'Aunt Cath', my mother had once walked across the beams for a dare. I asked my mother about it, one time, but she denied all knowledge.

"Don't you dare go anywhere near that old mine shaft, it's too dangerous" Mum's words echoed in my ears as I stood above the old timbers that made small pretence of covering the cavernous hole beneath them.

Hefyn held the rock high above his head, and then threw it as hard as he could onto the rotten beams. Hitting one of the beams, the rock only bounced off the decaying wood, dropping into the deepening darkness below. We started to count with the sound of the rock banging from side to side as it fell through the darkness. "Five, six" Still tumbling with the noise it made echoing back up,

"Twelve, thirteen!" The noise of the rock hitting the brick walls was getting fainter. "Eighteen, nineteen, twenty!" The rock falling silently; too far down for us to hear. "Twenty-four, twenty-five!"

The sound of the rock hitting the cage at the bottom came echoing up the shaft. A shiver ran down my spine as I thought of my mother, walking the beams high above where the rock had fallen, and I wondered how many ghosts lived in that dank dark hole?

CHAPTER SEVEN

The stream tumbled ever on with trout visible in the shadows of the pools. Shafts of light piercing through the leaves of the trees danced on the shimmering surface of the water. A blackbird flew from the bank, singing its chattering warning to the woods.

As we approached the Ruby Pool it was bathed in sunlight.

The Ruby Pool was a large pond, but it was like no other pond I had ever seen. One of its ends was open to the stream, but the streams waters did not flow in. Instead, crystal clear water flowed out, although I had never worked out where it came from, because there were no other waters that flowed into the pool. Maybe there was an underground spring somewhere along its bank, which would also explain how crystal clear its waters were.

 Shallow at the end where we stood, watercress grew, covering its mouth. At the far end it was deep, with steep banks held up by large rocks and boulders. A large area of dark black mud covered the bottom towards the far end, which I estimated to be at least fifteen foot deep. Surrounded by fir trees and woods, it was beautiful.

With its right bank drenched in sunlight the pool was transformed, in my imagination, into a miniature Italian lake; just like a picture I had seen in a travel book. It was like our own little Italy, in the midst of the Italian Woods.

"Let's go swimming!" Megan said, with a wry grin on her face. I had been skinny dipping there before, but only with Hefyn. It would be a little tricky with the girls there, but gradually my mind warmed to the idea. Looking at Hefyn, I knew he hadn't brought anything to swim in, but there again neither had the girls. I wouldn't put anything past Megan, but I was slightly surprised at the encouragement Anne gave to the suggestion.

"Wild swimming!" She said, with a playful smile edging out onto her face.

"All right then!" Hefyn and I said, almost simultaneously.

We made our way along the bank to the far end of the pool, but on looking back the girls were nowhere in sight. We both called out.

"We're not getting undressed in front of you two!" Anne shouted, from somewhere in the bushes. "You get in… and then you can look away when we get in!"

We quickly stripped down to our pants and, standing facing each other, we pondered our next move. I could almost read Hefyn's mind. Taking hold of his pants by their waistband, he pulled them away from his stomach looking down then glanced back up at me.

'Don't do it!' I thought to myself, but I didn't say anything; although I think he got the message because looking back down he let the waistband go. I heard the sound it made as his pants snapped tightly closed.

Stepping onto a large rock high on the bank, not even having considered what Hefyn had, I braced myself and dived out towards the centre of the pool. The water was freezing cold and the shock of diving straight in took my breath away. Struggling to control my breathing, I started to pant like a dog, with my body slowly getting used to the cold.

Hefyn stepped onto the rock then dived in the pool next to me. Both of us were treading water, panting in the cold. We looked around for the girls and called out to the faintly chuckling woods.

"Come on then…we won't look…honest" Hefyn shouted out to the shy, hiding bushes.

"What are you waiting for?"

The bushes rustled as the girls stepped out high on the bank, their clothes held tightly in front of them covering their dignity. I couldn't quite believe my eyes; amongst Anne's clothes I could see her bra and a skimpy pair of lacy white briefs. They gingerly walked down the bank towards us and stood close to where our clothes lay in two discarded heaps on the ground.

My eyes quickly searched through the clothes Anne held tightly in front of her. Her jeans were scrunched up covering her waist. Her other arm was holding her 'T-shirt, which in turn was opened out across her top, covering her upper body.

Anne's hair tumbled down over her bare shoulders and I looked up at her with eager anticipation, my eyes having fixed themselves firmly on her stripped and naked flesh, which I could already imagine beneath her clothes. I started to shiver as Anne stared back at me. With my teeth chattering I tried to control the myriad of feelings washing through me. I didn't want to miss a thing.

"Come on then!" I said in a low voice, my eyes firmly fixed on Anne.

In an instant, they both dropped their clothes next to ours to reveal swimming costumes. I looked at Hefyn in disbelief.

Quickly turning my attention back to Anne, the sight of her dressed that way instantly warmed through me. They both pulled the straps of their costumes over their shoulders and in turn the girls stepped onto the rock. They were both laughing as they dived into the pool.

We all swam and played, enjoying ourselves in the water. The cold seemed to vanish in the afternoon sun as our bodies grew numb. After an hour or so, we all got out except Anne. She continued to swim and as she did so she teased us all, shivering on the bank above her.

I watched her swimming quietly around the pool. Occasionally she would look up at me, smiling as she did so. Once or twice beaconing for me to come back in. Swimming to the far bank she stood on a rock beneath the water line, near some large boulders that seemed to prop up the bank. Pulling her hair back, she combed it with her fingers, into a ponytail. Her eyes closed as the afternoon sun drained into her. Despite the obvious cold around her, she appeared to drift off to some faraway place, her own private world, where she alone dwelt in her dreams.

Time seemed to pause; hanging motionless in the haze of the afternoon woods as I continued to study her. There was something wild about her, nothing timid or dangerous; maybe a little quiet, but I imagined her as a big cat bathing in the afternoon sun beneath African skies and I wanted so much to be at her side wherever she wandered in her dreams.

The sun danced on the rocks and the water around her, highlighting the gentle line of her powerful arms as she pulled her hair tight. She was a living, breathing, moving watercolour, painted in a limited palette of only the most precious colours. The light on the water reflected in her face and soaked deep into the rocks that surrounded her, bringing out countless shades and colours on their surface.

Anne looked up at me as though my stare had somehow called her from some distant land or dream. Smiling she leaned forward, parting the water with her hands as she swam back across the pool.

The sun was still beating down where we sat on the grass bank and its amiable rays warmed into us. The girls had even brought towels and they laid them out on the ground. We lazed in the haze of a hot mid-summer afternoon. I lay next to Anne, looking up at the sky. Holding her hand; still cold and damp, I could feel warmth from somewhere deep inside her body and I allowed it to seep into me.

Anne gently squeezed my hand and then rolled over, half lying on my arm as she placed her head on my shoulder, her lips touching my skin. I could feel her damp hair on my arm and side, teasing at my feelings as she slowly moved her head while kissing my neck. At that moment I imagined we were the only two people in the whole world.

Her lips caressed my shoulder and I could feel her warm breath drifting over my helpless body. Brushing her fingers slowly across my stomach she rested her hand on my chest, her fingers finding the first few faint young hairs that grew there. In that moment I became the trout lying mesmerised in the palm of her hand, gulping for its last breath.

I watched as lazy clouds floated past and half dreamt, fancying that I had spent my whole life travelling towards that moment. A traveller through time and space; an explorer; searching, scouring the universe, never dreaming or imagining, in the wildest times of my life, where the journey would take me, or how it would end. I thought of the 'power of generations', conspiring with time and the eternal nature of things, to bring Anne and I together in that one moment. I lay there lost, somewhere in that droplet of time, never wanting the moment to end. They were strangely new feelings and yet I had somehow felt them all my life, maybe even since before my life. Maybe I had followed her through more than one life time.

After what seemed an eternity, Anne sat up and I slowly sat up beside her. I wanted so much more and started to kiss her shoulder as she stared down into the pool. The water was settled and calm; crystal clear again. Dragging myself from her side, I picked up a small flat stone and tossed it out into the centre of the pool. The ripples spread out like feelings across my mind, over the surface of my life.

My eyes searched for the stone and I caught sight of it as it sank into the darkness. I followed its meandering path, but it disappeared into the expanse of black mud.

I thought of Anne, falling like the stone through the deep clear waters of my life and that thought slowly swam through me. We had known each other for less than a week and I couldn't quite believe the feelings I felt for her. The touch of her hand or a smile would send my heart racing and when we kissed, it took all other care from me.

The sunlight caught something in the darkness of the pool, possibly a trout; a spark of light flashing from its scaly skin. I moved my head from side to side, but the light flashed at the same point each time; it wasn't a fish.

"Can you see that?" I whispered to Anne almost excitedly.

"It's a trout or something!" I turned and looked at Anne with the thought of her still swimming through me.

"You what?" She said with a perplexed look on her face while gazing deep into me, obviously puzzled by what I was saying. I could sense I had dragged her from her own daydream and I cursed the trivial nature of my thoughts, but I continued to talk in the vain hope that she would become faintly interested.

"Down by the black mud!" I said.

"What mud? What thing?" Anne said, almost in a whisper, seeming to understand how awkward I felt and not wishing to embarrass me.

"Nothing…it's probably nothing!" I said, disappointed, feeling isolated in the very prickly world I had just created for myself.

"I saw something that caught the sun, down by the patch of black mud!"

"What black mud?" Anne said, looking back into the pool, with a puzzled expression on her face.

"You've really lost me this time David."

I pointed towards the black patch of mud, with my finger tracing its outline deep underwater.

"That mud!" I said, wondering whether it was just me being stupid.

"Oh that mud!" Anne eventually caught what I was talking about as the paradigm shifted. Anne looked over to where Hefyn and Megan sat wrapped up in each other, smiling and listening intently to our conversation.

"I've never seen mud quite that colour before!" I said relaxing slightly, no longer feeling like the village idiot.

"It almost looks like oil, doesn't it?" I turned to Anne, looking for some encouragement, but she just sat there smiling with that look on her face.

"I bet you couldn't swim down to it?" Megan called over, knowing I wouldn't be able to resist the dare.

"Of course I could!" I said quickly without giving the matter any further thought or consideration. I looked at Anne and she smiled as she said.

"Go on then!"

"I've got to see this!" Hefyn said, butting in, with Megan getting to her feet, wrapping their towel around her and saying, "You'll never do it!"

I leaned towards Anne and whispered to her, so Megan and Hefyn couldn't hear. "What is my bid for a handful of black mud?" Anne smiled again trying to encourage me.

"A handful of mud, for your love?"

She nodded, looking straight into me drawing me in once more. I could see she was puzzling it out in her mind and she whispered back to me quietly saying,

"All right then; a handful of black mud for my love!"

"Forever" I said.

"Forever?" Anne breathed the words in my ear, warming every part of me.

"Forever" And then almost as a second thought she said,

"Maybe!" as she smiled.

Rising to my feet, I prepared myself for my dive into the deep. I was a strong swimmer and could easily reach the bottom. Turning back to look at Anne, I smiled.

Stepping up onto the rock, I felt like a knight in olden days sitting astride his trusted steed, readying himself to ride out and win his ladies colours. Megan and Hefyn both stood grinning and looking across at Anne. There was definitely something going on, but in my eagerness to win Anne's affection, I couldn't see it and in any case a dare was a dare.

"Diving is cheating!" Anne called out, but ignoring the jibe I dived into the pool and immediately felt the cold water stabbing into me again. I swam out to just above the patch of black mud and controlled my breathing sufficiently to execute a perfect surface dive. I was soon heading down into the depths of the pool, swimming towards the mud, pulling with my arms and kicking with my legs, which propelled me further into the deep. The water was getting colder and colder the deeper I went. Darkness soon surrounded me. Holding my nose, I blew against it, altering the pressure in my ears, to that of the water around me.

There it was again, something flashed in the dim light of the water off to one side. It certainly wasn't a trout, but I kept my eyes firmly on the dark task in front of me, groping for the black mud I knew was somewhere just in front of me. Again I pulled with my arms as my legs grew numb and tired. My head was bursting, but I couldn't give up. Again I pulled at the water, but with my head tingling and my lungs bursting, reluctantly I turned and started back towards the surface.

I couldn't quite believe what I saw; shafts of light blazed in front of me and I found I was in what looked like a tunnel leading up to the world above.

Whatever it was stuck in the wall of the mine shaft, I had just swam into, it caught the light of the sun again as it penetrated down into the deep, but with lungs collapsing and limbs drained of all their energy, I struggled desperately to swim back up to the spluttering surface.

Gasping, I exploded out on to the top of the pool, to the sound of the others laughing and taunting me from the bank.

"It's a mine shaft!" Hefyn shouted towards me.

"You idiot" Anne shouted, her words piercing through me, cutting deep into my heart.

Dragging myself from the pool, drained of all my energy, I took a bow, but then, picking up a large flat grey-slate rock, I stood ready to dive back in. Anne walked towards me her arms open, as if to comfort and console me, but I ignored her advances, turning my head away. I caught the slightest look of hurt on her face and I turned back towards her and winked, smiling at her, drawing a smile back, but I quickly looked away again.

High on the rocky diving board, I composed myself; Megan and Hefyn's laughs subsided as they all wondered what I was doing. I had a different task on my mind and using all my strength I pushed off from the bank, diving out towards the centre of the pool, holding the rock firmly in front of me. It quickly took me back down into the depths of the mineshaft, which had become strangely visible to me. The slab of slate found the depth easily, dragging me deeper into the endless darkness.

When I had reached what I thought was the required depth, I dropped the rock and watched as it rapidly disappeared into the unfathomable depths of water that oozed up slowly from the centre of the earth. I had enough air left in my lungs to search the ledges for whatever it was that had caught my eye. Light once again blazed into the depths of the mineshaft as I turned towards the surface with time to hunt in the deep.

I saw a glint of light again and turned to one side. Reaching out I took hold of whatever it was and could feel it firm and almost sharp in my hand. Quickly running out of air, I put it straight into my pants for safe keeping, hoping that whatever it was couldn't bite. Then pulling with my arms, I struggled back to the slightly troubled world above.

A different reception waited for me at the top and everyone helped me from the pool as I searched in my pants for my prize. Anne and Megan both gave me funny looks wondering what on earth I was doing. My hand gripped firmly around what felt like a small sharp stone and I held my clenched fist up and out towards the others. I opened my hand to reveal a large almost perfectly formed quartz crystal that I had just tugged from the wall of the mineshaft. Taking hold of it between my thumb and forefinger, I held it out for everyone to see.

Anne gasped and Hefyn exclaimed,

"Boy, will you look at that!"

In the sunlight the crystal glistened as the light caught its many facets. Still wet from the water it was completely transparent and I looked through it. Inside, I could see what looked like strands of golden wire shooting through it in all directions.

My grandfather had told me of his cousins who once owned the goldmine further up in the mountainside and of how the hills were full of gold. He once showed me some calcite; with a bit of discoloured metal embedded in it, telling me it was gold. I can remember looking at it in amazement, but it was nothing compared to the crystal I had just recovered from the mouth of the huge mine shaft, where it must have lain in waiting for years.

They all stood admiring the crystal not quite believing what they had seen or what I had done. Looking closely at it, I could see a small cloudy patch just above the golden strands of wire, with tiny flecks that glistened in the sunlight.

Hefyn and Megan stepped in closer; staring hard; looking and admiring, but Anne remained slightly aloof, feeling awkward for teasing me.

"That never came from in there" Hefyn said, nodding in the direction of the pool. But checking his thoughts, having watched me strip off down to my pants, his mind turned over and over, considering everything in sequence. Standing, combing his fingers through his hair, he muttered something in Welsh under his breath as his mind eventually slotted into place.

"Iesu!" Hefyn said out loud.

"Sorry David!" He immediately apologised, knowing 'Nain Hughes' would not have approved, of his language, and that I never really cared for such language myself. "It's unbelievable though!" He continued.

"You never found that there?" Megan said, almost indignantly as she folded her arms waiting for my defence, but I just smiled with smug satisfaction glowing on my face.

I looked at Anne, still standing back slightly. She was straight faced and I smiled at her. Anne looked back at me with puppy dog eyes, wondering if she had hurt my feelings as she hesitantly returned my smile. We both edged back into the space between us; lazing in the renewed warmth that we found there.

Holding the crystal up towards her, it reflected in the catch light of her eyes. Light piercing the crystal shone on her skin in all the colours of the rainbow. I took hold of her hand and placed the crystal carefully in it, folding her fingers gently around its exquisite beauty. She looked into me and then threw her arms around my neck and whispered in my ear.

"Forever" I felt the power in her arms as she hugged me and once again I felt her body close to mine.

The sun dropped below the tree line and long shadows swam out across the pool. Feeling the chill of the late afternoon drawing in we all got dressed. In our own little world for the afternoon, we had forgotten our surroundings, but as we prepared to leave, we started to look and listen to the woods.

I heard the squawk of a magpie somewhere off in the woods. Hefyn took hold of my arm and with a worried look on his face, he pointed to the bushes at the other side of the pool. My eyes strained as they searched the shadows beneath the pines. I could see something, but what it was I couldn't make out. There was definitely a crouched figure in the shadows, but a breeze blew through the trees and a moment later it was gone. I looked and looked again, but there was nothing.

Anne had seen something too and Megan was getting worried. Anne pulled on my arm, for us to leave, saying she had a bad feeling about it and I remembered her father rushing down the field that morning, with his shotgun in hand to protect his daughter. We didn't have a shotgun, but Anne's father, I was sure would have rushed to protect us had he known the danger we were in.

We carefully gathered our things together with Megan quickly buttoning up her blouse. Walking slowly along the bank, back to the stream, we followed the path, making our way back towards the bottom end of the Italian Woods. We didn't rush or run, that would have caused panic and fear and would probably have encouraged whatever it was on the other side of the pool to chase us.

I could hear something off in the woods. Whatever it was it was following us. Its footsteps were soft, but clearly discernible as it stalked through the thick undergrowth. I didn't say anything to the girls and although my eyes searched constantly in the shadows, I didn't catch sight of anything. It was undoubtedly the same creature that had followed me through the woods that morning. I settled in my mind that it must have been a stray dog, as Anne's father had thought.

The girls jumped at every noise and there was some comfort in not being isolated in my fear. Hefyn walked in front while I walked slightly behind. I checked the woods constantly until we came to the bridge near Old Gwennie's, where the others climbed down into the bed of stream. I waited, crouching on the bank, looking, my eyes searching, ears listening, my heart jumping at every alien sound as the others made their way under the bridge. Hefyn helped the girls, fussing and being understandably protective. Then, when I could see they were safe, I quickly joined them on the rocks in the stream on the other side of the bridge.

Moments later we were out in the clear, calming ourselves and comforting each other with nods and smiles. Walking quickly, I placed my arm around Anne with Hefyn putting his arm around Megan, checking, looking, reassuring.

We had all calmed down by the time we climbed over the fence into bottom field. We looked out across the valley at the lengthening shadows and then up at the maternal mountain, which called us home, as a ewe calls her lambs, to be suckled for the night.

CHAPTER EIGHT

Whist was Nain's game. So after my younger brothers and sisters had been put to bed, we would beg her to play a few hands with us. It was one of the few times Nain let her hair down, so to speak. The game would always have to be played properly and she would start the session encouraging us to follow the strict etiquette of the game, having to apologise when we didn't follow the rules: Second player play low etc.

Nain would always start off the evening, quietly instructing us in the niceties of the game. But it was as if the game and playing it with us, was a drug that was drip-fed gradually into her and by the end of the evening she would be rolling around laughing and telling jokes with us. Andy would let-rip and everyone would go quiet, waiting for Nain's response. Nain would look straight-faced at him then slowly breathing in the repugnant smell, that only Andy could produce, she would turn up her nose saying "Burnt egg on chips" and then, laugh aloud and we'd all join in.

That evening had been no different to any other and the card game had deteriorated into the usual riot, but being tired from the adventures of my day, I excused myself after two full hands and went to the front room to make up my bed, meagre as it was. My father had returned home for the weekend and had brought with him some camp beds, which would be a sight more comfortable than the floorboards.

Andy joined me some time later and we settled down for the night. I lay staring into the coal fire as the flames flickered and danced, giving way to red-hot embers. Looking deep into its blaze, I lay, listening to its spit and crackle. As I looked, I imagined a strange shape crouched in the blackened shadows of the chimney. There seemed to be a pair of dark menacing eyes staring back at me from across the Ruby Pool and I wondered if I had imagined it all.

Trying desperately to think of Anne I couldn't settle. My mind wondered, remembering a story Taid once told. Sitting me on his knee he began his tale, of a young man called Jack - my grandfather's name – who'd got lost while walking in the woods.

"As I went to open the gate!" he said,

"I heard someone call from the cottage on the other side of the stream.

"There are wolves in the wood Jack" Old Gwennie said to me, as she opened her window.

I sat silently on his knee, caught up in the web of the world he created around me. "You be careful now Jack" He would say, changing his voice to mimic the different characters in his story.

"What, Old Gwennie" I had said quickly at the mention of her name.

"Is Old Gwennie a witch?" I can remember asking, but ignoring my question he continued with his story.

"I wasn't afraid of no wolves," He said, sounding brave.

"So I opened the gate and walked right in. I followed the path by the brook, but it soon led deep into the darkest parts of the woods." His voice built the tension as he spoke and each word would be spoken almost individually as they sank into my mind.

"I could then hear something following me, just out of sight, in the shadows under the trees" My heart began to pound.

"It was too dark for me to see, but something was there all right, I could hear it."

Taid would hold me tight, making me feel the tension in his arms as he lowered his voice to a forced whisper, his words creeping up on me.

"The trees became thicker and thicker, the woods darker and darker, until I could barely see the path in front of me. The footsteps continued to follow me, closer and closer. I could hear the pad, pad, of giant paws on the ground. With twigs cracking under them and the rustle of the leaves, I became frightened and wanted to run away. I was too scared to go on, so I turned back and there it was."

He would raise his voice and say the last few words quickly as he suddenly opened his knees, letting me fall almost to the floor before catching me; making me jump and squeal. Then pulling me back close to him he would whisper in my ear again, making his voice low and serious, building the tension once more.

"With its eyes on fire, it was the biggest, wildest, most ferocious wolf I had ever seen. Its teeth were drooling as it growled and snarled; creeping towards me." Taid would make the actions of the wolves' mouth with his hands, opening and closing, his fingers interlocking them as if biting.

"It opened its mouth wider and wider, moving closer and closer! There was nothing I could do, so I took my hand and stuffed it into his mouth!" He would throw his arm forward, mimicking the actions of his character.

"I forced it down his throat, pushing it right through his stomach and catching hold of his tail, I pulled him inside out." I watched Taid as he gripped hold of the wolf's tail, pulling as hard as he could.

My grandfather would laugh loudly teasing us, saying how strong he was and that he used to be a boxer; 'Boxing Kippers.' Asking to see the muscles on our arms he would squeeze them saying that they were nothing more than 'knots on cotton'.

I smiled to myself, thinking about him. Half in my sleep, I thought of the many years since I had heard his stories and the tremendous pain it must have caused him; us sitting on his bad leg, but I never once heard him moan or fuss about it.

The door opened, with Nain entering the room and both Andy and I sat up. Dad would be sleeping on the settee that night to save waking my younger sisters, but he wouldn't be coming to bed for a while. Starting into the room on her nightly ritual, Nain kissed me on the hair and then she went over to Andy.

"Nain" I said.

"Yes, cariad?"

"You and Taid once told us a story about a wolf in the woods"

"Ooh, no story was it then," she said, as though I had accused her of telling tall tales. "My grandmother saw it, she did" she said, almost dreamily, but with great emphasis as her memories wandered back through the years.

We begged her to tell us the story, Andy tugging at her arm. We both considered ourselves far too old to listen to children's stories, but for some reason we both longed to spend time with Nain, listening and feeling secure in her presence. Eventually she relented and with Gareth fast asleep at our feet we all sat down, sharing the sofa between us, staring into the fire, but those menacing eyes only stared back at me. We settled down getting comfortable, Nain placing her arms around Andy and I, pulling us close into her side.

"When just a little girl" she started. "My grandmother took me on her knee, just as Taid used to with you and told me of how she had met a wolf in the woods."

Nain's storytelling was in total contrast to the way my grandfather used to tell his stories. She would speak calmly and quietly, never trying to dramatize what she was saying. Her words were serious and never raised any doubt in my mind as to their authenticity. I believed every word that fell from her mouth, but her words built exactly the same excitement in me, just as if my grandfather had been whispering into my ears, building the tension with his voice.

"Walking to school one day, with her books in one hand and her dinner in the other; my Grandmother slowed at a place near the old tumbledown wall, halfway through 'Coed Du' woods. Hearing rustling in the bushes ahead, to her great surprise out stepped a huge she-wolf. It stood on the path staring back at her, each one wondering what the other would do"

Nain's voice never changed inflection, stating each word as though it were fact, leaving me in no doubt that it was. She continued

"My Nain opened her sandwiches and started to take a large chicken sandwich from the paper. With the she wolf starting to growl at her she threw the sandwich onto the path in front of her. Stepping forward, the Wolf sniffed at it for a while, then opening its huge mouth, it picked up the sandwich swallowed it whole. A second sandwich went the way of the first. The she wolf lay on the ground; it's snout between her front paws to let my grandmother pass, but there were still noises coming from the bushes. Her curiosity got the better of her and she looked under the bush. There she saw five wolf cubs, all painfully thin and hungry. So opening the wrapper, containing the rest of her lunch, she fed each of them in turn."

Andy and I listened intently not moving or making a sound.

"Passing that way after school, my Nain looked by the tumble-down wall, but the she-wolf and her cubs were gone" Silence spread through the night in the old front room as Nain paused slightly, allowing Andy and I to catch up with our feelings.

"She told no one about the Wolf in the woods, but a few days later, she was walking home from school on her usual path, when a man stepped out in front of her. His hands and face were dirty and he had long scruffy hair, with no collar on his grubby white shirt. My grandmother was frightened by the mere presence of the stranger, who stepped forward, saying,

"Come here, don't be frightened little girl!" But before he got close enough to grab her there was a commotion in the bushes to one side of the path. The she-wolf jumped out of the bushes hitting the stranger, with full force, square in the chest. The man fell to the ground with the she-wolf standing over him, growling. Spittle from her snarling fangs dripped onto his throat, which was just below her huge mouth!"

The air in the front room seemed to be dry and I couldn't swallow, I couldn't move or make any sound. I just sat in silence, waiting.

"My grandmother was allowed to pass in safety and was never afraid in the woods again. And although she never saw the wolf after that, sometimes while walking through the woods, she would imagine that she could hear something following her in the shadows of the trees. But she never worried, knowing it was only her friend watching over her."

Nain kissed us both on top of the head and blowing out the night-light she left the room. I lay somewhere between the sitting room and that nether world, once more feeling Anne's presence. I sensed her lips on my shoulder and her warm breath moving slowly over me. I lay there hypnotised by the flickering flames of the fire dying in the grate. Lying close, I could feel presence warming through me and we drifted off into the night together.

CHAPTER NINE

The following week I spent more and more time with Anne. We longed to be together; mostly hanging around with Hefyn and Megan and only occasionally did we find time to be alone. It would generally be at the end of the day, while waiting for Anne's father to pick her up, and as we waited we endlessly kissed, continually pushing at boundaries. I didn't really understand those boundaries at the time. I knew they were there, I could feel them deep inside. My understanding of them was growing, but how to overcome them, I didn't quite know.

We arranged to go walking one day, on the mountains. The following day we walked along the Leet, a path that led by the river Alyn. We walked all the way to Loggerheads and back.

We stayed away from the 'Italian Woods', our imaginations having run wild, telling us of the dangers that lay in wait for us there. Our fear of whatever was hidden in the woods had firmly barred our way along its rock strewn path.

In those first few weeks of the summer, my feelings for Anne, at times, threatened to overwhelm me.

Sitting here these years later, I'm still not sure I understand, but those things I felt in your presence and more tangentially when I was away from you, I knew was love; a deeper more profound feeling than I had ever felt before. I was certain of it then and am more certain of it now, if that is possible.

I think one such feeling began the day we went to the zoo. Hefyn had to go with Uncle John to the market and Megan had arranged to go with her mother and Anne, shopping in Mold. My mother and Nain were going to Chester Zoo and needed me to help with 'the kids'. I begged Anne to come too and so she made some feeble excuse to Megan.

My younger sisters were all over her. Anne was good with them; they loved her easy ways and I did too. We both took sketch pads and pencils and managed to lose the rest of the family with a little help from Nain. We visited all the main attractions; the monkeys and reptile house, bison and wild pigs. Paul Simon wrote, 'It's all happening at the Zoo; well it wasn't that day. The big cats looked a bit sad cooped in their cages, one tiger in particular, and at the end of the day nothing had inspired us.

With about an hour to go we came across an open pen which housed a shallow round pool that looked a bit like a doughnut, or at least the imprint of where a giant donut had lay. A jet of water was squirting around and down its side and bathing in the sun were two sea lions. There was something about the way they lay side by side, the smaller sea lion having her flipper over the male's stomach. She was nuzzled up next to him and appeared to be kissing his neck and face. Anne and I instantly took out our pads and began to sketch. We spent some time watching and scribbling eagerly as the two young lovers caressed and fondled each other. I still have the sketch and look at it from time to time. Its lines have faded now, but the memories of those feelings it evoked inside me haven't.

The day after going to the zoo, we all arranged to go climbing and I walked up to meet the others at the farm gates. Anne's mother had dropped her off before I arrived, so I still hadn't met her.

We started down Parry Lane. In the winter, Parry Lane was nothing more than an impassable quagmire, with water draining off the fields and trickling slowly down its muddy track, but in the summer it would dry up, providing a cut through to the Italian Woods and the Ruby-Brick.

Hefyn had a rucksack with him that I could see was full of slings and Carabineers, with a long length of what looked like brand new climbing rope slung over its top. The four of us walked along the main road passing Old Gwennie's, which was set well back from where we walked and it couldn't be seen unless you knew what you were looking for.

Before we reached Hendre and the quarry, we climbed over a small stone wall and walked across handkerchief field, a small meadow adjacent to the main road. Crossing the field we headed towards the quarry stream, which quietly flowed from the end of the tunnel under the old disused railway line. Carefully stepping from rock to rock, we crossed over its waters, with startled trout flashing and darting to the imagined safety of their rocks.

The stream that ran in front of the quarry flowed by the side of the main road, joining the stream from the Italian Woods just after Old Gwennie's. Her old, almost derelict cottage stood in the fork between both streams.

There was an abundance of trout in front of the quarry, but 'Mogg', the grumpy old foreman, would chase away anyone he saw near the stream. Most of the lads from the village wouldn't fish there, but sometimes Hefyn and I would walk through the long brick tunnel leading under the old railway line and, keeping out of sight below the banks of the stream, we would quietly fish all day in front of the quarry.

Crossing the stream near the entrance to the tunnel, we climbed over the old railway line, then up the steep hillside towards the cliffs hidden by thickets of hazel trees. In effect we were entering the far end of the 'Italian Woods' but we reasoned we would be safe, with the darkest parts of the woods, cliffs and steep walks between us and whatever it had been staring from other side of the Ruby Pool.

The path led steeply up towards the bottom of a tall cliff where Hefyn threw the rucksack on the floor and we all sat about on the boulders that were strewn about at the base of the sheer rock-face. We sat there looking out between and over the trees, down into the world below.

The day was hot and beat down on the rock, which in turn reflected its heat onto us. As we sat there, watching small cars winding along the thin track of the main road far below us, we relaxed in our new surroundings and slowly began to soak up the atmosphere of the day.

Hefyn opened the bag and got the slings out, fixing them around our waists and legs, joining the ends together with carabineers. Hefyn and I had climbed there before, Megan had done some climbing at school, but Anne had never climbed before. So we sat for a while talking to Anne, explaining some of the procedures and technicalities. No 'free climbing', purely 'top roping'. We knew our limitations and had no wish to take any risks with the girls there.

I took time to help Anne, wrapping the slings around her legs and waist, joining them with a carabineer at the front.

"I'll help Anne!" I heard Megan say, from somewhere behind me.

"It's alright, I've got it!" I said quickly, as I was placing the sling around Anne's waist. We were both enjoying the attention I was paying her. Looking around I saw a grin on Megan's face and as she saw me looking she laughed.

The cliff was about seventy feet high and for the most part was reasonably easy climbing, but close to the top you could split your climb into three different routes. The climb straight up led past what looked like a large crack in the rock, big enough to fit yourself in; like a chimney with one of its sides missing. It stretched up for about twenty feet, opening out at the top. The chimney got wider the higher it went and it took good technique and some strength to wedge yourself inside it sufficiently to climb out onto the top ledge. On the other side there was an overhang, which leaned out from the rock face, just below the top. The overhang had good handholds and a reasonably accomplished, technical climber, would find it easy to climb, although it would quickly sap your strength if you took too much time or deliberated too long.

Hefyn scrambled up around the side of cliff, holding onto the branches of the trees to help him out onto the top. He fixed the slings around two large fir trees just back from the edge, joining the ends with a carabineer. Feeding the rope through it, he dropped it over the edge, where we sat waiting.

I climbed first, with Hefyn belaying me and as I climbed I could hear him talking to Anne, explaining to her the techniques I was using as I quickly made my way up the rock face, towards the chimney. Climbing inside, placing my back hard against one of its walls, I pushed one of my feet onto the opposite rock face with my other foot firmly on the rock just below me. I must have looked like some giant grasshopper, wedged in the crack of a wall. Changing the positions of my hands and feet, pushing against both rock faces, constantly keeping my body and limbs taut, I quickly climbed to the top.

Once at the top I leaned back on the rope, with Hefyn holding it tight across the Italian hitch running through his carabineer. I held out my arms and he lowered me, the rope smoothly passing through the carabineer and I walked back down the rock face to where Anne anxiously awaited her turn to climb.

In those days we didn't possess even the simplest of climbing equipment, our belay loops were formed by tying an Italian hitch through our carabineers. It was a crude adaptation, but very safe and effective for the type of climbing we did, besides which, we knew no different.

Anne was a natural climber, with her feet and fingers finding good grip and purchase in the small clefts and faults in the rock. She seemed at home on our almost sheer, little rock face. Stepping carefully into the chimney she made the climb to the top look easy. She was slightly more hesitant when leaning out on the rope to come back down, but once at the bottom it was all we could do to stop her going straight up again. We took it in turns to climb and on Anne's second attempt she climbed across to the overhang. I was amazed at her strength and natural ability as she pulled herself up and out at the top.

We exhausted ourselves on the rock and with our forearms throbbing, Anne and I scrambled around to the top of the cliff. I pulled the rope up, tying one end into the slings with a re-woven figure of eight. Attaching it to the carabineer at my waist with an Italian hitch, I prepared to abseil back down the cliff.

Leaning out from the rock face with all my weight purchased against the rope, my body was almost horizontal. I paused as I stood out on the cliff face, looking straight into Anne's eyes as she sat on the ground in front of me.

Whispering quietly, I said,

"See you in a minute". She smiled and gave a little wave. Jumping out, I let the rope run loosely through my hand and Anne disappeared from view.

I dropped to the bottom of the cliff in large bounds, looking constantly for my next footing. Once down we spent the next half hour taking turns to abseil down the cliff. The last person to abseil would wait at the bottom, holding the rope ready to put on a brake in case the person following ran into difficulties.

With our hands red-hot and raw and with large patches of sweat seeping through our T-shirts, we all sat at the top looking out over the world once more. It was beautiful. We were almost too high for the sounds of the cars on the road beneath to reach us and could only hear a slight drone. Gazing out over the tops of the fir and hazel, we could clearly see Hefyn's farm high on the other side of the valley, with his father out in the fields. Carlo, Hefyn's dog, was trotting alongside the tractor following Uncle John up and down the field.

Looking carefully across the valley, my eyes strained to pick out details of the cave deep in Graig-y- Jingles, whose thick trees rose up on the opposite side of the road.

Hefyn looked at me with a smile on his face and said

"Let's run down the cliff" I looked back at him, knowing what he meant and he could sense my hesitation as I smiled back at him.

"Come on then." I said,

"Who's going first?" He pointed at me saying,

"You can," Grinning as he said it.

"You fall better than me!" Anne gave me a questioning look, but seemed to relax a little when I smiled back at her. We were showing off, but it felt good, and the girls were enjoying it.

I retied the slings around my waist and over my shoulders, so the carabineer was positioned at the back. I also tied a sling around my chest for extra protection, joining both at the rear of my waist. The girls looked at both of us as though we were mad, not knowing what we were about to do. I stood at the edge of the cliff, adjusting the slings higher onto the fir trees and making sure they were fully secure as the others climbed back down to the bottom. I tied myself onto the rope with the carabineer at the back.

I could see Hefyn down below tying the rope to his waist, making sure there was enough slack and then looking back up at me; he walked slowly backwards, testing the brake. Walking forwards again placing his hands on the rope above his head, he called up to me.

"Ready?" Still looking down at him, my eyes carefully following everything he did, I called back down,

"Ready"

I paused, looking out over the world with the adrenaline and anticipation rushing through me. In that moment I was invincible; an Eternal Warrior this world could not contain and I knew without any doubt, at that moment, I could not be taken. Standing there with the breeze on my face, I knew that if I leaned forwards spreading my wings, I would've been lifted high into the air to soar on the back of the wind.

Looking back through all the uncertainty of this life, I still think of how I felt in that moment, so sure of myself, nothing shaken. It was a feeling I often had as a child and when growing up; a feeling of being able to go anywhere, conquer anything, climb any height and run any distance.

Looking back down at Anne, who was standing next to Hefyn, I raised my arms like wings and leaned forward. Hefyn pulled the rope taut, applying the brake, prevented me from moving further out. He then released the rope slightly and with my feet firmly on the rock face he lowered me, until I was standing on the rock face, parallel to the ground.

I was staring down the cliff-face at the girls and Hefyn, all of whom were looking back up at me. Spreading my arms out again and I nodded at Hefyn and he raised his hands. The rope instantly ran slack, allowing the brake to fall free. I plummeted down the cliff face my legs running as fast as they could, the only control over my speed the friction of the rope running through the carabineer. The wind blew through my hair as I sprinted past branches and rocks in my vertical world. Hefyn gradually applied pressure back onto the rope, causing me to slow and eventually stop, just above him.

I was shaking as I untied myself from the rope and although I hadn't exerted any effort or energy in the fall, I was sweating profusely and I baulked at myself, the 'Eternal Worrier' shaking in the valley below. Hefyn went next, Megan refused a turn, but Anne was eager to have a go. She wanted me to be the brakeman and so Hefyn went up to the top to make sure she was tied in correctly and explaining to her precisely what to do.

She leaned trustingly out as I started to lower her into position, until she was standing out from the cliffs edge. Then slowly releasing the brake she walked down the rock face. As her confidence grew, I increased the speed until eventually she was trying to run faster than my care for her would allow.

When Anne was almost at the bottom, I pulled firmly on the rope and she stood, suspended in mid-air just above me with her feet firmly in place on the cliff. Her hair hung free and still keeping the rope tight, I stepped underneath her with her hair falling all around me. Gradually I lowered her towards me. Anne placed her arms around the back of my neck and pulling me into her, we kissed and slowly letting the brake off, Anne's feet gradually dropped to the ground and we stood there tightly entwined; tied one into the other, kissing as if it would last forever.

"You two!" Megan trotted her tongue against the roof of her mouth.

"Have you seen this Hefyn?" She called out.

"Leave them alone!" Hefyn said as he reached the bottom of the cliff. Megan began to pack away. Anne and I reluctantly dragged ourselves from each other's arms and scrambled to the top, untying the rope and slings. We dropped them down to the others, who packed all the kit back into the bag. I watched as they walked off down through the trees towards the stream. Calling back up, saying they would wait for us near the brick tunnel.

Anne and I sat looking at each other and then out across into the world. I could clearly see the breast of the mountain from where we sat and I thought of my grandmother's family, living, working, laughing, crying and dying; safely suckled in the bosom of their own little mountain home.

Sitting there, I wondered how much of my life would be spent under its careful gaze and more importantly, how much of it would be spent with Anne? In a few short weeks, she had begun to mean so much to me and already I desperately wanted more. More than either of us could give at that time.

Anne leaned towards me and whispered,

"This is my place; I didn't want to say anything with the others here". I looked at her and she looked straight into me, saying,

"I come here when I want to think and be alone". I looked around and orientating myself within the landscape, I realised, we were only a few hundred yards walk through the woods from her farm.

"It's a lovely place!" I said quietly, thoughts turning over in my mind.

"I don't think I have a place…not like this, anyway!" I said at a whisper, putting my arm around her. She smiled her safe, warm, comforting smile and I could see that Anne knew what I was thinking.

"You can share my place then!" Anne said, taking my free hand in hers, interlocking her fingers in mine.

"Why didn't you say something earlier?" I asked, looking up at her.

"We could have climbed somewhere else". I felt an almost tragic sense of reverence, as if our climb had trespassed into somewhere sacred.

Anne smiled.

"That's all right," she said understandingly and thinking far beyond my thoughts.

"I think it will probably add something new to my dreams and memories here"

I thought then, of how many times Hefyn and I had climbed the cliff before and of how Anne had been drawn there.

After a while we rose without having kissed and walked down to where Hefyn and Megan were waiting for us. Megan was sitting in front of Hefyn on a large boulder in the middle of the stream. Hefyn had his arms wrapped around and through Megan's as though they were tied in some sacred knot. Megan's head was leaning back on Hefyn's shoulder. She looked almost disappointed to see us, as if we were intruding into their space and time together.

"Let's go through the tunnel towards the quarry" Hefyn said, rising from their perch. He hid his bag behind the wall of the tunnel, but before he left it there, he opened the top and, reaching inside, brought out an old, chipped, white-enamelled tin plate.

"What on earth is that for?" I said, with a puzzled look on my face.

CHAPTER TEN

"There's gold in them-there hills!" Hefyn said, making a half decent attempt at an American accent. I laughed, catching how his mind worked.

Hefyn was right; my grandfather had often told us of the quarry men and miners finding small bits of gold, but their finds were few and far between. Two of my mother's cousins had owned the gold mine on Moel Fammau. They ran there mining consortium from the White Horse, in the village of Cilcain, but it never made their fortune and only mined enough gold to keep their families, the mine, and the men in drink for the weekend.

"Mining was a young man's game" Taid used to say.

We started to walk through the long tunnel. It was pointless trying to step from rock to rock. It was too dark, so we just waded through the water with it immediately soaking into our pumps and jeans.

Reaching the far end of the tunnel we quietly crept along the stream, stopping just in front of the quarry offices, the place where Hefyn fancied his chances at 'panning for gold'. Where better to plonk yourself than right under Old Mogg's nose. Sitting on the large rocks surrounding the pool, we watched in amazement as he scooped plates full of mud and small bits of gravel from the bed of the stream and rinsed it under the small waterfall at the head of pool, he would scour through his plate, looking and fingering at his imagined treasure trove. Sighing constantly, he washed the plate off and went digging in the stream again.

We sat there grinning, sometimes laughing at his sighs. His growing frustration showed as he fingered each plateful of mud and gravel, with disappointment written all over his face at his empty platter. He continued in this fashion for about ten minutes, when all of a sudden, he picked something off the plate and forgetting where we were, he shouted.

"I'm rich!" Throwing the plate up in the air he walked across the pool with water splashing as he did so. He came to where I sat on a large rock with Anne snuggled up close to me. Holding out a dark piece of shiny faceted metal about the size of my thumbnail, he said,

"I've struck gold mate!"

I examined the piece of metal. It was certainly heavy, but it was almost black in colour with small shiny facets. The gold Hefyn had found was almost identical in colour and texture to the chunk of lead my grandfather kept on the mantelpiece.

"I think its lead" I said, trying to show some sympathy in my voice.

"It looks the same as that piece of lead Taid Hughes keeps on the Mantelpiece." His shoulders dropped at my words.

It was enough to get our attention though and we all enthusiastically looked, scratching through the gravel in the clouded waters for whatever we could find. Anne found a small piece of iron pyrites, which looked a little more authentic. Then Megan called out and showed us all a large chunk of calcite crystal. It was almost perfectly formed and after she had washed it in the stream we all stood around admiring it.

Hefyn continued to work frantically, digging and washing the enamel plate with Anne and I moving further upstream; turning our attentions to the trout, but it was almost impossible with the noise Hefyn was making.

"I've got some!" he said out loud. I walked down to him as he picked something up from the plate and holding it between his finger and thumb, he dipped it in the water, raising it up for me to examine. It was certainly more the colour I expected gold to be and was about half the size of the piece of lead he had found.

"It certainly looks more like it!" I said, the girls gathering around us. We spent the next hour looking frantically for more, but the claim we had staked was all panned out.

"YOU LOT!" A voice boomed out from the quarry. It was Mogg, running full tilt towards us. We quickly ran downstream, to where it led back through the thick undergrowth of the woods and we were soon out of sight walking through the damp darkness of the tunnel again. Collecting Hefyn's bag, we walked back across the field towards the road.

Hefyn suddenly called out.

"Megan, be mine". He got down on one knee and holding the piece of gold out and up towards Megan. She said,

"Forever!" Clutching at the gold and then his hand; Megan held both tight against her chest.

They did the whole Romeo and Juliet routine, in a sarcastic charade, re-enacting my giving the crystal to Anne. But Anne just held my hand tightly and looked straight into me. She smiled and then kissed me.

"Can you sneak out tonight?" She asked me. Pulling slightly away from her, I looked straight into her eyes and could see she was serious.

"Maybe!" I said softly.

"Maybe isn't good enough," She said, sounding assertive, but a large smile inched onto her face drawing me in.

"My place…on top of the cliff…tonight." My mind was racing and my whole body tingled with those same feelings I had felt rising inside me as we both sketched the sea lions. The thought of meeting her that night mauled at my mind and I vowed to myself that, no matter what the cost, I would be there.

"All right!" I said, whispering, so the others couldn't hear,

"I'll be here as close to eleven as I can make it!"

CHAPTER ELEVEN

The last remnants of light were being brushed from the sky as I climbed the hill towards Hefyn's. I looked out at the breast of the mountain just before turning down Parry Lane; it was nothing more than a looming shadow, but its presence brought me some comfort in the night. I felt a sliver of guilt being out of the house without anyone, but my brother Andy, knowing. Of course Nain would know, somehow, she always knew.

I looked up at the moon, which was full and bright, and like a 'moon man', I stole down the back lane; a thief in the night. Dodging shadows, I ran, straining to see my footfall. At the bottom, I paused, looking across at the 'Italian woods' and the 'Ruby Brick.' There was a single dim light burning at the edge of the woods. I looked closer.

'Old Gwennie's' I thought to myself.

Quickly crossing the road, I made my way to Handkerchief Field with the occasional passing car lighting my way.

Walking through the meadow, towards the stream, I could hear the rush of its waters, singing eyrie songs to the haunted night. The moon reflected across its surface, painting a halo of white on the uppermost edges of the damp rocks. Too dark for me to see, trout flitted to and fro, hunting moths that had been tempted by the moons reflections. They fluttered frantically, caught in the net of the Moon's light fantastic. Struggling, drowning, dying, they flickered across the moon soaked surface of the stream. A trout sipped then rolled, splashing and with a flick of its tail, the moth was gone.

I looked up into the already sleeping woods, which opened one eye to see who was walking by. I could just make out the top of the cliff highlighted by the silver light of the moon between the trees. The sky was clear with stars thronging its galleries. The silver apple of the moon seemed to distil its light on everything it surveyed.

Stepping from rock to rock, I crossed over the stream into the darkness of the woods. I began to climb the steep slope, past fir, hazel and beech, until I stood at the bottom of the cliff where we had climbed that day. Moving to one side, I started to scramble around the edge, clinging to branches and stepping carefully on large tufts of grass. My eyes were soon peering through the darkness, looking, searching in anticipation, wondering if Anne would be sitting quietly at the top.

"You're puffing and panting like an old man!" Anne called out and although still out of sight, I could see the smile on her face. Not getting any response from me, she baited her hook and cast her line out again.

"You took your time then, waiting for Mummy to kiss you good night, is it?" She dangled the bait in front of me, putting on a pronounced Welsh accent, as if somehow it would lure me closer. In my mind, I could see the smile broadening on her face, as she continued to tease me.

I was desperate to warm myself at the fire that glowed in the catch-light of her eyes.

We had all been playing whist again, and I couldn't get away until everyone had gone to bed. I paused near the top with Anne still out of sight.

"I always seem to be waiting for you" Anne continued, the bait too tempting and I bit, feeling the hook barb into me.

"What do you mean?" I said rather defensively, but not really wishing to hear the answer, half realising what she might say.

"A whole week I had to wait for you to kiss me!" She said curtly, still out of sight.

"Well I was..."

"Scared…Hefyn told Megan!"

"Hefyn…!" I sighed,

"Some mate he turned out to be" I continued, as I wriggled caught fast as Anne started to reel me in.

"Even then I had to kiss you!"

"What do you mean, I kissed you!" I said, righteously.

"Oh yes, but I had to lead you by the hand, didn't I?" I was dumbstruck, remembering how much I had hesitated to hold her hand for the first time. I was still caught fast and Anne's words, barbed deeper into me. I was trying to swim to the safety of the rocks at the bottom of my pool, not wanting to hear anymore.

"You were walking that close to me, pushing me closer and closer to the hedge, I had to grab hold of you to stop myself being run into the ditch."

Not making the rocks at the bottom of my pool, she hauled me up, keeping my head out of the water, as she dragged me across the surface of the pool towards her.

"I virtually had to throw myself at you!" I remained silent as Anne continued.

"I even asked my Mum why you hadn't kissed me!"

"Your Mum…oh great, this just gets better!" Outraged, I blurted the words out. Anne guiding me into her net and with her catch securely landed, I heard her laughing, as she surveyed her prise, gasping for water.

"Very funny" I said, pulling myself out on top of the cliff with the help of a large branch from the Hazel.

Anne sat on a Welsh-woollen blanket with a smile on her face, immediately drawing me in, quenching any hurt feelings.

She was wearing a long, thick, patterned cardigan and her faded jeans. The cardigan was wrapped tightly around her, tied at the waist with a thick woollen belt. It had a large collar, which Anne had pulled up around her neck in the nights chill. Her arms seemed to be entangled inside it as she hugged it tightly to her body. Seeing her sitting there, with her long hair drowned in the moons silver glow, I was overwhelmed. A Pre-Raphaelite vision and a sudden tremor ran through me. She looked incredible and those new feelings quickly swelled inside me. Anne patted the blanket next to her and opening the front of her cardigan out, I sat down, snuggling up to the warmth of her body.

"I'm sorry," I said, whispering to her.

"Have you been here long?" I asked trying to sound genuine, but the uncertainty I had felt as she teased crept back in.

"Not long, Dad was up doing his books."

I lay back on the blanket and Anne cuddled up next to me, under my arm, spreading the lip of her open cardigan over me, as if to keep me warm, but the fire burning in her eyes was enough.

"It was quite scary walking through the woods" she said, quietly turning to look up at the sky. I then realised that she would have walked through some of the darkest parts of the Italian Woods, with the thought of a wild dog stalking her.

The silvery moon spun its light, draping it across the breasted mountain. Innumerable stars looked down where we lay, amid the spires of the mountain's rocky temple. The wood sat quietly behind us, watching intently as in turn we pointed up at different stars and constellations, naming each one as we did so, Orion, the Big Dipper and following over to the North Star, which was barely in view above the trees.

A small streaking glow tore across the sky, burning brightly then fading as it dwindled and died. A shooting star, we had both seen it. The brilliance of its short life struck us with awe and I thought of how many billions of light years it had travelled through space and time, only to end its existence in one fleeting moment.

I don't think I had ever felt so calm, and yet at the same time, my mind was so stirred and I struggled, as trying to comprehend my own feelings.

I gently took Anne's hand in mine and she wrapped me in her arms. I was helpless, a willing captive, and I had the overwhelming feeling that Anne and I had been born to live in that moment. It felt as though our being together was fulfilling promises we had made to each other, way back on the path, in another time, another place, long before our lives here ever began.

I looked at Anne, lying on her side next to me with one of her legs hooked over mine. She was already looking back at me as though she could hear and understand what I was thinking. She smiled and my feelings tumbled down stream and I knew we would find our very own path through the forests of life.

Anne took the crystal out of her pocket and held it up in front of us. The light from the moon filtered through it, catching its many facets. The white flecks inside the crystal glistened like stars. I could see a whole universe revolving within it, as Anne slowly turned the crystal around. The stars in the heavens seemed to glow from every facet.

"I've never seen anything like it!" she said, softly to the patiently waiting woods.

"It's beautiful."

I turned towards her brushing her hair from her face with one of my fingers and in a whisper, I said,

"And so are you!"

"I look at it, at night, before I go to sleep and I dream of you!" Anne said softly, causing the stream inside me to tumble over its rocks once more.

The trees seemed to crowd in around us, not wishing to miss a word. Anne sighed with her breathing becoming shallow and rolling over, half on top of me; we looked into each other. All the stars in the night sky seemed to reflect in her eyes. I pulled her towards me and we started to kiss. I could taste her, as our tongues played and explored. I could feel her hands as they tightened around me. Her soft lips plucked at my face as I kissed her neck. I continued to kiss her neck and then drowned her under a sea of kisses. Our kissing became unquenchable, as our tongues once more found their mate. I pulled her closer into me and I could feel her body close to mine, the cardigan and her thin T-shirt not concealing anything from me.

I held her desperately close, feeling every part of her as our bodies explored distant possibilities. The stream inside me surged forward, pushing me, ever closer to her and I could feel her wanting me, as if the two streams inside us would burst their banks.

We kissed for what seemed like hours, exploring unspoken feelings, searching, wanting. I wanted more, more of Anne Jones from the farm above the Italian Woods, and I could sense that Anne's feelings were swimming down the same turbulent river. We were wrapped up in each other, two pieces from different jigsaws, which seemed to fit perfectly, each inside the other and if it had been possible, I think I would have climbed inside her.

I slowly worked my hand inside her cardigan, feeling her warm body through her T-shirt. I moved my hand slowly across her back, fingers gently rubbing, massaging and caressing. I ran them down her side, slowly tracing the outline of her body. Rasping the backs of my finger nails along the seam of her T-shirt. And as I did so, I felt a tremor run through her.

My hand cupped around her hip, lingering and exploring tempting possibilities, but strong currents from the river of feelings inside me were too much and I turned to go but, in my turning, I stayed.

Anne was pulling me closer and our kisses felt as though they would never exhaust themselves. The trees that had crowded in around us held their breath, turning their heads to quietly slip away; leaving us in our private and secret moment together.

My fingers retraced their steps up Anne's side and around to the top of her back. They stumbled over her bra strap where they fumbled through her T-shirt and it was undone with a twist of my fingers.

Our kisses became almost desperate as I found her soft warm skin in the gap between her T-shirt and jeans, causing a tremor to quickly run through, both of us. I had anticipated and longed for the moment since those uncertain feelings had risen inside me, while sketching the inseparable and unlikely lovers at the zoo. I had thought of how her skin would feel next to mine, how my hand would cup over her hip. I had watched her the day we went swimming in the 'Ruby Pool', with my feelings surging inside me, but that night on the cliff top my feelings were running out of control.

My hand moved gradually over her flat taught stomach, tracing her forbidden wastelands. My head was pounding, my hand shaking, as I placed it on her flat warm stomach and I felt her wriggle in a spasm of delight, but the bolt of feelings inside me was too much.

Holding my hand still, my heart beat a retreat. In the confusion my mind, I mulled over further possibilities. I could feel her taut firm muscles under her soft belly skin. My fore finger found her belly button and I traced an endless circle around it. I was tempted in that moment to lift her belly-skin and roll it back, to explore all her sunken treasures.

Arching her back, she pushed herself against me. We both wanted more. She pushed again and again. We were lost in each other, lost forever, with Anne laying on her back sighing and breathing low as my hand moved further up her stomach. Feeling her ribs beneath them the rush of blood in my head made me dizzy. I whispered softly in her ear,

"I love you, Anne Jones, from the farm above the Italian Woods!"

We were both trembling as we kissed. Anne started to whisper quietly in my ear as she gently pressed herself against me again and again. I couldn't make out what she was saying, but her whispering was like the rhythm of a poem. I heard something like, 'you're here inside'. It didn't matter. Her words silently rushed through me and I thought I was going to burst under the pressure.

My hand moved higher and froze as it touched the edge of her bra. An ocean of waves pounded and crashed inside me; over me, through me, but the pressure from the surge of the stream was too much and my hand turned away, moving around to Anne's back, where it hid itself, not daring to move again. It lay there quiet and still, frightened of losing the touch of Anne beneath it, but it didn't dare to explore those distant possibilities again.

"Sorry…" I whispered.

"I so want this to be right!"

Her smile filled the void between us. She lay silently in my arms, with both our feelings settling.

My senses slowly woke and I realised I had fallen asleep. Anne was still sleeping and I lay there listening to her breathing.

We lay under the stars with the soft moonlight draped over us. I tried to imagine the thrill of falling asleep together for the rest of our lives. Anne stirred slightly and then opened her eyes.

"Hello sleepy head!" I said and we smiled together.

"I want to fall asleep with you at my side for the rest of my life!"

"We will!" The thought seemed to empty from us and one thought followed another as we whispered words I cannot write.

The relentless press of time forged ever on with the slow grey light of dawn seeping into the sky as the moon faded and slowly set behind the trees of the wood.

We moved and sat on top of the cliff with our legs over hanging the edge. Anne lent forward slightly, and reaching behind her, she clasped her bra back together. I tentatively smiled up at her. She smiled back and said,

"When the time is right we will continue this conversation!" I breathed the thought slowly in and held her gaze.

"David, I think I'm falling in love with you…" She paused slightly,

"If we take our time, I know we will get this right!"

We began to talk, slowly at first. We took our time and shared our hopes and dreams between us. Nothing would get in our way. Our journeys towards each other were complete; leaving our journey together, ahead of us.

Hand in hand we walked back through the quietly waking woods. We followed a familiar trail up to 'bottom field' under the old beech. Holding each other, looking, wanting, but in our wanting there was time. Our hearts were wet with the morning dew.

"You're beautiful…!" I said, I meant so much more. The words were there, but I was lost in my thoughts and dreams.

"How I wish…I wish we could be together, forever!" I almost stuttered the words out.

Anne looked deep into me and buried her head in my neck, as she whispered, "Forever!"

We had just spent our first night together, and I wanted more; I wanted more than my young life could give. I stepped back from her. She smiled, looking back at me, gently taking my hand in hers, she placed the forefinger of her other hand gently over my lips. Leaning forward we kissed, a long lingering slow kiss. Eventually our lips parted and she turned to go, but then turned again. We stood there, only her eyes disturbing the silence. She looked majestic, almost stately, with the blanket wrapped round her; like some Celtic Princess. I was transfixed in the moment, unable to move. The morning mists seemed to surround her in a halo of light.

I can't remember you turning away, but I do remember watching you walking back up the field towards the farm and in that moment, I realised how hopelessly and desperately in love I was. But somehow it seemed our youth was conspiring against us. Standing there, watching, I wondered if I had the strength to hold it all together. I thought of the night and my thoughts gave way to dreams and in my waking dreams, I was wandering up the field at your side. There was only one way to end such a night and that was arm in arm, as lovers. I pondered on my dreams and slowly came to the realisation that they would soon be a reality.

I remember, you turned, and looked back at me, before disappearing between the Shippon and the barn. You smiled that warm, soft, smile of yours' and then turned to go with a little wave of your hand.

I climbed the wall back into the woods. I didn't yet have the power to order my own life; I was too young, too young to stay, as the night ended.

I ran through the woods, down the rocky staircase of the stream, feet quickly stepping rock to rock, as I cursed the strong currents that swirled around me in the waters of life. At the bottom of the woods, I stepped slowly under the bridge past Old Gwennie's, not daring to look back.

The morning broke into the backyard of Nain's bungalow, with Nain waiting for me on the back step, a welcoming smile on her face.

"Your mother's not up yet, Cariad" she said, placing her finger to her lips. I helped her to set the fire and fell asleep over breakfast, in the middle of the wide-awake house.

CHAPTER TWELVE

I had become an instant celebrity in the village. Anne had told one of her friends about my dive 'into the deep' and shown her the crystal. She had told Rhiannon not to tell anybody, so, of course, everyone got to hear. Even I had to admit that it was an incredible find, but people were talking about 'pearl diving' and swimming to the bottom of a mineshaft with only a stone as ballast.

Tebbutt seemed to be avoiding me, which didn't bother me one bit.

One morning, I got Taid's old bike, a boneshaker, out of his ramshackle wooden shed. Both tyres were flat and one of them was slightly perished on its edge, but it looked like it would hold. My brother Andy and I had been eyeing it up for years, but I was the first to it. By the time Andy saw it, I had mended a puncture, blown up both tyres and was fiddling with the brakes. Andy was watching me and suggesting places we could go on it when Anne came round the corner of the yard. The first I knew of her presence was her laugh.

I looked up at her through the spokes of one of the wheels and smiled. I spun the wheel to check it was true. She was wearing jeans, with a white lacy top - broderie anglaise I think she called it - and a pair of brown, round-toed, covered sandals. Although the top was baggy, its thin material didn't hide the outline of her figure and my imagination did the rest. I couldn't take my eyes off her. Her hair tumbled down the centre of her back where it had been tied with two thin strands of hair she had plaited from the side of her head. In her hand she carried a sketchpad and a small box, which I assumed carried pencils or paints or maybe both. Anne's face shone in the sunlight.

"You look gorgeous!" I said, stopping what I was doing and standing for a moment.

"You always say that!"

"Well you always do!"

"I think you would still say it if I was buried up to my neck in muck" Her eyes sparked as she spoke. The thought was tantalizing and I grinned back at her.

"Well…!" I thought twice before saying nothing, especially with Andy there and I looked across at him.

"Don't mind me!" He said with a smile.

"Don't even go there!" Anne finished the conversation raising a finger towards me.

Turning my attention back to the bike I asked,

"Coming for a ride?" Andy made himself scarce.

"You don't think I'm going on that thing…I wouldn't be seen dead….!" I smiled again, knowing she was open to the idea.

The hill outside Nain's was very steep and down was the only real option until I was a little surer of the bikes capabilities. I had placed our sketching stuff in an old gas mask pouch of Taid's', which I had hung over one shoulder. Anne made a token protest, but willingly climbed up behind me. The saddle was one of those old fashioned leather ones and I had spent about half an hour polishing with saddle soap until it shone like knew. There were one or two small areas of rust, but they had cleaned up quite well.

"They don't make bikes like they used to!" Nain had said while passing one time in the yard and I repeated her words to Anne.

"Thank goodness!" I heard her whisper under her breath.

"You what?" I called out, teasing her as the bike began to pick up speed.

The hill was steep and I had miscalculated the adjustment on the brakes. I had tested them in the yard, but with Anne's arrival, I had been distracted. We had quite a head of steam when we hit the corner and coming out the other side we were facing our first obstacle, two land rovers, parked side by side in the middle of the road. It was Uncle John and Megan's father, one going down to the village and the other coming back up. Both drivers' windows where down. They were both deep in conversation and they didn't see us. I don't know if Anne had seen them, but I guessed from the way she gripped onto my sides that she had.

I pulled on the brakes, but nothing happened. I pulled on them some more; still nothing.

"Hold on!" I called out, but Anne already had her arms, clasped tightly around my waist. I dropped forward putting one of my feet on the floor to try to assist the brakes, but steering was the only thing that would save us and at the speed we were travelling steering was nigh on impossible.

How we missed them, I don't know. I think at the last moment I closed my eyes and somehow we squeezed through. My shoulder hit Uncle John's wing mirror as we careered between both vehicles and I could hear the dogs barking at us, but I hadn't seen them as we went sailing past.

Bet was waiting at the bottom of the hill, her arms hanging over the gates of Schoolhouse, with a concerned look on her face.

"You alright there, Anne?" she said while opening the gate and stepping towards us to check if she was.

"I never saw anything like that in my life!"

'Never mind strangers, what about your dear nephew?' I thought, but Anne seemed to be every one's darling.

"David Bach looking after you then?" Bet asked giving me a look, knowing the danger I had just placed her in. Bet had some tools and after some running repairs we were on our wobbly way again.

"Now you be careful! I don't like…!" We were out of hearing before Bet could tell me off again.

I was gaining confidence and pulled on the brakes a couple of times to help Anne's'. We made our way past Kath's and out towards the Stat meter and the river. I turned over the bridge and started the climb up past the Twm-path towards the built up hedges and thin, winding lanes that led past the common. In the end the steep hill got the better of me and forced us to dismount and walk.

Anne was full of the summer, full of life as she skipped up the hill. Bon vivant; the French seem to have the words for every occasion, certainly where the fairer sex is concerned. I watched her while pushing the bike up the hill. She disappeared around a corner and as she came back into view, I found her picking at something in the hedgerow; wild strawberries. The banks of the Twm-path were full of them and we spent a while, picking and eating great hands full of them. When the strawberries dried up we spent some time standing in the middle of the lane, sharing strawberry flavoured kisses, with my hands exploring the lacy frills at the edges of Anne's top.

On top of the common we took out our sketchpads and paints and sat painting the mountain, with farmyards and fields in the foreground. Anne was indeed an excellent watercolourist, keeping her landscapes simple, without any clutter; letting the water do most of the work. Her painting seemed to be full of light, capturing the full majesty and atmosphere of our mother mountain, the Mitchell's farm and the fields. Having exhausted the view we then turned our attention to each other and I tried my best to capture Anne's wild beauty, in a pencil sketch. I spent as much time on it as I could; trying to make it perfect.

My eyes worked from the paper to Anne and back to the paper. I allowed myself the luxury of long pauses: staring for long moments. I stopped drawing momentarily, and told her how incredibly beautiful she was. My eyes followed the contours of her skin, her mouth, her nose, and her eyes; always looking, searching, losing myself in her image and the sketch began to breathe life onto the page. I can remember being slightly embarrassed about how much I stared and how little I drew, but she seemed to wallow in the attention and smiled as I told her how lovely she was. The finished drawing was pretty poor, but Anne said nice things about it and begged me to give it to her.

The following morning I had to baby-sit while Carole, Mum and Nain went into town. Anne called around to help, with my younger brothers and sisters immediately falling in love with her all over again. We sat on the settee in the front room, with my sister Ann, Katie and Gareth surrounding her constantly, leaving me struggling to get close. I sat with her at arms length, my sister Ann between us. I stretched my arm over towards her with my fingers at the back of her neck, gently rubbing and playing with her hair. She always had an easy way about her and nothing seemed to fluster her.

Anne told the children stories of giant's, witches and fairies that had once inhabited the woods around Rhydymwyn. She started to talk quietly, with great emphasis and concern, as if the children's very-lives depended on what she was saying.

"Old Gwennie is the meanest, maddest, ugliest, most evil Witch in the whole of Wales!" She drew great gasps and deep breaths from Katie and Anne, but Gareth just said,

"I don't believe in Witches!" He always was an awkward child.

The girls were caught, captivated, they surrounded her and getting slightly impatient, even protective, I tried, in vain, to keep them at bay, but Anne just smiled, saying, she didn't mind.

"Is Old Gwennie really a witch?" Katie asked, while placing her thumb in her mouth, hooking her forefinger over the top of her nose as she settled down. Katie's long blond hair was a stark contrast to Anne's rich dark tresses.

"What does she look like?" My sister Ann asked, with a worried look on her face.

"No one in the village has ever seen her. They even had to get the police from Denbigh to go to her house when she chased Tebbutt through the woods. 'Old handcuff' in the village was too afraid!"

"Really?" Gareth asked. She had even drawn him in and he was caught up in Anne's world of magic and make-believe.

"What people don't realise is Old Gwennie had a son. Some people say he was a giant, but a more perfect looking young giant you couldn't have found anywhere!" Katie was sucking merrily on her thumb while Ann was snuggled in between us. Gareth sat on the end of the settee, fidgeting and scratching, but even he remained caught up in the web of the tale Anne steadily spun between us.

"Old Gwennie, the meanest, maddest, ugliest, most evil Witch in the whole of Wales, was so jealous; she used to keep her son, Hugh the giant, chained up in the backyard. She would constantly tell him how ugly he was and that he should hide in his face in shame."

"He wasn't really ugly, was he Anne?" Katie said, not taking her thumb out of her mouth.

"No he wasn't!" Anne continued,

"In fact, Old Gwennie was the ugly one and when he was a young man, he became big and strong like David" Gareth laughed and they all looked at me. Anne had a smile painted on her face and she turned her head to look at me. I continued to play with her hair at the back of her neck, my fingers searching for the warmth of her soft pale skin.

"So when Old Gwennie was out foraging in the woods one day. Hugh took hold of the chains around his neck and pulled them clean out of the wall. He ran out of the yard, stepped straight over the stream in one bound and ran up the path, through the woods."

"Did he run away?" Ann asked.

"Yes, and as he ran through the wood, Old Gwennie was standing on the path with moss and toadstools gathered in her basket. Hugh shut his eyes as he ran straight past her, bumping into her as he went, knocking her to the ground!"

"Did she die?" Gareth asked, knowing full well that she lived down by the Ruby Brick. I wanted to 'call him', but I could see he was just enthralled, too involved in the story to realise the stupidity of his question.

"No, but she was angry and shouted, cursing after him.

" Everyone had questions. 'What happened?' 'How did he live?' 'What did he do?' 'How did he eat?'

"He lived in a cave, deep in the darkest part of the Wood, feeding himself on berries and mushrooms and sometimes fish from the stream."

"David eats mushrooms; he brings them back for breakfast!" Katie said still sucking on her thumb.

"And he catches fish!" Gareth said eager to be included in the conversation.

"Not very well though!" Anne said, with a grin on her face, I smiled back.

"And the mushrooms he eats are funny looking, aren't they?" Everybody laughed as Anne started her story again.

"Hugh the giant lived happily in the woods. He explored, climbing the cliffs and trees, some of which he cut down to make a table, chairs and a bed to sleep on. He was happy and never wanted to go home to be chained in the back yard again."

"Does he still live up in the woods?" My sister Ann asked,

"I'm going to tell you. Just wait and see!" Everyone settled down again.

"One day he was playing with the rabbits near his cave, when he heard something down on the pathway through the woods. Creeping as quietly as he could through the bushes and undergrowth, he lay on a ledge just above the path and waited in the bushes to see who was walking in the woods." I could see my sisters getting excited, Katie stopped sucking on her thumb, but it still remained in her mouth as she held her breath waiting to see what would happen next.

"Hugh lay quietly on the ledge, without making a sound. Then, down the path in the woods rode the most beautiful young lady, anyone had ever seen. She rode side-saddle, on a grey mare. Her hair was long and flowing, tumbling wildly down her back. It was the same blonde, almost white hair that hung down on her horse's mane and they appeared to flow together. Hugh the giant thought she looked like a fairy princess. She wore a long white flowing dress that draped over the dark leather saddle and down both sides of the horse. The saddle was decorated with gold and there were golden bells hanging from the bridle held delicately in her hands."

"Who was she?" Ann asked, excitedly. Ignoring her question, Anne continued with the story.

"She was beautiful; the sun shone through the trees and glistened on all the gold decorating the horse's saddle and bridle. The bells jingled, ringing as she went. Hugh the giant couldn't take his eyes off her. He was madly in love, from the moment he first saw her. He followed her as she rode through the woods, keeping quietly out of sight, hiding in the bushes and dark shadows beneath the trees, but when she had passed the old mine shaft he stopped following, not wanting to go too close to Old Gwennie's."

"Did he see her again?" Gareth asked

"She would often go riding through the woods and each time, Hugh the giant would watch her, falling deeply in love with her. Then one day, Hugh heard a commotion higher up in the woods. He made his way up the path to investigate. The fairy princess's horse came thundering down the path, galloping out of control, but the princess was nowhere in sight."

No one spoke a word, Katie had stopped sucking on her thumb once more and I could even feel the palms of my own hands perspiring.

"Hugh went running through the woods, searching for his secret love. He found her struggling to get out of a thicket of thorn bushes. She was crying with blood on her face that dripped into her eyes and down onto her flowing white gown. Her hands were stretched out in front of her as she blindly felt her way down the path through the woods. Remembering how Old Gwennie had told him how ugly he was, he kept just out of sight, but followed her to make sure she was safe."

"He wasn't really ugly, was he, Anne?" Gareth said, apparently quite concerned. "Shush!" The girls said almost simultaneously, and then Ann asked.

"Was she blind?"

"No, but she couldn't see with all the blood in her eyes. Hugh followed her through the woods and to his horror he realised she was walking straight towards the open mine shaft!"

"Hefyn and David throw rocks into the mine shaft, don't they?" Gareth half asked, sounding righteous.

"They certainly do!" Anne said, looking at me as if telling me off, in front of my brothers and sisters.

"It's dangerous isn't it, Anne?" Ann said, raising herself up from her cosy position between us.

"It certainly is!" Anne said, again looking at me, telling me off once more, and then continuing.

"Now, Hugh knew that the mineshaft was covered over with big wooden beams. But he also knew there was a gap between two of them, big enough to fall through. So not knowing what else to do, he ran down the path and holding his arms and legs out he put his huge body in the gap between them. Even though he was big the gap was bigger and he hadn't been able to fill the whole of it as he struggled to keep his grip on the damp beams."

"Did he fall?" Katie asked with the others grumbling at her interruption.

"The Princess stumbled closer and closer to the gap." Anne's voice became nothing more than a loud whisper, putting that same urgent emphasis on her words, which she had done at the beginning of the story.

"Hugh could see that the Princess was about to fall into the gap, so forgetting how ugly he was, he called out for her to stop. Holding up one of his arms from where he lay, he took hold of her delicate hand and guided her around the top of the mineshaft. She called out to Hugh for help, unable to see where he was. But all of his strength was gone and he started to slip on the beams and his body slid further down. He held on with all his exhausted might, frantically gripping the timbers."

I could hear Mum and Nain in the next room, but Anne continued.

"Hugh couldn't hold on any longer, his hands slipped on the damp beams and he fell into the mineshaft!"

The room was silent and as Anne said the words Mum opened the door, causing everyone to jump, including me.

"Here you all are then. Have they behaved themselves for you, Anne?" Mum said with a smile on her face.

Gareth and my sisters grumbled and begged Anne to tell them the rest of the story. Asking whether Hugh lived and whether they ever got married, but Anne just said, "I'll tell you next time I come!" Then to the protests of my brothers and sisters we left to go up to the farm.

It had been hot for a few days, really hot, and as we climbed the hill towards the Fechlas I could feel the pressure building.

"Boy its close!" I said, half to myself.

"You're not that close!" Anne said, smiling at me. She pulled at my hand and I let go of it, wrapping her up under my arm. I felt the sweat on the back of her t-shirt as my hand moved across her back. I could feel myself sweating, but it didn't seem to bother either of us.

On top of the hill we could see the storm clouds gathering above the mountains; electrifying stuff; great billowing clouds rising high into the wild blue yonder. We could almost smell the storm, mixed with the dry heat of the ripened crops, which lay suffocating in the fields on either side of the road. I wanted to stop; to climb the fence in the field and lie down with Anne in the long summer grass and drown beneath her sweet summer sweat. I wanted to make love to the symphony of the storm with the rain beating down on us.

On the brow of the next hill, Megan's farm came into view. The storm was quickly rolling in off the mountains and if we didn't put a spurt on, we would get drenched. We started to run together when the first drops of rain fell and as we raced across the yard towards the house, the skies opened up. Megan's father called to us,

"They're in the hay loft!" Changing direction slightly we missed the back door and made our way round the corner, to the back of the house; towards the hay loft. I followed in Anne's footsteps, as I hadn't been to Megan's before. I could remember seeing Megan as a child – her red hair was hard to miss – but had never spoken to her back then.

Placing my feet almost exactly where Anne's had fell a split second before; we sprinted the last few yards towards the open door. The heavens opened at that moment with the rain bouncing off the cobbles and blinding my eyes. Anne was just a blur in front of me. I was so close behind her; I didn't see what it was that tripped me, but I hit the floor below the hayloft with a thump.

Anne was half way up the ladder before she realised I wasn't behind her. She stopped, looked back down at me, and asked,

"You alright?"

I nodded. I was all right; I'd fallen well, if that's possible. At least, I had fallen in the dry of the barn and some loose straw had broken my fall.

"You've cut yourself!" Anne said, still standing half way up the ladder that lead up to the hayloft. I got up, opened my arms out and looked down. I could see nothing.

My face was wet and my tongue instinctively licked at my lips. It was then I tasted the blood.

"Is that you two down there?" Megan's voice bellowed out in the dim light, from somewhere above us.

Turning herself around, Anne sat half way up the ladder and held her arms out towards me. I was already on the bottom rung of the ladder and I climbed slowly up towards her. As I got closer, she leaned forward.

"Let me see!" She said, looking at my lip.

"There, it's not too bad!" She leaned further forward draping her long wet hair over me. The mixture of hair and rain on my face excited me. I was totally shrouded in the nest of her tangled hair as we gentle felt our way forward with our lips.

Anne's lips meet my forehead and I could feel her gentle kisses raining down on me. She kissed my eyelids, my cheek and down towards my lips. I was overwhelmed, as her lips met mine and I could feel her tongue gently caressing the small cut on my bottom lip. The faint taste of blood seeped between us as our tongues met and we kissed, kissing as though it would be our last, kissing as though we would never part, kissing as lovers do, all tangled up in each other.

"You two coming up, or what?" Megan's intrusive voice was ignored and we continued to kiss, long kisses that went on forever. I could hear Megan grumbling to Hefyn, above us.

"What on earth's going on down there?"

"Leave them!" Hefyn said, quietly. I half went to pull away from Anne, but she held me close to her. I was drowning beneath her arduous lips as her teeth tugged at my cut lip. Again her tongue, with her lips on mine; I thought I would die in the heady throes of her kissing. I don't think, in all my life, in all the pleasures and pain I have ever tasted, that I have ever felt anything as sensual as you, gently sucking on my bottom lip and then kissing me, over and over again, your tongue on mine and then your lips, and all the time the faint sweet taste of blood between us.

Eventually our kisses exhausted themselves and we parted just long enough to breathe. We were still tangled up in the net of Anne's hair. She leant her head to one side and her arm swept underneath it as she dragged it on top of her head and it tumbled down her back. In the darkness, I caught the fire in her eyes as she smiled, tempting me to linger longer in her gaze. The rain hammered on the metal roof of the Shippon. It was one of the most sensual moments of my life. Anne had never looked so beautiful to me; with her tangled wet hair thrown over her head, down the centre of her back, her eyes smiling, and the taste of warm blood on our lips.

She slowly rose up and turned to continue climbing the ladder. Her rear was in my face; it filled every inch of her faded Levis. I couldn't resist, its presence, its shape, its curve. I leaned slightly forward and kissed her on one of her cheeks. Anne stopped climbing and looked back down at me; her smile radiated through the damp dusky shadows of the loft, as my eager eyes followed her every move.

We climbed out into the loft, where Megan and Hefyn were lying warm and cosy on a bed of hay with a bale for a pillow. They were discussing what we could do for the rest of the day. They looked so comfortable.

We had only been in the rain for a few seconds, but we were both soaked through to the skin. Anne shivered slightly, as she started to put some order to her hair, combing it back with her fingers.

Her wet T-shirt was almost completely see-through. I could see she was wearing a thin cotton bra, with what looked like small flowers on it. It didn't hide much and I could see the shape of her breasts clearly defined through the damp material. She shivered again. I nuzzled into her side, my mouth finding her ear.

"You cold?" I knew I had said the wrong thing the moment the words fell from my lips and she looked straight up at me, feeling vulnerable and slightly embarrassed, but she managed to smile.

"She looks cold to me!" Megan had heard. Her words were almost cutting.

"Sorry!" I half smiled, feeling as awkward as Anne, and then I shrugged my shoulders. I mouthed, "Sorry!" again and then opened my arms and she buried herself inside. As she did so the whole loft lit up and almost instantaneously a deafening crack of thunder made the air shudder. Anne jumped in my arms. A bolt of lightning must have hit the ground, somewhere very close; probably a tree in the Sand Pits on the other side of the road; it was the high ground.

We all moved over to the bale-hatch high above the yard and we sat on the sill, in the lee of the roof, watching the storm, counting the seconds between the lightning and the sound of its thunder. It was a huge storm with great forks of lighting. Its thunder rolled over head, crashing from cloud to cloud all around us, but it soon passed over, leaving its rain dripping from the leaking gutters. We sat quietly, Hefyn and Megan, Anne and myself, arm in arm, watching the storm over Moel-y-crio. Blue skies were already reflecting in the rain on the yard and steam started to rise off the cobbles and fields as the rain stopped completely.

Hefyn broke the silence, suggesting that we should all go night fishing. After our experience in the 'Italian woods' the girls were sceptical at first, but he went on to explain that it would not involve the woods, but he was never the less unusually secretive about the precise details of what we would be doing.

CHAPTER THIRTEEN

I told Mum, I'd be home late and that we were all going round Megan's. The others told similar stories, but all had said, they were going to Nain Hughes; knowing she didn't have a phone for anyone to check out their story. Anne had arranged for her father to pick her up outside Nain's bungalow at eleven and whatever Hefyn had planned, we had to be back by then. She had tried for midnight, but her father had thought that would be too late. So instead Anne just pleaded for ten minute extra to say our goodbyes.

We met at the gates to the Fechlas and walked down Parry's Lane to Bottom Road. Megan started to grumble when Old Gwennie's came into view, but soon stopped as we carried on walking up the main road by the Italian Woods.

Hefyn had brought a landing net and I could see he had some type of grain in his jacket pocket. Before we knew it we were out of the village, through Hendre, past Star Crossing and heading towards the 'Rising Sun'. The stream followed the road for about a mile and we were able to scout out pools full of trout for future fishing.

The sun was heading towards the breast of the mountain, painting a watercolour sunset in large brushes full of raw sienna mixed with light red and French ultramarine. As dusk fell into evening we turned off the main road and up towards 'Afon Wen' and the fisheries, with my ideas of what Hefyn had planned growing in my mind.

The fisheries at 'Afon Wen' were beautiful. A manmade lake with a clay dam at one end was surrounded by fir covered hills that seemed to have come to the lakes edge, to drink. A restaurant and small hotel stood at the head of the lake. One night dad had taken the family there for a meal. I remember sitting at the front of the restaurant, eating a freshly caught rainbow trout stuffed with prawns and mushrooms, watching the setting sun at the far end of the lake. I watched a lone fisherman standing in a boat in the middle of its waters. He was fly-fishing, casting his line gracefully over the water, slicing through the dusk until eventually he laid it gently on the surface of the water, waiting patiently for a trout to rise.

As we left the restaurant that night, I noticed the fish tanks, where they bred the trout. Ifor was in the process of feeding them. I watched intently as he took a handful of fish pellets, throwing them onto the surface of the water, which almost turned white and bubbled as the trout fought for their last supper. Driving out, I looked down and could see fish three or four times bigger than any I had caught in the local streams.

We had left the relative security of the road and started walking through the woods. Quietly creeping forward, we almost tiptoed as the lake got closer. Eventually reaching the top edge of the wood, we lay motionless on the ground peering through the trees in the dwindling evening light, which seemed to have crept through the woods with us. I looked across at the lake; it was even more beautiful than I remembered. The sun was casting its light into the sky from below the horizon where it still burnt, having quenched itself in the stillness of the water. The dying light glistened across the lake, reflecting its 'water-coloured' sunset in brilliant colours that silhouetted the hills and trees.

We lay there for about ten minutes, taking in every sound and movement, getting comfortable with our new surroundings. Then without a word Hefyn crept forward, his belly only inches from the ground, like a cat stalking a bird, down to the edge of the fish tanks. I could hear trout jumping and breaking the surface as I joined him.

"Is this a good idea," I whispered. Opening the landing net and ignoring my warning, Hefyn extended it into the pool. Then taking a handful of grain from his pocket, he threw it out onto the water in front of him.

The fish came biting out at the hard course food and the top of the pool boiled in the frenzy. Hefyn forced the net up through the water and pulling it towards him, its handle bent under the strain. I could see the net bulging with our catch. Glistening rainbow trout wriggled and thrashed, caught in their greed. Hefyn dragged them to the edge of the pool. It would take two of us to lift them out and I could see five or six fish, all of them well over a foot and a half long. As I reached down with my hand almost touching the net; the silence of the lake was shattered.

"You two!" Ifor called from the other side of the pools.

Hefyn dropped the net and was on his feet running before I realised what was happening. I quickly got to my feet and looking around, I realised I couldn't see Hefyn or the girls. The girls had seen Ifor long before we did and in their efforts to attract our attention, Ifor had seen them first and eventually found our position.

Ifor was fast bearing down on me. Running into the trees for cover, I tripped in the darkness, hitting the ground with a thump. I lay motionless and winded, listening to Ifor's footsteps on the ground behind me.

He called out to the deep, dark, hiding woods, from where I could hear the others running and laughing through the undergrowth.

"I know who you are." He shouted.

"Rhydymwyn boys! I'm calling Old Bill on you!"

I listened as his footsteps faded to a safe distance and raising myself up, I slowly made my way through the woods to where the others were waiting. Hefyn and Megan laughed uncontrollably in all the excitement, but I was pleased to see Anne was looking slightly more concerned, and she threw her arms around my neck.

Turning for home, we would have to be careful. So as we walked, we kept watch for car lights. Each time we quietly hid in the hedgerows or over gates and walls. We laughed and joked together as we walked, still excited from the rush and commotion of our adventure.

We couldn't go home empty handed, so after we had passed the 'Rising Sun,' we jumped over a small wall, down to the pools in the stream we had seen earlier. The darkness didn't matter; fishing with your hands is all about touch. Within a few minutes both Anne and I had caught three trout between us. Hefyn was lying on a rock, his arm almost up to his shoulder in the water.

"I've got...Ouch!" He moaned, as he jumped up, shaking his hand. A freshwater eel had bitten his finger. We all fell about laughing as Hefyn danced from rock to rock, trying to balance as he exaggerated his pain, acting the fool, shaking his hand and arm vigorously. Chuckling we climbed back over the wall and onto the road.

Still laughing and joking, we walked up Parry Lane. Looking across we could see the warm security of the Fechlas lights. At the top of the lane, we said our goodbyes. Hefyn walking Megan up the hill towards her farm and before Anne and I walked down the hill to my grandmother's. I looked across towards the Mother Mountain, waiting patiently to suckle us, once more, for the night.

Standing, waiting for Anne's father at the front gates of the bungalow, we held hands. Looking up through the chilled air, beneath the clear dark endless night, we could see stars without number staring back down. The more we looked, the more stars we could see, out past galaxies and universes, travelling through time and space, we both stood in awe. A shooting star streaked across the sky, just as one had done the night we had spent together. Anne saw it first out of the corner of her eye. Hefyn had said there would be a meteor shower that night. So we searched the heavens for more. A few minutes later a second one tore across the night sky. Our eyes caught its glow. Another glowed and died and we waited, watching, eyes straining. Two others shot in front of us; one seemed to break into two then three pieces like a firework.

"Make a wish!" Anne said quietly. But looking deep into her eyes, all the wishes I had ever wanted were already coming true.

We began to kiss. Slowly at first, then long kisses and gradually we fell into each other, tumbling through the universe each one, inside the other.

Silhouetted in the headlights coming down the hill, we stopped kissing and Anne's father pulled up beside us.

"Before breakfast tomorrow!" Anne whispered in my ear and as she hugged my neck, I understood her invitation.

I watched as they drove out of sight, imagining her smiling and looking back through the darkness at me and then picking up the trout off the grass, I walked through the gates of the bungalow.

I sat down with Nain to a late supper of trout stuffed with wild mushrooms and thought of night fishing. We sat either side of one corner of the table; each with a fork in hand, slowly picking at the trout and mushrooms, the space between us growing warm, secure in the love, I always felt in her presence.

"No wolves tonight, then?" She asked, smiling.

"No, not tonight" I said quietly, as I returned her smile. Mum was settling my younger brothers and sisters down for the night in the back bedroom and I could hear Carole playing the piano in the front room, where I assumed Andy was also.

"Old Gwennie?" I asked, looking up at Nain, to watch the expression on her face. It didn't change, but I had her full and undivided attention.

"Yes Cariad!" she said quietly.

"People say she's a witch!" It was a statement, but I was really asking her a question.

"Witches are many different things, David bach!" she said quietly and then changing the subject, she asked me about the crystal I had found. How she knew, I didn't know. She seemed more concerned about my dive into the deep than whether Old Gwennie was a witch or not.

My mother entered the room interrupting Nain and what she was saying. With a concerned look on her face; apparently having heard the same people talking around the village, she sent me to bed, telling Nain not to fill my head with nonsense about witches and crystals. Mum was uncharacteristically short with me and seemed to have misunderstood our conversation; Nain hadn't seemed that concerned about what I was asking, but Mum obviously was.

Climbing into bed, my sister having finished her practice, I watched the fire and listened for the conversation from the room next door. I heard Nain's voice echoing through the chimneys,

"You don't understand Pam!" The conversation from the other room seemed to be about Old Gwennie. I could hear the concern in Mums voice, but Nain's voice fell silent and she remained quiet. Nain never argued with anyone; nothing was ever worth the upset. If something was that important, she would revisit the subject at some other time, when people were more receptive.

Lying in bed, looking into the smouldering fire, I pondered my mother's concern, contrasted against my grandmother's calm, trusting each one as implicitly as the other.

I fell asleep dreaming of you lying in your bed, no more than a couple of miles from where I lay and I could feel the warmth of your hand, resting on my chest and I lay mesmerised by your touch.

CHAPTER FOURTEEN

My grandfather's shed, which housed the Boneshaker, was like Aladdin's cave. Tools of every imaginable kind were stacked in corners with others hanging on nails hammered into the wooden walls and posts. Jars of every description lined shelves, which contained every button, nail, screw, nut and bolt saved by Taid over the years. Nothing was ever thrown away. Old pennies, farthings, pretty beads and sometimes old bits of broken jewellery could be found in them.

The flickering torchlight added a touch of eeriness, but I picked a jar off the shelf and emptied its contents onto the large wooden bench. Searching in the dim light through the bobs and buttons strewn across the work surface, I found what I was looking for after emptying the third jar. Holding them in my hand I examined the old broken earrings held together with a small piece of wire Taid had fed through the loops and twisted at the end.

As I had remembered, they were quite delicate. Two Celtic Knot earrings, one broken at the top with the hanger missing, the other slightly bent and both tarnished from being kept in the jar. Studying them, I could see they would be perfect.

Quickly cramming everything back into the jars, I rummaged through the drawers to find the old tubes of resin Taid had kept there.

Placing everything into my pocket, I quickly ran up the hill and down the back lane towards the Italian Woods. It was still early, with the sun not yet up, but its light was brightening the sky. I could hear the song thrush deeper in the woods and then its shrill chorus was echoed by a second. Summer love, I imagined, as I paused to listen. My eyes began to well for some reason, memories of Taid I guess, the song thrushes, the shed, his old jacket on my back with the earrings and glue in its pocket. It was as though he was still there and I fancied I could feel his presence.

I stood looking at the woods, hesitating, slightly nervous at the prospect of creeping past its malevolent places and prowling phantoms, but the alternative was walking around the lanes, a good two miles further after only managing a few hours' sleep. Hurrying, I picked my way towards the bridge by Old Gwennie's, my heart racing and throat becoming dry. With eyes scanning every shadow, my heightened senses picked out every detail. I was beginning to take more notice of my surroundings. Still very tired, I tried to rouse myself, checking and checking again. Mist lay thick on the ground. I looked at where I had trod and could see what looked like smoke or mist slowly rising out of my footprints, as though my very presence was alien to my surroundings and it was purging me from the ground.

Thick fog flowed down the bed of the stream, almost hiding the large slab of rock in the middle. Jumping down onto the rock I found myself waist deep in its mists. A stream of fog flowed past and I could barely see my feet.

Pausing, I took a deep breath. Nothing stirred in the woods; even the song thrushes were silent. The woods were still, waiting in the darkness, no sound, no movement. I couldn't even hear the hum of cars on the road. Bowing my head slightly and stepping onto another rock, I touched the bridge in an attempt to steady myself. Instantly my hand froze to it. I could feel the cold welding my flesh to the metal. Quickly snatching my hand away, I examined it, but there wasn't a mark on it. I reached out to touch the railings with my fingertips, but they were no longer deathly cold. My imagination was strangely stirred by an unseen presence, and fear started to creep into me.

Although I knew the morning wasn't that cold, my breath blew great clouds in front of me. Looking under the bridge, I could see Old Gwennie's cottage floating eerily in the mists and decided to be as quick as I could. Picking my way carefully through the tunnel of the bridge and emerging on the other side, I found myself shivering. Stepping slowly from the rocks to the bank, still looking across at the cottage, a light came on and I heard the squawk of a magpie. Too early for magpies I thought in an instant, 'but maybe not for witches'.

It was as if I had been hit by a bolt of lightning. I stood unable to move, except for my chest pounding. The ground was covered from the dust and evil of a thousand years and I could feel all my energy draining into the un-consecrated earth. An awful stench pervaded around me and the smell of death was in my nostrils. Dead miners, having climbed from their bottomless graves, were crawling, unseen, across the decaying woods towards me. I could smell my fear. The stench of evil was sapping my energy and I wondered if a place could be inherently malevolent.

The door to the cottage opened and Old Gwennie stepped into my fear. She was dressed in an old dark flannel dress; long grey matted hair straggled all the way down to her waist, covering her face. Darkness seemed to gather around me, black tendrils creeping towards me with the lips and the tongues of a thousand demons, that bit and vipered into my heart. Mustering all my energy, I tried once more to move, but couldn't break free from the chains that held me bound. Gwennie slowly raised her head and parting her hair looked straight into me.

With her eyes and face on fire, her stare pierced my very soul and I knew I was doomed to a sudden and awful destruction. I closed my eyes to rid myself of this awful nightmare, but as I opened them again Gwennie was standing immediately before me; the furnace of her face froze solid any resistance inside me; the stench of her breath seemed to poison the air as her hand clawed out towards me. Ink black blood spewed from her mouth over her bottom lip and down onto her chin. Her bent and crooked fingers beckoned towards me as she extended out the talons of her long black nails. Then quickly clenching her fist, I felt my heart give way as her talons ripped into it. I slowly sank to my knees in submission and just as I thought my life would end, to my surprise the image of my grandfather stood in front of me and I reached out in desperation. Taid held out his hand, catching hold of me and I immediately found myself free from her shackles.

Gwennie no longer stood before me. Looking across the stream, her cottage was in darkness. I looked around for Taid, but he was nowhere to be seen. My strength returning second by second, I started to move quickly upstream. Running past the Old Winding House, the brick tunnel, then Ruby Pool with mist rising from its mirrored surface, on and up towards the Rabbit Warrens, where I rested awhile as I tried to catch my breath. I couldn't work out what had happened. I had never been so frightened in all my life.

Looking around I could see someone had set snares and netting at the rabbit holes. I would have normally removed them, but still dazed and confused, I just got up and continued to walk towards Anne's. By the time I had reached the top end of the woods and was crossing the fields towards the farm, I had convinced myself that it had all been nothing more than a bad dream; an imagined nightmare conjured up in my exhausted mind.

Thinking of how fear had taken hold of my whole body, creating the illusion. I was cross with myself. Purging the feelings from me, I charged myself never to let fear take over my body in such a way again.

It was still cold and I began to shake as I walked round the corner of the Shippon.

"You all right? Anne asked with a genuinely concerned look on her face.

"You look like you've seen a ghost!" The dogs were concerned too, circling around us, in between us and nudging me with their snouts. Not telling Anne what I had just experienced, I shrugged my shoulders.

"I'm all right…!" I said.

"I've just run all the way…I'll be fine in a moment!"

We hugged each other.

"You're late…!" Anne said when she was sure I was fine.

"I was expecting you much earlier!" I looked straight into her.

"I had to get something before I came,"

"What?" She asked inquisitively.

"Has your Dad got any tools?" I said, deflecting her questions, smiling. Anne took me to the far end of the Shippon where her father had a small lean-to workroom with a bench in one corner and boxes of tools lined across the back wall.

Feeling for the old broken earrings in my pocket I asked,

"You still got the crystal?" I knew she had, I'd seen the small bulge in the money pocket of her jeans and knew she kept it with her night and day. Digging deep into her jeans pocket, she brought the crystal out and held it in the palm of her hand. Picking it up between her thumb and forefinger, she held it up into the space between us. Again I saw the warm glow from the crystal reflected in the catch-light of her eyes; caught in the early morning sunlight streaming in through one small window. Taking it, I held it out towards Anne, pausing and looking at her for a few moments.

Reaching for the old earrings in my pocket, I quickly went to work taking the loop from the top of the one good one. Using all my care, I cleaned and fashioned them to the shape of the crystal, with the top of the Celtic knot standing proud to form an eye. Opening the tubes of resin, I mixed equal amounts together. Spreading the mixture over the top of the crystal I pushed the earrings into position so the crystal would hang beneath them; a bit like a clasp over its top. I then placed the crystal upright in the vice to keep it secure as the resin set.

Anne could see what I was doing and moved to the back corner of the workshop where I could see a small metal hook screwed into the wall with leather bootlaces hanging from it. One of the laces slipped easily away from its companions and moving back across the workshop, Anne stood directly in front of me. Lassoing the lace over my head, she pulled it around my neck and holding both ends she pulled my head forward and we started to kiss. My body was no longer full of fear and I bathed in the warm pools of affection Anne created between us. Throwing her arms around my neck and with her mouth so close to my ear I could feel her lips against my skin, her breath warmed through me.

"I think I'm falling in love with you, David" she whispered. "Deeply, madly, uncontrollably…...." Easing my head back from her slightly, I placed one finger over her lips interrupting what she was saying. I loved Anne more than I could say, more than mere words could express and I started to speak, slowly at first, drowning in her deep green eyes.

"No matter where I go… no matter where our lives take us" I paused slightly trying to find the words; words I had rehearsed in my mind, over and over again; like an unwritten poem.

"No matter who stands at my side, or how much love surrounds me, I will never love anyone as much as I love you right now; and if the sky fell down on me, crushing me into the dirt, I would still love you!" My words stumbled as they tumbled into the back of my throat where they toppled backwards into the deep.

My thoughts were mixed up in something I once heard Taid quote. I had thought of his words the night before, as we looked up into the endless star clustered night time sky. I couldn't remember all he said, but during the night I'd remembered and for some reason I quietly quoted his almost forgotten words.

"Guided by the stars of the night,

We dream by the moon's silver light,

Until (by the grace of God)

Our dreams take flight"

She bowed her head and rested it on my shoulder. We stood there for what seemed a lifetime. Time paused as all the stars of the crystal sphere danced around us. The dogs lay still and quiet on the floor, not wishing to intrude and sensing the moment.

Taking the lace from her hand and testing the resin was dry, I threaded it through the eye I had created at the top of the crystal. Tying a neat double-fisherman's knot through the loop at the top of the earrings so the crystal hung in the centre of the knot; I placed it over Anne's head. It hung neatly between the top of her breasts, over her heart.

I had once been told how the ancient Celts would decorate arrowheads with feathers and small precious stones, threading them onto a hide lace. They would hang them around the neck of their true love, the arrowhead resting between their breasts pointing straight to their heart. I looked at the crystal as it pointed down between Anne's breasts, straight to her heart. I was suitably satisfied and Anne continuously held the leather lace in her fingers, playing with the crystal, examining its every detail. She would touch the gold Celtic knot at the top of the crystal, rubbing her fingers across it feeling the pattern beneath. Anne looked dreamily down at the floor and then back at me and smiled.

Lifetimes later we walked out into the fields, the dogs trailing behind. Making our way down to the Beech Tree we sat on the wall. The chanterelle mushrooms were still growing on the tree stump, but they were beginning to turn. Sitting, talking quietly as the dogs explored the hedges and undergrowth, I watched as one of them sniffed eagerly at the loose earth by the roots of the tree. It then started to paw at the ground, sniffing again and again. Jumping down, I knelt by the dog.

"Good boy" I said patting him on the back. I started to move away the soft earth with my hands and underneath touched the dark, blue-black warty body of a truffle.

"What's that?" Anne asked turning up her nose.

"It looks like a truffle!" I said excitedly, holding out my prize as I showered more praise on the dog, patting him as I did so.

"My Dad likes rum truffles!" she said, tilting her head back and laughing,

"You do find some funny mushrooms, David!"

Anne's father called from the top of the field,

"Come on you two, breakfast" We walked slowly up the field towards the old, dark, grey-stoned farmhouse, with its slate roof turning green with moss.

Entering the kitchen, the warm smell of breakfast sizzled in the pan. Anne's mother looked across the table with a warm smile spread across her face. Tilting her head slightly she beckoned me to move closer to her as she half asked,

"So you're the David I've heard so much about, then?" I should have said.

"All good I hope!" But instead I just smiled nervously and nodded saying 'Hello', I think.

Any embarrassment faded and both Anne and I were told to get ready for breakfast. I washed the truffle at the kitchen sink, examining it for grubs and returning to where Anne's mother was standing half holding the frying pan at the stove, and I asked.

"May I?" While lifting the truffle and pointing to the pan.

"I've heard about your strange mushrooms" Anne's mother said, staring at the truffle in my hand.

"Don't you dare poison us then!" She gave a little laugh and then stepped to one side giving me room at the pan. Taking a knife from the draining board, I sliced the truffle into the hot fat. It sizzled as its yellowing flesh drowned in the scolding heat.

Anne's father asked me what it tasted of and I told him that it had its own unique taste, but that on its own it was nothing special. I explained further that it would bring out the flavour of everything else cooked with it in the pan, or at least that's what my grandmother had always told me, although they weren't really meant to be fried and my grandfather would have shuddered at the waste of such a precious find. I felt a little unfaithful. Nain was a fantastic cook and would have given her right arm for the truffle and in putting it in the pan I felt I was wasting its full potential, but youth will be impetuous. At the time, I think I was showing off a little.

I explained to Anne's father that my grandfather used to take me over the fields and through the woods mushrooming. He knew every bird by its feather, flight or call, every tree, by its shape, leaf or bark, every animal by its track and every mushroom whether edible or poisonous. If a game bird or chicken had been killed by a wild animal in the woods or on the farm, with careful study of its feathers and the way it had been killed, he could tell you if a fox, weasel or polecat had killed it.

"Old Jack Hughes" Anne's father said,

"I remember your Grandfather. I was a very young boy when he used to hunt in the woods and I would sometimes see him talking to my father. Da had said he was the best shot for miles around and we would often see him with his old shotgun, shooting pigeon and rabbit or any other game-birds that flew his way. He was a fine old gentleman; what he didn't know about the woods wasn't worth knowing".

'A fine old gentleman' I thought to myself. He had been that all right, but to me he had been so much more.

Anne took me upstairs to the bathroom where we washed and cleaned ourselves down. Anne's house was a large old farmhouse and the stairs to the landing creaked slightly as we climbed them.

On the landing, waiting patiently between two doors, stood an old grandfather clock, almost identical to the one that stood in Aunty Catherine Anne's hallway. It had a large face with great roman numerals marking each hour. There was a cut away at the top, which had a revolving dial with the sun, the moon, and the stars, enamelled on it. The stars were sinking out of sight and the sun was rising on the dial. A cock crowed in the yard as if to confirm what was in front of me.

The door to the left hand side of the clock was open, it was Anne's bedroom. She took my hand and led me through the doorway. Streams of sunlit watercolour brushed past the white lace curtains and seeped into the room, washing itself onto her eiderdown and laying subtle watery washes of ultramarine and alizarin crimson on her pillow.

The room smelled soft and comfortable. There was a dressing table and mirror standing quietly to one side of Anne's bed, covered with a large lace doily, with a brush, comb and mirror set, neatly laid out at its centre. They looked almost identical to one Nain had and I supposed they had been handed down to her from a benevolent grandmother. Her large single bed was draped with white-cotton bed linen, the edges of which were decorated with the same pattern of lace that was on her dresser. I looked on the floor at the bottom of her bed to where a plain white nightdress lay discarded and empty, cold without her warm body inside.

That thought seemed to move through me, tingling, with strange sensations, somewhere deep inside me, and Anne, somehow, standing next to me, following where my eyes moved, could also see and feel everything I felt and thought.

My eyes wandered over Anne's bed to above the ornately decorated metal bedstead, where, in an old pine frame was hung the sketch of her I had drawn the day we spent painting the mountains. It was better than I'd remembered, but I still hadn't caught her to my satisfaction and I wondered if that was possible. Below the picture was a piece of paper pinned to the wall, with what looked like a poem written on it. I pointed to it and asked

"May I?" She hesitated slightly, but then nodded her head and smiled. I walked over to her bed, placing one knee carefully on her pillow and leaned across to read the poem. It felt strange, my knee on her pillow and being that close to where she lay at night.

Looking at the poem I recognised it straight away. It was the poem I had only half heard as she whispered its words in my ear, as we kissed, the night we spent together on top of the cliff. I hadn't understood her at the time. But I immediately recognised the flow of its verse and their rhythm. Taking a deep breath, never daring to imagine that the poem might be about me, I read it quietly to myself, with Anne standing close behind me.

'And you are here'.

'I dream at night and you are here.

I wake in the morning and you are here.

Washing my face, I look in the mirror

And you are here.

I walk in the woods and you are here.

I climb to the mountains and you are here.

Lying in bed, I imagine and you are here.

Love is a stream that flows through my heart

And you are here

Deep inside.'

I struggled to contain my feelings. I was full, a dam straining under the pressure. Pausing a moment, trying to control my feelings, I closed my eyes before looking around at Anne. We stood entwined together, dwelling in a place where words dare not tread and wishing we could both live there forever. Time slowed to a crawl, locked in a perfect moment that seemed to pause, absent from the race towards its end. The pendulum on the old grandfather's clock on the landing stopped swinging as it waited patiently for permission to move again.

A voice called from downstairs shattering the silence, dragging us back to reality.

"What are you two doing up there?" Anne's father called and although out of sight, I could see the grin on his face and could hear Anne's mother quietly saying,

"Leave them alone…why don't you?"

Breakfast was lovely, with Anne's younger brothers sitting one either side of me, questioning and pulling at my arms.

"Leave him eat his breakfast" Anne's Mum would say. Her hair was dark like Anne's, but greying slightly at the front. She was lovely though. I could see where Anne got her looks from and like Anne her mother had an inner strength and beauty that shone from somewhere deep inside.

"Well your truffle worked, that was the finest breakfast I think I have ever tasted" Anne's father said, smiling at his wife as he took hold of the crystal hanging freely around Anne's neck.

"Your work David?" indicating the mounting.

"No," I replied.

"I just put it all together,"

"I've heard about your dive into the deep…the pearl diver!" I winced slightly as he tilted his head back and laughed with Anne telling him not to tease me.

"I'm sorry, it's impressive…it really is" he said as he continued to talk and question.

A few people around the village had called me 'the pearl diver!' I recall watching a programme on telly about sponge divers using heavy weights in their hands to take them quickly to the depth of the sponges. So it wasn't an original idea, but I was still quite proud of how I had found the crystal.

Anne had arranged to go with Megan into town for the day and I would miss her desperately, but our love, I felt, was strong enough to bear the endless separations we suffered. She went upstairs to get ready as her father drove me home.

The dogs climbed in the back and again snouted and barked at the scent of the sheep on the breeze. Anne's father chatted to me about my grandfather, which brought back good memories and between the rise and fall of his conversation, I thought of Taid. We passed the old quarry, where Taid had once worked and I was lost in my memories.

CHAPTER FIFTEEN

With the girls away, Hefyn and I decided to venture back into the woods. We both had reservations and none more so than me after my experience that morning. Walking down the fields and over Bottom Road, I began to get nervous, but as we approached the woods, none of the fear I had felt that morning returned. The sun was beating down and we talked as we walked beneath a cloudless sky. We passed Old Gwennie's without incident, although I looked across at her front door, expecting it to open at any moment.

We were soon hopping and stepping, rock-to-rock, watching the sudden shadows of wild trout darting to and fro beneath our feet. Small eddies and waterfalls sang chuckling tunes to us as their waters danced and spilt across the glistening pools.

Wearing pumps and cut-off jeans, I took off my old rugby top and tied it around my waist. Hefyn wore much the same, but he didn't take off his top until we reached a large pool near the old winding house. We saw a huge trout, dart from the centre of the pool to its imagined safe haven, under a large rock at the bank. A second boulder jutted out from the opposite bank, both meeting in the centre of the stream with a small waterfall tumbling between them.

The rock was big enough for both of us to lie belly down on its rounded, damp surface. I felt its cool exterior beneath me as its cold heart seeped into my body, a stark contrast to the sun's amiable rays, which pierced through a thousand quivering leaves to warm my back. We lay side by side peering over the edge with my head just above the pool, which was about three feet deep at its centre. I was nearest the waterfall and it continuously spat at me; the sensation, although cooling, was quite unnerving.

Not seeing the trout beneath the lip of the boulder, we lent further out looking for the entrances into its secret chambers. Both of us dipped our hands into the water, watching carefully to see if the trout fled. We felt our way under the immense limestone slab, counting five entrances into the trout's secure hideaway. Picking up pebbles from the bottom of the stream we blocked up two of the holes. Then putting our hands once more into the water, I placed a hand in one hole with Hefyn placing an arm in each of the other two.

"Can you feel anything?" Hefyn asked, straining to get his arms further under the rock. I could feel something, but I wasn't sure what it was.

"I think I've just got its tail!" I said, extending my arm further under the rock. Hefyn had the trout's head. I leaned towards the water with my shoulder half immersed in the pool, but I had to lift my head away from its surface to keep my hair from getting wet, with the waterfall splashing on my back. Working together we started, one from each end, to rub the trout's belly with our fingers meeting in the middle. My ear was touching the water with my hair drowning in the pool. I was in a precarious position, leaning so far out. Hefyn definitely had the shorter distance to cover and the rock was more rounded where I lay with less purchase.

"I've got it!" Hefyn said eagerly.

"I can feel it in my hand…its huge!" I could hear the excitement in his voice. Slowly the trout slipped from my touch as Hefyn gently eased it towards himself. I looked across through the clear water to where a large brown trout rested hypnotised in the palm of Hefyn's flat hand. Gradually he brought it to the surface of the pool. Straining my neck to see, I twisted my shoulders around and up, but with no handhold my fingers slipped on the damp rock. My other arm was trapped under the boulder, preventing me rolling to the side. There was only one way out and that was head first.

I would have loved to have seen the splash I made. It half drenched Hefyn, but I was too busy thrashing about under water, trying to free my arm. When I eventually escaped, I was sitting in the mud at the bottom of the pool, my chin only just out of the water. Mud and silt were dripping down my face. I spluttered slightly and then coughed.

"Tell me you got the trout?" I choked the words out. Hefyn pointed to the bank, where the trout was struggling and gulping, amid the suffocating scent of wild garlic. It was, as I thought, a huge brilliantly coloured brown trout, which Hefyn of course claimed as his.

"Well…you were splashing about that much…I'm surprised I landed it at all!" We both laughed.

We walked further upstream as the sun began to dry my clothes. My pumps were squelching every time I put them to the floor, so instead of stepping rock to rock I just waded through the water. I looked at the trout in Hefyn's hand; it was almost as big as those we were forced to leave behind at The Fisheries. We had snared two more trout before we got to the Ruby Pool, although they were minnows compared to 'The Brownie'.

Edging further along the bank of 'Ruby Pool', something caught my eye. A large grass snake was sunning itself, draped across the branches of a sapling Ash growing out of the bank, just above the water line. Raising my hand to stop Hefyn, I indicated for his eyes to follow mine. He stopped and stared, and then we both edged closer. The snake was quite large. I estimated over four feet long, with its little tongue flicking in and out, searching the air for the presence of danger. I had never seen a grass snake that large before. Sensing our presence it slipped quickly into the water and slithered across the top of the pool, its head protruding, like in those old photographs of the Loch Ness Monster. It seemed naturally at home in the water and I imagined it hunting and stalking the edges of the pool for small fish or young frogs or any other juicy Grass Snake type morsels.

Laying our trout on the grass, we stripped off and dived into the pool. I was covered in mud, my hair, ears, even up my nose. I washed myself down as I swam. Knowing the mineshaft was below me gave me a hollow feeling in my stomach and I was quite nervy at the time.

We lay next to the trout, drying ourselves in the sun, talking of the summer and of the adventures we'd had, including running from Ifor at 'the Fisheries,'

"You could have brought my net back with you!" Hefyn said, quite indignantly. I laughed as I lay there imagining Ifor landing some gigantic fish with the aid of Hefyn's net.

"Why don't you ask him to give it back then?" I said, confident of his answer.

Conversation led to the girls. Hefyn told me how lovely Megan was. I knew she was full of fun, her prank with the ewe, squirting me in the face with its milk, showed that. There was a continuous grin on her face and her bubbly red hair matched her character. Her freckles did little to hide her mischievous personality, but Hefyn told me of a more serious side to her. A side that was caring, tender and loving.

"Tender?" I said, with a surprised tone to my voice,

"Yes!" He said, trying to sound hurt.

"There's no need to sound so surprised…I'll tell her…and then you'll be in trouble!" But most of all she was good fun and he loved just being with her.

Thinking of Anne and what we had shared that morning, I tried to remember the poem on her wall. I could see her face clearly imprinted on my mind and I vowed that I would do a painting of her, to capture all her dark and wild beauty; the greatest painting I would ever paint.

I stared up at my cut-off jeans hanging in the branches to dry just above me. The sun warmed into me with a soft breeze whispering through the leaves. A song thrush was in the branches of a thicket of bushes and trees, behind where I lay. Its shrill call was almost hypnotic. I closed my eyes and listened. It sang a little ditty, repeated it, changed the ditty and repeated it again; it continued to sing and repeat its ditties as though its heart would burst.

A dog barked in a farmyard, near a field, by a stream, in a wood, by a pool, where I lay, drowning in my memories and the emerging love I felt for a girl I had known for a little less than a month. The warmth of the midday sun soaked into me and I drifted down stream, carried away by soft summer breezes.

The cool air made me shiver and I woke with a start. Hefyn was nowhere in sight. A cloud had crept into the sky and moving across the sun it brought a chill to the woods. I could hear something off to my right and my heart skipped a beat as Hefyn appeared through one of the bushes, parting its branches.

"You've been snoring mate" he said, grinning.

"Not me" I said, defensively, trying to drive the sleep from me.

"I don't snore!"

"You want to get to bed at night!"

"I do" I said.

"Tell Anne to leave you alone then…and let you get some sleep" Hefyn grinned and we both laughed.

"Have you and Megan…?" I paused.

"She says she wants it to be right…whatever that means.

I thought awhile then yawned. The morning was obviously catching up on me. Rising to my feet, I put on my almost dry shorts, but they were uncomfortable, feeling hard and damp as we walked further up the stream. We caught another large 'Rainbow' just below the Rabbit Warrens, where I had seen the nets and snares earlier that day.

As we climbed up the bank from the pool we heard it for the first time, a sound halfway between a large dog snarling and a cat spitting and hissing, almost like the last long mournful cry of a baby in utter despair. The fear I had felt in the morning started to creep back, but I exerted all the energy my tired body could muster and managed to stem the nightmares from rising inside me. Looking at Hefyn, we both stepped a little closer to the raised bank of the Old Rabbit Warrens. Creeping slowly forward with our senses heightened, we watched and listened for any signs of movement. I looked up towards where I had seen the snares that morning and saw it for the first time, caught in the nets. I couldn't make out what it was, half hidden by the great mound of earth riddled with rabbit holes; a mess of black fur struggling in one of the nets. One thing I was certain of though; it was big. I pointed towards it, but Hefyn already had it in his sights and was frozen to the spot. Climbing slowly up the bank I got to within ten feet of it. It stopped struggling and stared straight back at me; its eyes were slate grey and cold as steel. I couldn't say for certain what it was, but I was sure it was the same beast that had followed me up through the woods and Hefyn was certain it was the same animal hiding in the shadows on the far bank of the Ruby Pool, the day I found the crystal.

"Come on let's go?" Hefyn whispered. I have never worked out why, but I ignored him. All my concentration was on whatever it was trapped in the nets and I moved closer, as its eyes followed me. I honestly can't remember what was going through my mind. Looking back the only reason I can imagine, is that it didn't deserve to die; not like that anyway. Everything in my frightened body was telling me to turn away, but something deep inside me seemed to be pushing me forward. A long black tail flicked vigorously from side to side, with the fur on its back standing on end poking through the holes in the netting. It was well and truly caught, blood coming from the sides of its mouth where the chord had cut in, as it had tried to gnaw its way free. It was exhausted, panting in the heat of the day, wrapped up like a Christmas turkey in a string shopping bag with feathers poking everywhere.

'A wolf' I thought, and then I laughed to myself. One of its legs was caught in a snare; its paw was almost as big as my hand. 'A wolf?' I thought again. 'It couldn't be.' Despite Nain and Taid's stories, wolves had become extinct years before, even centuries.

'Pontblyddyn', a village only a few miles further down the valley; its name meaning 'the bridge of the wolf'. It was reputedly where the last known wolf in Wales had been killed. Taid had told me, of how the men from Rhydymwyn had tracked a huge she wolf from the Italian Woods, which in those days was called, Nant Ffigillt. They had stalked her for days; with the wolf continually trying to double back towards the Italian Woods, for some unknown reason. They eventually cornered the huge beast down by the old bridge, shooting it several times before it fell. Even then, when dying with three or four bullets in her, she struggled, clawing along the ground as if some primal instinct drew her back towards Rhydymwyn and the woods.

Taid told me that his great-grandfather, who was young at the time, or some other close relative, he couldn't remember exactly, was one of the men who shot the wolf, but when he witnessed her dying exertions, with the wolf looking up at him, he could take it no longer. He bent down and stroked her head and neck, bitterly regretting his involvement in the whole affair. Holding the gun against the wolf's head he squeezed the trigger for the last time. Handing his gun to another, he never took it in his hand again. Placing the huge animal across his shoulders, he alone carried her to her back to her beloved woods where he buried her.

One of the creature's hind legs was caught in a snare with its head and shoulders packed and twisted in one of the nets. It began to struggle again.

"Shussssh!" I whispered quietly, making what I thought would be calming noises, trying to sooth the beast.

Taking Taid's old penknife out of my front pocket, I opened the smallest blade, which I had sharpened like a razor with an oil-stone from Taid's shed. It would easily cope with the wire of the snare and the netting. Moving up close, the huge animal was just lying there, too exhausted to struggle. I studied how and where it was trapped.

It was held fast in the netting, so I determined firstly to free its leg from the snare. The wire had cut deep into its leg, just above its paw and I could see blood stained fur around the wound. I pulled at the stake, which had been hammered into the ground. I pulled with all my might and eventually it relented and came free. The wire of the snare immediately loosened its grip on the animals paw. The wire fell free and I threw it into the hedge with the stake.

Starting at the area around the beast's mouth, I gently cut the netting away. Its fangs were clearly on show as it shied away from me, giving a low growl as it did so. As I cut more netting away, I could see it was a huge dog of some sort. It looked like a cross between a Husky and an extremely large black Alsatian. Either way it was about nine stone of snarling death and I slowly retreated back to where my trout lay on the ground. The giant canine shrugged off the rest of the netting from around its head, with one sweep of its paw. It immediately got to its feet and slowly walked in a large circle, sauntering back towards me, with its hind leg held off the ground.

'Oh Hell!' I thought, and then I immediately repeated the words under my breath.

"Sorry Nain…!" I said, apologising for my cursing.

"But you've just got to see this" She was magnificent and frighteningly beautiful, or at least had been at one time. The dog's coat was getting shabby. She stopped and showed her fangs giving a snarling growl. We both stood staring back at the beast, transfixed; unable to move. I picked up one of the trout and threw it towards the wild dog, hoping it would distract it in some way, thinking it might be hungry. I could hear Hefyn trotting his tongue against the roof of his mouth, but didn't dare look. I knew what he was thinking, but it was the smallest of our four trout. He hadn't let me carry the big brownie.

The trout landed on the grass between the beast's paws and bending its head it sniffed at the fish. Again and again it sniffed, but apparently not liking fish, it stared back at me.

"What do I do now?" I spoke without moving my mouth and whether Hefyn heard me or not, I don't know.

The wild dog continued standing there, looking at me. It seemed to hesitate slightly, as though weighing up its options and then it just turned and walked away. Slowly and silently, without even rustling the lower branches of the hedge, it vanished between the trees, disappearing into the woods.

Hefyn had a few choice names for me, most of them in Welsh, most of which I couldn't understand.

Walking back through the woods, we chatted loudly, howling like wolves as the adrenaline slowly drained from our bodies.

"I'd have fed you to the beast if you'd thrown the big brownie to her!" Hefyn said and we both laughed.

We found the girls at Megan's and sat about in the hay while Hefyn told the story of how we had found and freed an enormous black wolf trapped in the rabbit nets, deep in the Italian woods. The girls listened in disbelief and ribbed Hefyn for telling such fanciful tales.

"Don't believe us then," Hefyn said, with disappointment rising and he made his hurt puppy dog look, trying in vain to gain some sympathy from Megan. They didn't know what to think or believe, but as I walked Anne back down the hill to wait for her father, she asked me if it was true and I assured her that there was indeed a large wild dog of some description in the woods.

CHAPTER SIXTEEN

It rained continuously for the next few days. Anne got a lift and came to tell my younger brothers and sisters more stories of how the giant had survived the fall, with the princess returning to save him from the mineshaft, oh, and of course, how they lived happily ever after. She knew most of the traditional stories, folklore, myths and legends of Wales. Her grandmother had apparently, like my grandfather, been a great storyteller; whether the story was fact or fiction or just somewhere in the space between, it didn't really matter; our lives were richer for their tales. Anne kept my brothers and sisters entertained for hours. They flocked around her so much I thought she would suffocate.

Nain sat in the old chair in the corner, listening in silence. Her softly greying green eyes gazed off into the distance as she drifted away into times past. Her head would drop as she fell asleep to the sound of Anne's stories and she snored, while Katie, Anne and Gareth begged Anne for more.

That evening, on her nightly ritual of kissing our heads and blowing out the night-light, she told me how lovely Anne was. Nain had said she thought Anne came from 'good people', who had also lived in the shadow of our mountain and I knew what she was alluding to.

We spent a day at Megan's. It was still raining and Anne and I found Hefyn and Megan lazing about in the hayloft. We crept up the ladder to where they were heavily engrossed in each other, half buried in a bed of hay. As we jumped out on them, Anne shouted

"What are you two up to then?" They both jumped and separated, pretty quickly. Red faced, Megan quickly straightened her blouse, pulling it together at the front. But not quick enough to prevent me catching a flash of Megan's loosened bra. Anne asked me later what I had seen, so she had obviously seen more than me.

"You know what farmers daughters are like" she said with a grin. I didn't, but the thought kindled something inside me.

The rain fell, heavily at times, but no thunder or lightning this time. I stood at the loft door, high above the farmyard, listening to the hum of conversation from the warm hay somewhere behind me. Somehow Hefyn, Megan and Anne's voices made me secure, even cosy, in my moist, musty world. Staring out of the door, I could see large towers of rain slowly drifting out across the valley and down over the woods. It was falling just a few inches in front of my face and I caught its sweet smell mixed with the heady scent of the hay.

Everyone was getting bored, so much so that we all helped Megan's father with jobs around the farm. We didn't venture out of the barns though. Her mother, who was a large woman with bubbly long red hair and freckles just like Megan, made us butties and we sat about once more planning our week.

Anne said her father was going to visit his brother who lived on the Lleyn Peninsula, west of Snowdon, and if we wished we could catch a ride and either, go to the beach at Black Sands, or to the mountains for the day. It would be a long day, starting straight after milking, or even before that, if Anne's mother got up to do the morning chores. We would be returning home late at night, but we all agreed it would be worth it and a day at the mountains was planned.

Megan mentioned the dance on Friday. We wouldn't usually go to the dance at the Institute, but 'The Crazy Line' were gigging there, and they played music more to our tastes. Besides which they attracted a good following, everyone would be there. The problem was that the trip to Snowdon would be next morning and we would all be tired little bunnies.

On the Friday afternoon I packed my rucksack with Nain saying she would pack some food for me before I left in the morning. Never in her wildest dreams would she have packed me up the night before. Nothing was ever too much trouble and she would not dream of kissing us goodbye without fresh butties in our pack. Once I watched her baking a cake and as she cracked the eggs into the mixture, she rubbed her finger around the inside of the shell to make sure, all the egg went into the mix. It was typical of the way she did things. Nain was precise and meticulous about everything she did: even down to getting up early and making my butties for the day.

My mother was taking my brothers and sisters to Auntie Mabe's for the evening, so I had arranged for her to drop me off at Anne's or at least at the end of the lane above the quarry from where I could walk the short distance to her house. My elder sister, Carol would walk down to Noel's, a lad from the village she had seen once or twice,(nothing serious' she said) and then they would walk to the Institute together.

The afternoon had been hot and steamed headlong into the evening, giving no relief from the hot humid air of the long summer days. I walked up the lane towards Anne's farm, excited about the evening ahead. I was wearing some old Levi's, which although they were not in holes yet, I had patched and put badges on. They weren't exactly smart, but I knew Anne liked them. She had made a comment about them earlier in the summer and I had barely taken them off since. On my feet I wore an old pair of comfortable Desert Wellies. A black T-shirt, which suitably showed off where the sun had tanned my arms and face.

Anne's father answered the door and showed me into the kitchen. As we passed the stairs he shouted up,

"Anne…David's here; Hurry then…you'll be late if you're not careful!" We stood in the kitchen chatting for a few moments, until he went to get something out of the Land Rover, telling me Anne wouldn't be long. I could hear Anne's mother trying to keep her two youngest in Pallor Bach, so they didn't disturb us, or get in their sister's way. It was somehow Anne's special night.

A few moments later the kitchen door opened. Anne walked in and I just stood and stared.

"Boy" I said quietly, half to myself on seeing her. She wore an eggshell blue, almost cerulean, smock dress, with lace around the low neck line; her long dark hair was pulled over one shoulder, cascading down the front. Loosely tied at the back the dress accentuated the shape of her breasts. The crystal hung just above the low neckline, pointing straight at her heart. The catch light in her deep green eyes seemed to light the whole room.

All of the feelings I had felt over the long weeks of that summer came flooding into me. A young, short lifetime of feelings welled inside me and I stood in the kitchen of her mother's dreams and fell completely and uncontrollably in love with Anne Jones, from the farm above the Italian Woods.

"You look…incredible" I half stuttered, stumbling with my words, struggling to describe my feelings. I had never seen her dressed that way before and she outstripped any dream I had ever dreamt.

"A Pre-Raphaelite vision" I said with more confidence.

She moved in close placing her hand by the side of my neck, slowly cupping her fingers behind my head, bathing in the balm of the compliment as I stood looking at a universe tumbling through her hair with its stars melting in her eyes. Anne was a Pre-Raphaelite dream that no Pre-Raphaelite had ever seen and I mourned their loss.

Hefyn and Megan were waiting for us by the gates of the Institute, as Anne's father dropped us off. Carol and Noel arrived soon after and we all paid at the door and went in. The Crazy Line rocked. We danced all night, sipping on bottles of cherry cola between dances. We chatted in loud voices trying in vain to raise them above the volume of the music. Occasionally I would beckon Anne to lean forward, whispering in her ear, telling her how beautiful she looked and felt as we dance close.

Towards the end of the evening I noticed Tebbutt standing at the side of the hall. He flagrantly stared in my direction. Ignoring him the best I could, I moved around, but he would alter his position so his stare could catch my gaze once more.

At the end of the evening the slow dances started and the 'Crazy Line' sang a slow ballad. I put my hand into the small of Anne's back and pulled her gently towards me and whispered in her ear in time to the music, the words of the song.

We held each other close. The 'space' between us, surrounded us, drawing us in. We stepped closer and closer, wanting, whispering, feeling, but that hunger burnt inside us. Wondering if she felt the same; every part of her seemed to tingle as I touched her and I knew she did. In the middle of the crowded floor we danced alone, again the only two people on the face of the earth, slowly turning through the night sky with the stars crowding in around us, watching and waiting for the moment to end.

We continued to sway from side to side, long after the music had finished; both locked into each other. The hall was almost empty as the lights went up, but we continued endlessly swaying, touching, slowly spiralling out of control. I could feel Anne's arms around my neck hugging me into her; I could feel every part of her body next to mine through the thin material of her dress; I could feel her head on my shoulder and the touch of her hair on my skin; I could smell the faint aroma of her fading perfume mixed with her sweet summer sweat. I wanted to taste her, smell her, to bury my head in her arms, to hold her, never letting go; I wanted to feel her naked in my arms, beneath my hands, to kiss every part of her, with my tongue and lips pulling at her heart.

We began to kiss still dancing through a universe of lights and stars. The band, who had begun to clear away their equipment, stopped to watch us. One of them gave a long low slow whistle and then called out.

"Now that's what I'm singing about" But another gave a shrill wolf whistle, dragging us from our dreams. Slowly we untangled our hearts and walked out to the others.

Tebbutt was waiting at the gate and if I wasn't careful he would ruin the evening. Hefyn was doing a good job of fending him off, trying to reason with him. Since a child I had never fought. I knew all the moves, had all the theory, but was short on the practice. My mouth seemed to reason far more eagerly than my fists would punch and I had always managed to sidestep trouble, only ever having hit two people in my life. The first was Andy, my brother. I got into an argument with him and he 'lost it'. He began to rage at me, milling like a windmill. I buried my head in my arms, preferring to defend than attack, and it was working up to a point, until one of his fists caught my jaw. He went down with one well aimed blow, but he was younger than me and it didn't count. The other was a bully like Tebbutt; a lad from my old school. I had been walking arm in arm with a girl; one of those puppy dog relationships. The lad started to follow us around, calling me, kicking at my heels. If the girl hadn't been there I would have dealt with him in the usual manner, but I lost it, and turned on him swinging out wildly. My fist caught him in the throat and he went down gripping at his throat. Wheezing and choking, I thought he was going to die.

Tebbutt had been wearing on me since that first day at school and that night, I could see my patience was about to be tested to its limits. I let go of Anne's hand and stepped forward through the gate with Anne trying to call me back, realising what was going on. Tebbutt grabbed me as he had done outside the school, placing his fist up against my face, again spraying out his twisted words.

"We must stop meeting like this!" I said sarcastically and seeing the rage in his face, I continued,

"I have no wish to fight with you Tebbutt…and if all you're going to do is talk me to death…then I'm going!"

I pushed past him, his grip loosened and I started to walk off. I heard his heavy footsteps on the path behind me, but it was too late. His chest hit me square in the back as he wrapped his arms around my body and clasped his hands tightly in front of me, interlocking his fingers; trapping my arms at my sides. The amount of strength he exerted in his grip surprised me slightly and I wondered if I had overestimated my abilities. I was helpless and felt my body forced forward, but stepping out with one foot; I bent my legs slightly and leaned forward in an attempt to prevent myself from falling face first in the dirt.

It all happened so quickly. One minute, Tebbutt's weight was completely on top of me, forcing me to lean further forward, but I managed to remain on my feet. His weight was too much for me, and I could feel how precarious he was on top of me, so certain of my balance I leant further forward and he overbalanced completely. Letting go, he toppled to the ground, landing hard on his back, hitting the floor with a thump. I could hear his strained wheezing and he started to choke slightly as the wind was knocked out of him. He had pushed me too far and I could feel the anger rising inside me. It raced through every muscle and sinew, and I wanted to fall on him, pounding on his helpless body, but instead, and much to my surprise, I just offered him my hand.

"Sorry mate" I said, shaking under the façade of my calm exterior. But he refused to take it. As he slowly got to his feet, I was ready with my feet planted firmly on the ground in a wide stance and my arms and fists flexing at my side. Tebbutt stared at me only for a moment, before he turned, walking off through the crowd that had gathered behind us. I hadn't really done anything; it was his own weight and force that put him on his back, but I wasn't going to tell anyone else that.

I walked Anne along Bottom Road to the end of Parry Lane, with the trembling inside me slowly seeping and edging from my body. We stood waiting for Anne's father, endlessly kissing; the music from the band still ringing in our ears. We began to dance, slowly smooching as we stepped from side to side. Holding each other close, we danced under a cloudless night sky.

With the gaze of the Land Rover's headlights catching us in their stare, I whispered. "I won't let you go…not now…not ever"

My words were futile, but Anne's eyes smiled her encouragement as she buried her head in my neck.

"I love you!" I breathed in her ear with the tantalizing touch of her hair on my face and neck.

Anne went to say something, but she seemed to change her mind for some reason. I could almost see what she was thinking.

"I'll meet you on top of the cliff in an hour!" I heard the words inside my head but knowing she felt the same. It's what we both wanted; I could see the blaze in her eyes, but she just smiled.

"I'll see you in the morning David!" She placed her forefinger on my lips, parting them slightly as she continued to hold my gaze, but then she turned to go.

CHAPTER SEVENTEEN

Anne's father dropped us at Llyn Ogwen, telling us to be careful, but trusting us enough to be sensible. We each wore sturdy, but comfortable walking boots that had endlessly stepped rock to rock on a myriad of mountain and forest trails. Each of us carried a rucksack with enough food and water for the day and waterproofs if we needed them. I also carried a small board, some watercolour paints, a sketchpad and a camera.

Nain had packed plenty of food for me telling me on the back doorstep to be careful, so as not to wake the whole house. Meeting Hefyn and Megan by the farm gates we walked down Parry Lane to wait for Anne and her father. The journey hadn't taken long, across the Denbigh moors, past the old hunting lodge; on past Betws-y-coed and up towards Tryfan.

Hefyn and I rode in the back with the dogs, while the girls rode up front with Anne's father. He had put the cover over the back of the old Land Rover and I imagined myself as an old American pioneer, riding in a covered wagon. Although we had put our waterproof tops on for the journey the weather was mild and promised to be good for the rest of the weekend. Care would be necessary though as the mountains have a weather system all of their own and walkers have often been caught out on deceptively good days.

All of us had walked the big mountains before, both with our parents and on our own, but never all together. That day we planned to walk over several mountains, finishing near Beddgelert, at the car park near the bottom of Watkins path, on the far side of Snowdon.

Looking up from Ogwen to Tryfan, the first mountain we planned climb, in the early morning light the mist was still creeping down its sides. The sun was bright, just above the mountains. Tryfan looked magnificent floating amongst the clouds of mist surrounding it. We walked along Ogwen on the road and then off on the track upwards towards the Canon and up and out onto the Heather Terrace.

The views from the terrace were magnificent; early morning mists giving way to the bright sunlight, with only the odd white cloud in the sky. With the extra weight, I could feel the rucksack cutting into my shoulders, but I remember thinking it would be worth it in the end. We chatted as we moved along the terrace, making good time.

We skirted around the top of Tryfan as all of us had jumped from Adam to Eve and Eve to Adam before. We chose instead to press on, giving us more time to make our rendezvous at the car park by half past ten that evening. We dropped down off the back of the mountain and then climbed up towards the Castle of Winds and the Glyders.

We stopped for a few minutes at the 'Castle', taking in some food and water while admiring the views as sitting amongst its spiny turrets. Every step brought a new watercolour to my eyes, changing skies and colours on the mountains reflected in the lakes. Off the rugged slopes of Glyder Fach, we climbed down towards Pen-y-Pass and the car park. We had made excellent time and l felt quite fresh although my legs were beginning to ache as we walked out of the car park and up onto the Pyg-Track leading to the top of Snowdon.

Climbing steeply up the track ahead, stepping rock-to-rock, we reached the gate where the first major decision of the day had to be made: the Pyg-track or Crib-Goch?

"Crib-Goch!" We had all climbed there before, but only with youth leaders, never on our own. Crib-Goch could be very dangerous, often walking a thin knife-edge of jagged rock with sheer drops on either side.

The sun hammered down, as we climbed the steep sides of the mountain at the beginning of the path, but the climb was worth it for the views at the top. Fanned by a cool breeze we rested awhile, puffing and panting and slightly red faced. Megan's fair skin was suffering in the sun, but other than that the girls matched us step for step. In the strenuous exertions of our climb we were all developing large pools of sweat on our T-shirts, under our arms and down the centre of our backs.

I smiled across at Anne, remembering all the feelings that had pulsed through me the night before. I moved a little closer and she smiled back.

Scrambling across the knife-edge of rock at the top, we watched people walking the Pyg Track down below. My eyes gazed further on, down into the lakes and across the causeway. Climbing behind Anne I watched her every move, muttering a silent prayer with every footstep she made. Climbing at such a height, I marvelled at her strength and quiet composure on the rock.

Anne turned and smiled at me. My eyes looked, carefully searching, tracing the shape of her body through her jeans; and tumbling with her hair, my thoughts slowly stirred distant possibilities.

We continued to walk the precarious mountain trail. Our climb was interrupted by the large edifices of rock rising up to block our path. One by one we scrambled over their rocky outcrops, until Glaslyn came into view, its water an opaque cerulean blue mixed with varying shades of olive green. Glaslyn was bathed in the suns golden glow. We paused to take in the scene and countless panoramas on every side.

"We'll not go swimming in there then?" Hefyn said. Glaslyn is the highest natural lake in Wales and there are many myths and legends surrounding it. Anne told us a story she had heard from her grandmother, of a fairy princess who once walked out of the lakes depths, took off all her clothes and after washing them and laying them out to dry, she placed them back on and walked back into its depths.

"Maybe we will go swimming there, then!" I said with a grin on my face.

"Steady Tiger!" Anne said, looking across at me.

I looked out through the clear early afternoon skies, past Snowdon, to where I could see the west coast of Wales as it stretched out above Cader-Idris, and on towards the hazy horizon. On the other side of the ridge I looked across to Anglesey with its comparatively flat landscape. Turning back on myself I looked back to the Glyders and could just make out part of the path we had walked that morning.

Each turn I made exposed a different view, a patchwork of layered landscapes, marching out to meet the misty mountaintops of distant watercolour horizons. The sounds of the mountain rose up to meet us. Mountain streams tumbling over high rocks, birds scavenging for the crumbs walkers had left and the breeze in our ears. My senses were full and a tremor ran through me as Anne took hold of my hand. She indicated to a small group of mountains on the Lleyn Peninsula and pointing to one in particular as she said,

"See the one on the left, that's standing almost alone?"

"Yes!" I said, quietly.

"My uncle lives just to the right of it" I looked out through the warm hazy day, towards his silent misty mountain home and wondered if everyone in Wales had their very own mountain to watch over and mother them. I thought of how my own family's mountain had watched over and suckled both our families for countless generations.

Continuing along the path, we followed the railway track for the last stretch. On reaching the summit we sat to one side, trying to avoid the groups of tourists. We drank and ate our pack-ups, as the sun soaked into our bodies and warmed our aching limbs. Our boots felt hot and awkward on our feet as the sweat on our backs cooled in the breeze.

A group of eight walkers sat off to our right. One of them was shouting his mouth off about places he had climbed and glaciers he had traversed; Alps this, Himalayas that. He had all the equipment, even crampons strapped to the back of his pack; although I had to wonder why in mid-summer. Even his ice axe looked like it had just come out of its box. It certainly didn't look as if it had ever done much climbing.

The group got up and walked off in the general direction we were heading. The man, who had been shouting his mouth off, was like John Wayne at the front of the U.S. Cavalry. We packed our stuff away and made our own way down towards the pinnacle of rock that marks the beginning of our descent, the top of the Watkins Path.

Following the group, I could see the two at the back weren't as confident on the mountain as some of the others. The man at the back, whom I would estimate was in his late forties, was wearing a pair of old, badly worn Doc Marten shoes that had little grip. They must have been size twelve at least, and looked more like brothel creepers than walking boots.

I couldn't believe what I was seeing. John Wayne at the front was climbing over the edge of the mountain, starting down before the beginning of the track. The Watkins path at the top is quite steep, traversing the side of Snowdon above large cliffs. The path is sharp at best and long scree slopes cross it, making climbing down difficult, even for experienced walkers. John Wayne, by cutting down early, was making a difficult job more dangerous. I ran forward waving to the group, concerned mainly for the couple at the back, and out of breath I said,

"It's just a little further" I explained that a pinnacle of rock marked the beginning of the path and that it was only a little further down the mountain. John Wayne looked at me. I could hear what he was thinking.

'What does a kid know?' He turned his back on me saying,

"Come on! I've done this before" Disappearing out of sight. He may have done it all before, but it was obvious that some of his group hadn't. We stood there, in disbelief.

"We'll go down to the path, you and Hefyn follow them" Megan said being serious for once. I didn't quite know what we could have done, if anything, but we did as Megan suggested. I watched as the girls walked off to the beginning of the path and Hefyn turned with me, to climb down after the group. They weren't difficult to catch, John Wayne charging off into the distance leaving the two at the rear to fend for themselves.

Hefyn started to help the woman climb down the more difficult drops and I helped the man with the old Doc Martins'. They both seemed relieved and grateful for our help. Approaching one of the larger scree slopes I looked down to where I could see Anne and Megan on the path off to our right hand side, just below us.

I climbed down a short drop at the top of the slope and was just about to turn around when I heard rocks slipping behind me. The man had lost his footing. There was a low thud and I heard him moan as his breath left him. He landed on his rucksack upside down, just beside me on the rock. He bounced and tumbled onto scree and curled himself up into a ball, doing large forward rolls as he went.

When you're falling, your reflexes automatically make you protect your head and you curl your legs in, to protect your vital organs. Of course on a mountainside heading towards a cliff with a drop of two hundred feet or more, it is the last thing you need to do. You have to fight against your instinct and spread yourself out, praying with every fibre and sinew in your body that you will stop in time.

Without thinking I started to chase the man down the scree, with small rocks and boulders moving like quicksand beneath my feet. Running down scree slopes presents its own hazards. You can easily twist or break an ankle or cause the scree to move so much that it sweeps you off the mountainside in an avalanche of granite. But I had sturdy walking boots on, with good ankle support. Hefyn and I had both run on scree slopes before and I was reasonably confident in what I was doing, but my confidence was relative to my proximity to the cliff's edge.

Hefyn had started down the slope behind me and as we both ran, we shouted for the man to keep low and spread himself out, but each time he landed on his back he tried to straighten his legs and as his feet hit the ground he would try to stand up, catapulting himself further off the mountainside. We were fast running out of slope and I could see the edge of the cliff gaining on me rapidly. I was managing to keep pace with the man as he did big forward rolls, both of us moving rocks and scree as we went.

His body seemed to go limp, flopping down onto the broken ground, as he came to a rest with the scree still moving beneath him. Both Hefyn and I were with him in moments and I could immediately see that he was still breathing, but badly dazed. The rocks beneath our feet were steadying slightly, but their movement still made me feel uneasy, with the drop about five yards further down the slope. As he came round, feeling the movement, he started to panic and like a scolded cat he clawed at the mountainside.

"You're not going anywhere" I said to him and placed my foot on the ground firmly between his legs, asking him his name. He looked up through his dazed and confused world, at me.

"Steve" he said, stuttering and shaking as he spoke.

Hefyn started to check him over, asking where it hurt and whether he could move different limbs, each in turn. I spoke to him and tried to raise his spirits. The scree was steady again, but it was twenty minutes before we could encourage him to move. Forty minutes later he was back on the path they should have been walking down, in the first place. The moment his feet touched the downward trail, John Wayne turned to him.

"All right mate, come on then" and off he went, blazing his trail again. Steve turned around and thanked both Hefyn and myself and then turned again to follow John Wayne down the mountainside. I watched as he scrambled down a few small drops in the rock and saw him struggling nervously to gain his composure.

Turning to Anne and Megan I could see their eyes were red and their cheeks were wet from crying. Megan was still sobbing quietly to herself, as Hefyn went to put his arm around her, wondering what was wrong. I could remember hearing screams as we ran down the scree, towards the cliff, but did not imagine for a moment that it would be them. I held my arms out towards Anne, and she hugged me close.

"What's wrong?" I asked, I felt her warm wet tears on my neck and gently kissed her eyelids, tasting the salty tears on my lips.

"Don't ever do anything like that again!" She whispered in my ear.

"I thought I was going to lose you!"

I had acted out of instinct, not really considering the consequences, but for Anne and Megan looking helplessly on, at a situation running out of control, it must have been terrifying. The thought of having to return without us and explain to parents why their sons were not with them was too much. Holding the thought we walked carefully down the path and I quietly contemplated how delicate life could be, turning to Anne at every step in the mountain, helping her down, much to her annoyance.

We followed the group down, but kept a discreet distance. When we reached the neck between Snowdon and Y Lliwedd Bach, we stopped, taking time to walk across to peer over at Glaslyn, from the opposite side of the mountains. I looked down into the depths of the lake from our pulpit perched high in the spires of our rocky vantage point. Standing with the ancient hills around me, I thought of a quote from Li Po, which always reminded me of walking down the lanes of Rhydymwyn and out on to the mountains with Taid. I was stood at the edge of the world, hand in hand with Anne, her head resting on my shoulder and I repeated the words out loud.

"We sit together, the mountain and me, until only the mountain remains."

There was a long pause as a mountain of thoughts tumbled through me.

"That makes me feel sad!" Anne said quietly,

"I don't know why!"

I remained silent, staring out over Glaslyn with Anne at my side, her hair blowing in the breeze. Hefyn and Megan sat on a huge rock, tangled up in each other, somewhere to our rear.

I thought of my grandfather and one thought lead to another.

A tear began to well in my eye; it broke free onto my cheek. I raised my hand up to wipe it quickly away, trying to conceal it, but Anne looked up and caught me.

"What's wrong?" She asked, turning to me.

"Nothing!" I said,

"Nothing…really!" Anne gave me one of those looks, as her eyes smiled up at me and I cracked.

"Just sad thoughts" I said, not wanting to explain further, but she would not let it be.

"Sad thoughts about me!"

"No, no!" I said, quickly,

"About…?" Anne held me in her gaze.

"About Taid" I said, hoping that would be the end of it.

"Happy sad thoughts" Anne whispered to me.

"I wish I had known him"

"Maybe, one day!" I said as we turned to find the others.

CHAPTER EIGHTEEN

The afternoon continued on its downward path and we descended quickly to the old quarry. We could see Steve's group in front of us, with John Wayne still charging off ahead, leaving the rest of the cavalry to bring up the rear. By the time we got to Cwm-y-llan we were drawing level with the main part of his group. Stopping momentarily, we asked Steve how he felt and again he thought to thank us for what we had done. I didn't feel we had done much, or that he had much to thank us for, and I felt slightly embarrassed. We hadn't prevented or cured anything, although I had desperately wanted to, and maybe it was for that thought he gave his thanks. We passed John Wayne in silence just above the waterfalls. He tutted while stopping to look back, making out he was waiting for the rest of his group.

We soon reached the mountain pools; they were beautiful; just as I remembered them. There's something about water running over rocks. The sound, the rush, the music of its cool waters calling on hot summer afternoons to bones and limbs that ache from stepping endlessly, rock to rock, over a thousand mountain trails.

The car-park was about thirty minutes away and marked the end of our journey, but there were hours before Anne's father would pick us up and our intentions were not to reach the car-park just yet. We had planned greater things for the rest of our day. So instead of following the path through the gate, we cut left and walked carefully down to the flat slab of rock spanning the tumbling mountain stream. Opening the small metal gate, we crossed over to the other side where we made our way to a secluded pool. It was beautiful.

Tucked away under the mountain, beneath the shelter of a few straggling, windswept trees; the pool was hidden away from the path and mountain above, so there would be no prying eyes to disturb us for the rest of the day. Its fresh mountain waters were crystal clear and numbingly cold. To the right of the pool the water fell about thirty feet from the pool above and to the left was a raised ledge where the wind swept trees took root. The rocks where the waterfall fell, shone in a myriad of dark colours and hues, glowing in a shimmering blaze of dancing reflections in the afternoon sun.

My legs ached as I sat down and we all eased tired feet from hot sweaty boots. Cooling our feet on the short sheep-shorn grass beneath us, we sat at the edge of the pool and soaked our limbs in its depths. The clamour of its bubbling waters massaged our legs, its foaming turbulence tickling our toes. The sun was still hot, reflecting and dancing on the surface of the water and it called us to bathe.

The girls changed behind one of the bushes. I wasn't getting caught out again and had been wearing my trunks all day so quickly stripping off; I was the first to dive in.

The shock of the cold mountain torrent hit me like a bolt of lightning. I came up gulping and panting for air, but its pure waters soothed into me. Hefyn dived in as the girls appeared from behind the bush and soon we were all enjoying a day at the pool. Swimming underwater and up into the waterfall, I could feel its power flowing through me. We sat on the rocks just below the surface of the water with the waterfall spilling and pounding on our bodies.

I held Anne's hand and we slipped off the smooth rocks into the depths of the pool, its power still rushing around us. I peered up through the clear waters at a sparkling phosphorescence of bubbles, caught in shafts of bright sunlight, as it blazed around Anne. The bubbles seemed to glisten as they surrounded us, dancing on their endless meandering journey to the world above. Anne's hair floated free, framing the perfect symmetry of her face, and looking into each other we kissed, long and slow. Everything seemed to pause, the bubbles, the waterfall, even time stood still as it waited patiently for the moment to end.

Taking hold of Anne's waist I lifted her from our watery bed. The crystal flashed past my eyes as the sunlight pierced its many facets. I pulled her close to me and kissed her belly. Then, cursing love for its shortness of breath, I too returned to the world above.

Climbing out onto the grass verge above our heads, the four of us took turns jumping into the depths of the pool. Diving, jumping, swimming and playing, we exhausted ourselves in the stream.

I climbed to the top of the waterfall and looking down, I watched Anne. My eyes followed her every move, just as I had done at the Ruby Pool. She swam to the far side of the pool where it was shallow, and standing near to the far end, she pulled her hair back into a ponytail. Twisting it, she laid it back over her head and held it in place with one hand. I could see the day soaking into her. Taking her other hand, she began splashing water over her neck and shoulders as if it were a sweetly scented perfume. I saw each drop of water trickling down her back, splashing and shattering across the surface of the pool. Once again, I was caught up in the magic of her as she wandered through that other world and I longed to join her in that private secluded place.

Exhausted, we lay in the sun at the side of the pool. The afternoon was a graduated wash of cobalt blue that brushed slowly by, with small white patches of cloud, lifted out with a sponge. The sun leaned low over the mountains, glowing big and bright in the late afternoon haze. I watched as it bled its colours into the sky, mixed with a little ultramarine at the horizon. Foraging in my bag I took out my mother's camera and created landscapes through its lens, catching their light at the squeeze of a button. The shutter quickly caught the scene, as I wound more film into place.

I had borrowed my mum's old 'Agfa Isolette' which dad had bought for her when doing his national service in North Africa, a hybrid of a box camera and an SLR. Mum was a reasonable photographer and she had used the camera as far back as I could remember and I was turning its intentions towards Anne. She stood in front of me with her hair still slightly damp, looking to one side or the other; the low sun casting its deep orange glow onto her face. Looking through the lens with the camera melting, I told her how lovely she looked, 'a crystal shining in black water; my Pre-Raphaelite. At my words, she looked straight into me with the shutter tripping over her beauty.

My pencils and pad lay waiting impatiently for their turn and I sat, drawing Anne, with endless lines quietly calling my Pre-Raphaelite from the white paper in front of me. Fingers, hands and eyes all worked quickly, but delicately, desperate to catch each detail. But no matter how hard I tried, I could not stop myself from gazing at her. My eyes lingered for long moments around her face and through her hair, tracing every line of her body. From where I sat, I could smell and feel her hair on my face from the night before and from when we both spent the night drenched in the silver light of the moon. The mountain slipped away and clouds drained from the sky. The heavens closed their mouth, holding their breath. The evening breeze stopped as the birds flew from their trees, mournfully singing their hymns as departing and we sat alone, the only two people in the whole world; with my eyes resting at her side.

High cloud bled across the sky, reflecting its light in deep washes of a water-colour sunset. Taking out the board I had prepared with paper taped to it and sitting next to Anne, we both took brushes wet with the colours of the evening skies and washed them across damp empty paper. Raw Sienna bleeding into light red, where French ultramarine waited to darken and subdue. Wet into wet, the vision appeared before us. Shadows creeping over the stone bridge that lay silently above the pools, reflecting an eternity of sky, which in turn fell into deep, dark waters. Hefyn and Megan came over to watch as we caught the tapestry of colours before they disappeared forever, in the miracle of their continuously rolling sunset.

The cool air of the evening called us to dry and dress ourselves. Hefyn and Megan went off to explore the waterfalls and pools that lay beneath us while Anne and I, sat together on the giant slab of granite, which formed the bridge, looking out over the ever-changing world below, each silently sharing the other, lost in dreams, trapped somewhere in time.

"This is our place!" I said quietly, looking into the waters rushing beneath us as they cascaded over the edge of the huge waterfall and out of sight; down into the world below.

"It's certainly beautiful, but it could never be our place" Anne said, as she slowly raised her eyes up to mine.

"Our place is that space we have created between us. It is a place where only we may dwell; a place where we can walk and talk of things only we could ever understand" Anne paused momentarily and then continued.

"Our place is a space deep inside us, a place that will always draw us towards each other, no matter where we are." She paused again, controlling the feelings welling inside her.

"I think you said it best, in my father's work shed, David! What was it you said?" She paused again,

"If the sky fell down…!"

My words were quiet and subdued.

"I think I said a little more than that… No matter where I go, no matter who stands at my side, or how much love surrounds me, even if the sky falls on me, crushing my body into the dirt of this earth, I would still be loving you"

"Can you feel Our Place and the space that has grown between us?"

I nodded, unable to speak as Anne rested her head on my shoulder and I began to whisper, in that space, of poems and dreams, of quiet thoughts and love. A tear rolled down her cheek, hanging close to her chin. I lifted my hand as the tear dropped and caught it as it fell. We looked in the palm of my hand as though I held some intricately cut, softly coloured, precious gem. Placing my hand over her heart, I felt the strong pulse of life beneath it and her soft warm skin beneath my fingers.

"Nain says this is where we keep fallen tears!" Anne smiled up at me with my hand over her heart and we kissed. Again and again we kissed, but eventually our kisses subsided and we began to talk. I wanted her to know everything.

"That first day at school, when I first walked into the classroom, something drew my eyes to you. It was as though I had been waiting all my life for that moment…maybe even longer. When I saw you, something happened to me; I think something happened to us both…I felt it…! Tell me I wasn't dreaming!" Anne shook her head.

"You weren't dreaming…I felt it too!" Her words raised a sluice deep inside me and the stream bubbled and surged through me.

"Hefyn had told me about you, and I didn't think much about it. Hefyn's a nice lad and all…but I don't fancy him and, I guess, I thought of you as being like him somehow…But when I saw you for the first time, something happened. You were nothing like I had imagined. Hefyn said I'd like you, but I couldn't believe the feelings that ran through me when I saw you standing in front of me that day!"

"…boy, I couldn't believe my luck when Mr Robertson led me to sit right in front of you. I couldn't wait till break to see you again; I had to turn around to check if what I had seen was real!"

"Twice!" Anne said quietly.

"Remember when you walked away, to talk to your friends at break; I followed every move of your body; I wondered who you were and what you were about. I longed to know more about you and I couldn't wait to talk to you again!"

Anne smiled.

"My friends all wanted to know who you were and how I knew you!"

"Since that first day, you've filled my life and being with you…I just can't think of anything or anyone else but you. You are constantly on my mind. My thoughts and dreams are only of you. I lay awake at night, turning to your heartbeat; I feel your fingers brushing over my stomach, just like at the Ruby Pool with your hand warming through as it rests on my chest! I think of you, lying in your bed, only a short walk through the woods from me…and I long to be there with you!" I paused, and after catching my breath, I quoted the Lady of Shalott.

"I'm half sick of shadows!"

I knew what I'd said the moment it fell from my lips, and I was worried about how she would take it.

"I don't mean… I just want to be with you, always and forever!" The surge of the stream built inside me again.

We sat, our hearts woven tightly together like an intricate tapestry sewn in subtle colours, and stretching out along the walls of the space between us. Nothing could touch us. We were invincible; the last of a band of Celtic Warriors, that this world could never quell.

We started to kiss again; long slow kisses and I could taste Anne on my lips. Again we felt as though we could climb inside each other, our kisses burning into each other. We were searching, wanting, needing, exploring each other, never wanting to let go. Anne sat between my legs, in front of me, on the rock bridge, leaning her head back onto my shoulder and I cradled her in my arms as we wrapped ourselves up, each in the others heart. Evening colours drifted off into the unbridled darkness of the night.

The rush of the water below us tumbled over the edge of the world and it dragged our feelings with it. We flew effortlessly into the velvet-graduated colours of the night as we soared up through the heavens, leaving the desolate empty void of the world far below us. It was as though the rock slab we sat on was floating free and we drifted out into the night, with warm breezes fanning the embers of our young passion.

I felt her breath on my neck, her soft scented hair against my skin. There was a rush of feelings inside us as my cold hand found the gap between her T-shirt and jeans; my fingers wandering over the flat lowlands of her stomach. She pulled me closer.

The clank of the metal gate, to one side of the bridge, and a forced cough, dragged furtive hands quickly from Anne's clothes. A climber stood to one side of us, on the bridge; a darkened silhouette waiting patiently to pass.

"I'm sorry!" A quiet voice whispered reverently into the stillness of the night as we made room for him to step over us. When he had gone, we laughed out loud in our interrupted innocence and watched the solitary figure walk off into the twilight and darkness of the mountain. With night falling quickly around us, we reluctantly rose and started to walk the path that would eventually lead us home.

Hefyn and Megan were waiting for us, sitting on a wall near the car park as tightly wrapped in each other as Anne and I had been on the bridge over the mountain stream. I still had some sandwiches and shared them out. I thought of Nain, carefully calculating the food I would need for the day and packing some extra. Sandwiches for one, times by the time I would be away, times-by the love she sent with them.

The lights of the Land Rover silhouetted our huddled figures on the low wall of the bridge and we were soon on our way back to the refuge of our own mountain homes, to be cradled once more for the night by our own misty mother mountain.

CHAPTER NINETEEN

Anne's father had arranged with her uncle, for Anne and her mother to spend a week's holiday on her uncle's farm during the last week in the summer holidays. That meant Anne and I only had two more days together before going to college and on one of those days, Anne would have to spend her time sorting things out for the holiday and getting ready for the new term.

College, the very thought filled me with dread, drenching me in the mixed memories of that last week at school. It hadn't been good, with 'Tebbutt' picking on me at every opportunity and six of the best on the first day, but Anne would be there, and that seemed to make all the difference in the world; and Tebbutt wouldn't. He had got a job working for his father in the family business as a driver, which I doubted because he wasn't old enough to drive a car, let alone a lorry.

Anne and I would both be going on for A levels; Art and English. It would be fun going to College together. I had scraped through my English, how? I don't know, but that would mean two classes we would share. I presumed we would have others, but something still nagged at me, insecurities I guess.

Mum and Dad had stopped looking for a house in the area, saying 'the time isn't right just now', and 'not to worry'.

Thursday it rained all day. I spent the morning working on the sketch of Anne, producing two further sketches and scribbling ideas for the painting, down the margins. Although I would miss her terribly, the week would give me the opportunity to complete the painting I had already planned out in my mind, each detail and wash scrupulously pored over until I could see it bringing life to the paper. It would be a masterpiece. I spent Thursday afternoon reading poetry and studying a Pre-Raphaelite book Carole had lent me.

My sister was brilliant at art and I had always existed somewhat in her shadow; she was going on to 'Manchester Uni', taking Graphics and Illustration. I loved drawing and painting. I was pretty good, I thought, but when you placed one of my drawings next to Carole's, my efforts paled into insignificance. She was my mentor though, and over the years I had continuously watched her, and with childish immaturity, I vowed that one day I would be as good as her.

It's different now. To me there's no such thing as good or bad, just like or dislike. You cannot judge something that someone finds attractive or pleasing to the eye as bad; just the same, as you cannot class something that has no meaning, beauty or poetry in its heart as being art.

On the Friday we decided to have one last day together in the Italian Woods, maybe to do a little fishing, maybe some swimming or maybe we would just walk through the woods. The girls had obvious reservations, but I pointed out, that after my encounter with the 'Hound from Hell' I was still alive. I think we all recognised that our lives would be changing in no small way following the summer and it felt appropriate for us to say goodbye to the woods, one last time; before stepping into the adult world that lay in wait for us. Who knows when we would get the chance to walk in the woods again?

I arrived at Hefyn's halfway through milking. After lending a hand with his jobs we walked up the road, past the old limekiln, towards Megan's.

Anne and Megan were sitting on the large beamed wooden table outside the farm gates, with milk churns standing like tin soldiers next to them. On getting closer the girls stood up and walked across the road. Climbing the wooden gate into the field we all walked off towards Griag-y-'Jingles' which led down into the valley and over Bottom Road.

The Italian Woods got its name from the Italian prisoners of war who worked there during the Second World War. Some of them had stayed on, even marrying local girls. Some of the older trees had Italian names cut into their bark next to the names of Welsh girls.

Earlier in the summer we had seen an old oak, up along the Leat, with 'Brio' and 'Megan' carved neatly within a heart. The old bark had covered over where the tree's flesh would have been exposed, but the inscription was still clear.

First we teased Megan, asking her who her Italian lover was. Then for the rest of the day we called Hefyn, Brio, much to his disgust. He eventually joined in the fun, talking with a ludicrously caricatured Italian accent. Turning to Megan he would say. "We makah' d'lurv?" Chasing her around as she squealed with excitement.

We took time to explore some caves and cliffs in Griag-y-'Jingles' before crossing over the road towards the 'Ruby Brick'. Hefyn had brought a torch; an old thing that rattled, but it was enough to light our way and we walked right to the end of one of the caves. There was a large pool of water, which seemed to be fed by what looked like a small spring that seeped from its side wall and we had to keep to the other edge as we slowly made our way to the caves damp dark end.

Walking back into the daylight I imagined generations of cavemen and their families living there, lifetimes before. Anne interrupted my thoughts, stating she had once been told that the Romans had mined rock out of the cliff for the villas they built in the area and that her grandmother had told her stories of the Celts who had lived there, which managed in some small way, to recreate my dream.

The day was almost perfect with small clouds only occasionally drifting in front of the suns warming rays. In the shadows it brought the damp from the grass and trees in little flurries of mist. We crossed the road and walked along the bank of our own little stream. A summer full of birds seemed to sing constantly amid the whisper of the breeze through the leaves of the trees as the green rhapsody of the woods tumbled off the mountain of tears. The chuckle of water in the stream trickled by, as it splashed across the surface of shimmering pools and the thick smell of wild garlic, saturated through us. The shrill chorus of a single song thrush filled my ears and as we moved closer to the woods I could hear a second answering its call.

We all had reservations as moving up towards the metal bridge, but we had left school and were going to college in a few more days. I distinctly remember the thought of having to be grown up about everything.

Carefully stepping down onto the rock in the middle of the stream, we picked our way under the bridge to pass out of sight of Old Gwennie's, which seemed to be fast asleep. But as we came out on the other side, a cloud passed in front of the sun bringing a chill to the air and a shiver ran down my spine as someone crawled over my grave, not for the first time that summer. I looked at the others. We were all too old to believe in Witches, but still something would not let me be and like everyone else, I had just picked my way under the bridge as I had done throughout my childhood. I had half thought of just walking over the bridge in full sight of Gwennie and her cottage, but I was gripped by strange irrational feelings that had compelled me, with the others, to jump down onto the security of our rock. It was somehow our passport into the woods. So much for being grown up and I balked at my insecurities.

The door to Old Gwennie's was open with a broken pane of glass in one of the dark bare windows. I could see another window was splintered and cracked, with a hole at its centre.

We jumped suddenly as something squawked at us from the branches above our heads. I looked up to see Gwennie's scraggy old magpie staring down at us with its one good eye.

"Shush, Maggie!" Hefyn said quietly with his finger against his lips, not wishing to wake the dead or Old Gwennie. Maggie squawked again.

"MAGGIE!" It wasn't Hefyn who called out the second time; the voice had called from the direction of Gwennie's garden. Like startled rabbits caught in the headlights of a car, we roused our senses and were all up and out of the stream running off as fast as lightning, passing the old winding house before we slowed our hearts or legs. Standing in a group, red faced and panting with all of us out of breath and laughing, we asked each other in turn, if anyone had seen Gwennie; we hadn't.

'So much for my brave new world.'

Excited by the rush of the chase, we continued to walk up the stream to the Ruby Pool.

It was too early for swimming and we sat talking, leaning against the trees on top of the bank. The song thrush was singing its heart out in the branches of one of the trees behind where we sat. It sang its song, repeated itself, changed its song and repeated it again. The morning was indeed beautiful and we all drifted away into our own little worlds.

Anne and I both looked down into the mineshaft at the bottom of the pool and I couldn't believe how I had ever dared to swim down into its huge gaping mouth and on into the jaws of the underworld. Anne whispered to me,

"When you disappeared into the darkness, we all stood staring at each other not knowing what to do or say! I couldn't believe it! Hefyn was the funniest; you know how he is. He brushed his hand through his hair, scratching his head, and just stood there, with his mouth gulping like a gold fish" She paused and half laughed then said, "I wondered if I'd ever see you again; maybe I could have sent a letter to Australia!"

Megan caught some of what Anne was saying and she and Hefyn butted in. We were all laughing and joking; none of us paying any attention to the woods, which were slowly waking around us. The squawk of 'Maggie' brought us all quickly back to the reality of our surroundings and although we hadn't seen or heard anything else, we decided to walk a little further up the stream with Maggie squawking her goodbyes in the dark woods behind us.

Further upstream, we walked past the Rabbit Warrens, where Hefyn and I had freed the wild dog from the netting and climbing the steep bank we showed the girls the remains of the snare and nets. Megan dismissed it all as an elaborately concocted hoax, and not even that elaborate.

Walking a little further, we came to High-banks just past the Old Wooden Dam, which because of the ravages of time just sat and watched as the stream's waters flowed under its timbers. The tall clay banks towered above us on one side of the stream. At the top of the bank there was an overhanging grass lip and an almost sheer graduated slope of damp clay pebbles, strewn into the stream at the bottom, like scree. We could see trout swimming in a pool to one side of the bank, but we had no wish to catch them so early in the day.

"Watch this!" Hefyn said, a sly grin breaking out onto his face as he climbed round to the top of the bank. He stood on the overhanging grass lip, fifteen feet or so above us. Looking down, we were all sat with large rounded boulders for seats. Spreading his arms out with his fingers outstretched, he raised himself onto tip-toes. He looked like one of those divers in the movies, diving into the ocean from the cliffs above Acapulco. The girls began to shout and cheer him on. Anne gave a shrill whistle right next to my ear, almost deafening me.

He jumped up slightly and landed again on the overhanging piece of grass, it immediately broke away. He dropped like a stone with the grass and earth still held firmly beneath his feet. The curve of the bank slowed his fall as he reached the bottom with his arms still outstretched. When he came to a stop, he stared across at us with a grin chiselled onto his face.

"I'm having some of that!" I said, running around to the top of the bank. It was the last summer of our childhood. We were all moving onto to A-levels and the adult world of further education. I felt quite mature, but I wasn't going to relinquish my childhood so easily. Standing as Hefyn had with arms outstretched, I gave a feeble Tarzan call, while beating my fists against my chest as I stamped eagerly on the grass beneath my feet. Part of the grass came away leaving my foot dangling in mid-air with the other foot trapped at the top. I overbalanced slightly and trying to regain my balance I was forced to jump. My feet alone didn't make a very efficient braking system on the clay wall and my landing was heavier than Hefyn's, and not as graceful. I winded myself slightly, but on hearing the others laughing; gritted my teeth and took my usual bow. Anne shouted across,

"Get over here you idiot!"

Anne suggested that we all went up to Top Pond. I had been up there before, but not that summer. The top pond was about level with the Ruby Pool and although it was only a couple of hundred yards away from the stream, it was hidden behind a steep climb and woods so thick that in places you couldn't see any light through the trees above you.

As we walked back down the stream towards the Ruby Pool I heard Maggie squawk again, somewhere off in the distance. We were all cautious walking back down to Ruby Pool. Megan occasionally jumped at imagined sounds, from deeper in the woods, while Hefyn and I tried rather unconvincingly to look calm. A cloud had covered the sun, bringing a chill to the air and dark shadows loomed out at us from beneath the trees. We were surrounded on every side. The deep shadows beneath the trees hid eyes and faces that constantly stared back at us. Hefyn cautiously walked in front with me, as usual, bringing up the rear.

I watched Anne as she moved steadily from rock to rock, occasionally pausing, holding her hair back from her face as she looked for her next footfall. Her hair tumbled down her back with the shape of her body clearly defined under her T-shirt and jeans. She walked with a certain grace and poise, and I could see the untamed power I knew she possessed, radiating from somewhere deep inside her. It was like a lighthouse shinning in the storm of the dark tempestuous woods and I thought of how little I really knew her and the same yearning; almost desperate feelings of wanting more of her, came flooding into me.

I didn't want to have or possess her; that would have meant taming her in some way. I wanted to be with her, watching, waiting, sharing in whatever wonders her life and mine would bring to us.

Hefyn stopped and raised his right hand with its fingers out stretched. We all paused, standing motionless behind him, straining our ears to hear, our eyes searching to see. I inched quietly forward, passing the girls and whispered to Hefyn,

"What is it?"

"I don't know!" he said, in less than a whisper, so the girls couldn't hear.

"There's something off in the woods!" he said, although I couldn't hear or see anything.

With all of us on edge we moved nervously forward. The sun was still blinded by a cloud and I could see goose pimples on Anne's arms as we stepped from the rocks in the stream and back onto the path. I put my arm around her to try to take away the chill.

We paused for a while just before the Ruby Pool, Megan saying something quietly to Hefyn. The squawk of Maggie once again pierced our ears and we looked up with a start and there she was. She had stepped out onto the pathway, from behind a thicket of bushes, about five yards from us; Old Gwennie.

Her grey matted hair, hung in rat's tails half hiding her face. She appeared to be exactly as I had imagined her in my nightmares that morning in the woods; all except her eyes, which were dim and grey and old. A dirty old-grey-flannel dress was covered in front by a grimy pinafore apron. And covering it all she wore an old dark blue hooded coat, which hung open at the front. Maggie squawked again and flew out from somewhere behind her, landing on Gwennie's shoulder. Maggie squawked continuously at us staring with her one good eye, but Gwennie apparently hadn't seen us yet. Slowly, Gwennie raised her head, her stare catching ours as we all stood frozen on the path.

I was petrified, unable to move, feeling the fear draining out of the air around me. Every breath I took filled me with more and more dread until I was eventually full, so full, I felt I couldn't move. I could see nothing, but the path and Gwennie standing on it. Darkness once again started to surround me and I remembered the vow I had made.

I quickly stepped in front of Anne, my body pulsing with the beat of my heart and my limbs heavy as lead. I was ready, ready and waiting to deal with whatever terror was about to befall us. But just at that moment, there came a rustle from bushes where Gwennie had appeared and out stepped the 'Hound from Hell'. It too, stood blocking our path, directly in front of Gwennie.

All my energy sapped away with the appearance of our new adversary. It stood, staring at us, drooling, snarling its teeth, fangs glinting in the dim light of the wood. Whatever happened, it wasn't going to touch Anne, and I stepped forward crouching slightly; all my concentration fixed on its stare. The dog growled louder and I could see its muscles flexing, the hair on its back and tail standing on end, its tail held rigid in the air. Then, apparently without reason, it turned and walked away from us to where Old Gwennie had been standing.

'Where on earth had she gone?' It was as if she had disappeared into thin air. Our attention had been so drawn to the dog we hadn't even seen her leave. We watched as the 'Hound from Hell' walked further down the path and quietly disappeared into the depths of the woods.

It took us several moments to recover. We stood in disbelief, looking at each other, our eyes still scanning the woods for any sign of Gwennie.

"Well we can't go forward!" I said, thinking I didn't want another confrontation with nine stone of snarling death. So we decided to walk to the Top Pond as originally planned, feeling slightly more secure in the knowledge that the woods were too steep and thick for an old Witch to climb.

We climbed the bank, bowing our heads as we started to walk under the trees on the opposite side of the stream. The woods were indeed thick and darkness gathered around us as we scrambled deeper and deeper into and under the thick fir trees. Brambles and briars snagged at our jeans in the darkness beneath our feet and I could only just make out the distant light from the clearing where the pond was. Small branches brushed our faces and I held Anne's hand as she crouched behind me for cover as we struggled up the steep bank.

The light in the clearing around the pond was a welcome sight. We were still not fully recovered from our confrontation. Sitting on a fallen tree-trunk next to the water we listened to the woods, breathing and living once more, its birds singing the all clear from the boughs of their branches. Resting awhile, my eyes took in all the detail of my new surroundings, the pond, the reeds and even gangly spiders, skimming across the surface of the glassy mirror of the pool. On the other side was a small cliff, half obscured by holly bushes and a large sycamore tree, looking as though it had grown there undisturbed for centuries.

Taking time to recover, we gradually regained our senses, moving around the pond and exploring the cliff, with thoughts of climbing. As we reached the bushes I noticed a faint path in the undergrowth leading behind a holly bush. Rabbits, I thought. Then I saw what looked like a heel mark from somebody's boot or shoe. Looking behind the bush I couldn't see any other signs, but moving to the cliff face a small cavity in the rock opened up to my view.

"Hey, look at this!" I called. Everyone gathered around and I stooped down to look in. The small hole at the bottom of the cliff led into a larger cave. Hefyn handed me his torch and I crawled inside. The cave opened out into quite a large space, which dropped away at the far end, with what looked like another passageway leading deeper underground.

"Come on in!" I called to the others who were waiting anxiously outside for me to reappear. Everyone crawled inside, our eyes steadily getting used to the darkness in the cave, which was lit only by the dim torchlight. We moved to the far end and climbed down the small rocky corridor which led, deeper into the mountain. It dropped quite steeply and, climbing down, it looked as if it would open up into a larger chamber.

"Moel-y-crio!" Anne said, quietly behind me, sending a shiver down my spine.

"The mountain of tears!" She continued and her words brought a reverent silence to our climb.

Hefyn broke the silence saying that if it got much steeper we should turn around and that he didn't fancy ending his life at the bottom of a mineshaft. I could hear the drip dripping of water, falling into silent pools deep underground and as I neared the end of the stone staircase its echoes dragged quiet cosy memories from deep inside me, of Taid taking us down the old lead mine. Our hallway and stairs opened out slightly and I could clearly see the entrance to a larger cavity. We climbed out onto a large area of level rock deep underground.

The torchlight struggled in the darkness, with our eyes straining to see. Stalactites hung in front of us like vast organ pipes in some ancient gothic cathedral. They pointed down into the darkness, where water trickled and ran, echoing all around the underground tomb. Everywhere I looked I could see stalactites and stalagmites. They reminded me of the snarling teeth of the 'Hound from Hell'.

"It's huge!" Anne gasped. It was like the chamber, my grandfather had taken us to, as children, in the lead mine. Although we couldn't see the bottom, we were standing on a ledge high above the watery grave where I had once stood with Taid on a different subterranean gallery.

We explored the ledge, which itself was quite extensive. Flat for the most part; with rocks and boulders strewn about, but where we were standing it was clear, almost as though some one had cleared it. Looking further over I could see it dropped away. At the far end there was what looked like steps which led further down into the enormous underground cathedral, with the path crossing back underneath where we were perched, but it was steep and we could not see properly where or if it ended. I describe it as a path, but it was little more than randomly positioned and convenient structured rocks that you could walk along with some security.

"Shine the torch over here?" Megan called and I turned pointing it in the direction of her voice.

"Not at me…down here!" She pointed to a huge rock she was standing next to.

We couldn't believe quite what we saw, an old photograph in a tatty old wooden frame. We looked a little closer; it was leaning against the wall of the cave, the huge rock almost looking like an altar, high up in the Gods of the rocky Cathedral.

An old soldier in uniform, I guessed from the First World War, with what looked like dark bandages wrapped around the bottom of his uniform trousers.

It stood between two candles whose wax had dripped down their sides, for what looked like forever. The wax had dripped over the rock and down to the floor of the cave, making its own waxy stalactites. A new candle lay behind the picture and what looked like a string of pearls hung over one corner of the frame. Megan went to touch the pearls.

"Leave it!" I said, quite abruptly.

"Sorry, I just think we ought not to touch it!" There was a certain reverence about the place, the past seemed to surround us, and a shower of mixed feelings fell lightly through me. Something of some importance, at least to someone, stood in front of us.

A box of matches was half hidden behind the frame and we decided between us that it would be all right to light a candle to help us illuminate our way. Anne took the box and lit the two candles, one on either side of the picture and, blowing the match out, she then lit the third candle from one of the others.

I could see footmarks on the damp floor beneath us and I wondered who had been there. It was obvious that someone visited the cave and I was anxious not to disturb whatever purpose they had there.

We decided to explore the path further into the cavern, but all agreed that if it became too steep or dangerous we would turn back. The path started down almost in steps with rocks and boulders strewn on either side. Hefyn turned off his torch to save the batteries that were dimming slightly and we climbed down by the flickering candlelight, carefully stepping and climbing over the damp rocks.

We turned with the path, walking underneath the ledge of rock where we had stood. I looked back up and could see the faint flickering glow of the candles we had left burning at the top. Standing at our new vantage point; a thin damp rocky ledge barely wide enough for us to stand on, we peered once again into the darkness, listening to water dripping endlessly into pools deep underground; droplets of water that echoed from the rock walls, far beyond anything we could see.

Suddenly everything went dark and I froze. Anne had dropped the candle, extinguishing its light. Hefyn turned his torch back on, bringing light once more to the cave. It seemed to dim slightly so he shook the torch and it brightened once more.

"We'd better hurry back" Hefyn said anxiously.

"The batteries aren't going to last much longer" He shone the torch directly up to where we had stood. There appeared to be a short scramble leading to just below our original ledge. A short climb at the top and we would be back into the light of the candles. "It's too far to go back up the path, the torch won't last!" Hefyn said and we all looked at each other nervously.

I started up the rock with the others close behind me. Leading the way, I was soon close to our original ledge. The torchlight was fading fast and I could barely see the flickering light of the candles on the roof of the cavern and it was most certainly not enough light to climb by. The last bit of the climb went up into a large crack in the rocks, a chimney. Not dissimilar to the one we had all climbed just a few weeks earlier; a little damper and maybe fewer hand holds, but not a difficult climb. In normal conditions we would have had no problems climbing out, but as I put my back to one side of the rock and my feet to the other, Hefyn's torch finally gave up the ghost. He shook it and the light came back, but a few seconds later it failed again for good.

The ambient light from the candles, still burning above us, was not enough, and I strained in the darkness with fingers fumbling, trying for holds that would secure my rising from our rocky tomb. There was a slight over hang I hadn't seen, just below the top that was pressing in the back of my neck, preventing me from climbing straight out.

Using all my energy, the others perched precariously, just below my position; I pushed with my legs trying to lift my back further up the rock, my head not yet close enough to the top, which was still out of reach. I could feel my leg starting to shake vigorously as every ounce of energy drained from it and I was unable to move my arms from their position, where they were clamped tightly onto the rock-face. I was beginning to sweat profusely; I could feel it gathering on my forehead and trickling down into my eyes. Things were getting desperate and I called to the others.

"Look out; I think I'm going to fall!"

'Please, please no!' I thought to myself; I didn't want things to end this way. I was meant to be the hero; not the catalyst of some unforeseen tragedy. No one would ever find us; even the person who came to the cave would not see our bodies. If I fell, I would tumble like a bowling ball, taking all the pins with me. My hands started to slip and I could feel one of my feet losing its grip.

The thought, that I might be the cause of Anne's death was unbearable and senseless images flashed through my mind. 'I could push out from the wall and hopefully only I would fall into the watery grave below.

Suddenly someone's hand appeared in front of my face.

CHAPTER TWENTY

It was knarled and twisted and looking up, I saw Old Gwennie's dull eyes staring down at me, with the Hound from Hell peering over the ledge, looking down at me. Old Gwennie shook her hand. Light from a candle she held in her other hand, lit my way. She shook her hand again, beckoning me to take hold. It was all I needed to steady myself, finding good handholds as she helped to lift me out at the top. In my relief I lay, exhausted and silent, unable to move. The Hound from Hell started to lick my face, reviving me slightly and looking up at Old Gwennie I said, quietly.

"Diolch yn fawr! Thank you very much!"

"Ooh, Welsh, is it then?" she said in a heavy North Walian accent. I shook my head and lowered my eyes, as if in shame, not quite understanding her meaning.

Gwennie tapped my leg with her foot, awakening my thoughts. She held out the candle in her hand, beckoning to me, not saying anything as stepping back from the edge. Peering into the flickering void below, I could just make out everyone's worried faces. They only half realised what had happened, knowing only that someone had helped me climb to the top.

In turn, I helped pull the others from the darkness of the desolate grave that surrounded them and one by one they sat at the top staring in disbelief at Old Gwennie, not knowing what to do or say. Eventually we all sat safely at the top looking through the dim light into her face. We sat as if in our guilt, children caught with our hands in the jars of penny sweets at the 'post office shop' and we all stared in silence at our accuser.

When all was safely gathered in, Gwennie took a long deep breath as she looked back at us and said.

"Ooh, what'ou doin 'ere, then?'Ey? Mine place it is! Mine, ess now!" She spoke quite abruptly, her English wasn't good, but I could just make out what she was saying.

"I'm sorry!" I said,

"We were just exploring" We all felt awkward there, as though we had intruded into something private. Hefyn said something to her in Welsh; I recognised his apologetic tones and some of the words he spoke. Gwennie was staring at me as she spoke to Hefyn. I couldn't understand a word she was saying, which was unusual because I would generally pick up a few words of Welsh in a conversation and would often get some direction or hint as to what people were saying. But her accent was too pronounced and I couldn't make out a single word.

Gwennie was still staring at me, making me feel rather uncomfortable and I was about to apologise again and suggest that we left, when I heard her say what I thought was my name. I couldn't be sure, but I became seriously worried and desperately wanted to leave. Instead of leaving though, Anne turned and asked Gwennie something in Welsh, pointing at the picture in the old frame. I heard the word 'Milwr' and wondered what on earth she was saying. Of course he was a soldier, I thought and I balked at the triviality of her questions in the delicate situation we had found ourselves in and wondered again why we weren't making our way, quickly out of there. But the others seemed to be getting a little more comfortable in her presence.

Anne had spoken in a gentle caring voice, but I was most embarrassed at what I thought was a pointless and obvious question.

"Ooh, Will, it is then, my Will y'no Ess now" The others gathered around her as she spoke, but I was more hesitant, getting to my feet with Gwennie still watching my every move. She seemed to be studying me, almost as though she knew me and it was making me feel very uneasy. She sat down on one of the larger rocks on the cave floor and I could almost see the years flowing through her, as she spoke to us. Anne was asking her more questions in Welsh and I was beginning to get a little lost and out of depth.

"Ooh, my Will now is it, yes now! Udy Udy. I tell 'ou if 'ou list'n, then, ess now? Listen good mind 'ou?" I was concentrating hard trying to understand her, often having to keep her words in my mind long enough to sort out the Welsh from the English, straining to understand both.

Hefyn leaned across to me and quietly whispered in my ear saying,

"She knows you can't speak Welsh…you know?"

"How?" I whispered back. Hefyn shrugged his shoulders,

"And how does she know my name?"

"Ssshh!" Anne said, almost at a whisper, holding her finger up to her mouth. Gwennie was still looking at me, but her eyes somehow seemed warmer and they brightened as her mind drifted back. As she spoke it was as if a sluice had been opened somewhere way back along the stream that flowed inside her.

At the time, I couldn't work out why she told us all she did. I often think she was compelled or restrained in some way; at least that's how it felt at the time. Now, even knowing all I know, I still cannot comprehend fully her want or need, although I can see some of her purpose. It was though her vision was clear; perhaps as clear as it had ever been. It was as if she saw clearly, all that had gone before and those things that were yet to be, but her words fell into us as she began to tell us of her lost love, Will.

She rehearsed how they had met. He had been standing in his uniform at the old station in the village, ready to leave for war.

"Ooh, handsome, he was then! Ess now!"

Hefyn leaned against the wall of the cavern next to Megan, while I sat on a large rock to one side with Anne kneeling in front of Gwennie, who looked at Anne as she continued to speak. The Hound from Hell slowly nuzzled between them, placing its head on Anne's knees.

Will was off to fight in France, after he had finished his basic training and had been trying to look brave, the way young men do on such occasions. Gwennie told us of how she could sense his nervousness and had walked across to talk to him. She had never seen anyone as dashing and handsome in all her life. He had deep, blue within blue eyes and as he looked at her they pierced straight into her soul, holding her gaze.

We were all captivated, sitting on the rocks around her in the cave, as we listened to the witch of the village telling us of soldiers, the war, of love and magic. She spoke almost excitedly as she described how they had talked forever sitting next to him on the train, each minute seeming to last a lifetime, and of her disappointment as the train approached Mold.

She scribbled her address on a scrap of paper and the following week received her first letter. It had contained the photograph in the frame. Her dim eyes gazed back through the years, to when he called on her, having a few days leave in the middle of his training, and she told us of how they walked through the woods, sharing silent moments together.

We were riveted. Sitting motionless, we listened patiently, catching each word that fell from her mouth. My understanding increased and I was caught in the web of the story Old Gwennie spun.

On one walk in the wood, they had stumbled across the cave and using an old miner's lantern they borrowed from her father, they had stood hand in hand unable to move, surrounded by the unbelievable splendour of the cavern where we were sitting. She told us of a dance in the village, where they danced all night in each other's arms, with romance and sweet kisses leading quickly to love.

"Ooh, kiss he could then, Ess indeed!"

It wasn't the same in those days she had explained, almost as if she was justifying falling in love so quickly. Time had been against them from the beginning. They spoke about a wedding with her parents and arrangements were made for them to be married during his next leave, which was due to be about six months later.

Her eyes welled with tears, the years flooding from her and she sat, like some seer, gazing through the eternities, her stare fixed firmly on his distant image, as he stood, locked in the corridors of time, caught in her memories.

Gwennie told us of how they had come to the cave the night before he left; down to their special place, deep underground. She had loved him that night with all she held precious, giving herself to him, holding him close, never wishing him to leave.

But the morning chugged along, steam puffing and blowing into their station and its train dragged Will off to war. He had given her the string of pearls just before he got on the train, telling her they were his grandmother's and that it was her dearest wish for him to give them to his wife when he fell in love and got married. They had no money for a ring and Will had given the pearls as a sign of their engagement.

Gwennie paused with her voice breaking, tears running freely down her cheeks, dripping to the floor of the cave as she struggled to hold on to her feelings and she cried uncontrollably. Sobbing, she spoke through her tears,

"Ooh, leave 'e did ess now!" Tears fell like black rain in the darkness.

"Ooh, too young you are then, ess indeed, too young, I was too, 'ad 'is baby inside me I did an' when I got that letter, Naw, Naw, I cried, didn't believe it, ess now!" Trying to control her sobs, she struggled to continue,

"Ooh, 'at letter, told me it did, told me of his death, out there 'n France, ess indeed!"

Tears were starting to well in my eyes as I fought to control my feelings, desperately trying to stop them from falling on my face. I could see Anne had tears streaming down her cheeks, although she wasn't sobbing or crying out loud. Looking over at Hefyn I could see he was getting misty eyed, with Megan holding his hand, the tears rolling down her face.

Anne took hold of Gwennie's hand, placing her other hand lightly on her shoulder. All the years, all the memories of her lonely existence flooded from Old Gwennie as she paused in her grief, struggling to gain her composure.

Her parents had hid her away in their shame and her baby was stillborn a few months later.

"Ooh ess, died inside me it did, my baby! Ess now! Died he did. I did, an' all, somewhere 'n 'ere I died!" Gwennie pointed as if to indicate to her heart and she explained that feeling numb and unable to cope with all the emotions running through her, she had come to the cave, where she stood at the edge, looking down into the darkness below.

Her legs trembled as her eyes searched through her tears looking to find some meaning or make sense of it all. Will had whispered gently to her, with every fibre in her body wanting desperately to lean forward and be with her Will again.

She described how she had found herself walking through the woods, not quite knowing or understanding how she had got back there, but she explained that Will was still whispering in her ear, calming and reassuring her, pouring balm on her broken heart.

The girls both sighed and I moved closer, taking hold of Anne's hand on Gwennie's shoulder and placing my other hand on Gwennie's back as she continued to tell us of how her father had died with consumption a few years later. Her mother had been sick with 'The Croup' and Gwennie had nursed her until, she too died three months after her father.

Keeping herself pretty-much to herself, she rarely visited the village, not wishing to be with people who didn't or couldn't understand. A few knew and understood, but most didn't and were just unkind.

"Ooh, a Witch I was, then! No good as a friend, ess now! 'Ey? No good as friends, Witches, ess indeed, 'ey?" Gwennie's tone was almost abrupt as she pointed the questions towards us, partly in bitter accusation, but then her tone mellowed in the quiet understanding she could see in us.

I could see what the others were thinking and I felt that same guilt, the guilt of a village too blind to see or care about the 'lonely stranger' living in their midst. I thought of how unkind and cruel people can be to those they do not understand or deem to be different. Without understanding they use words that cut and tear at hearts already broken by life.

"You're not a witch are you then?" Megan asked. I could see she regretted the question the moment it fell from her lips.

"Ess no, but 'ats what people calls me, is'n it, ooh?" Her voice became calmer and more settled.

We all gathered around her, silent in our shame. The witch, Old Gwennie, having just saved our lives. Her eyes seemed more caring to us, as she wiped away the tears; with the sleeves of the years she had spent crying. Old Gwennie then shocked us, by saying.

"T'wasn' 'til Will B come home 'an told me, 'at I found a truth out then! Ess now," She tutted,

"Brave death? Isn'it?"

"Will B?" Megan asked, with a perplexed look on her face.

"Ess now, Will B!"

She told us how Will had been a good friend of Will B's, in fact, from an early age they were inseparable. It was the same when they fought in France, and he had been there when Will had died.

Old Gwennie explained to us that her Will was the oldest Will in their class, Will A, and that both he and Will C had died while fighting over in France, leaving only Will B.

"Will B from the village?" Megan started again.

"But I thought..." Megan, realising what she was about to say, let her words fall silent into the darkness of the deep, but Gwennie understood her confusion, and said,

"Gave 'im back the pound, I did then, ess now!" Megan smiled as we all realised she had given back the pound note that Maggie had stolen.

We could feel and hear the hesitation in her voice over what she was saying, but the words kept coming, a river flowing forever on. She told us how much she owed Will B. It was more than she could ever repay in this life and probably even in the next. Will's death had been a travesty, which had cut deep inside her, haunting and tearing at both Will B's and her hearts. He had dealt with it the best way he could and Gwennie, well, we could see how well Gwennie had coped.

I stood there listening, barely able to comprehend, with my own limited experiences of life and I imagined myself drowning if I had to live a life such as hers. The grief, the pain and the sorrow flooded into me, but I felt that impression again, that she was fulfilling some overwhelming need to tell us, or even me, what had taken place all those years ago. Almost as if it were her life's blood trickling from the wound it had caused and we were the bandages that would stem its flow.

She went on to explain why they were both inseparable, saying her Will and Will B were distant cousins or something. When the war started they followed its progress, talking of its politics and discussing its rights and wrongs. Many of their friends in the area had already enlisted and so, seeking adventure they both joined the Army.

The training had been hard, but it was made almost impossible by their commanding officer. She could remember Will telling her how cruel and needlessly sadistic he was, to all his men.

"Ooh, killed 'im ee did! Ess now!" Gwennie told us of the voyage to France in the troop ship and of how Will and his company were up on deck, when their commanding officer came up from the officer's quarters for some evening air. He started bawling and yelling at a young soldier, who, in the relaxed atmosphere had inadvertently left his top button undone.

As he bellowed and shouted, six of the men from his company jumped the officer from behind, throwing a large sack over his head and tying it around his waist. They quickly bundled him overboard, never to be seen again. No one who witnessed it seemed to care or worry about his early demise, although all of them in some way felt they were participants in the crime, whether by action or complacency.

Their new commanding officer had been no better than the first; having heard rumours about his predecessor's sudden and awful end. He lived in a state of constant fear, ruling his men with a rod of iron.

She described what Will had told her of their awful life in the trenches, mud, squalor, rats, always having to contend with the constant shelling and fighting. No sleep for days on end compounded by a life of living knee deep in death, that lay in wait, like a wolf, silently at their feet. He had spoken of the senseless slaughter imposed upon them as they charged into Hells Mouth, which spewed deaths wake before them.

Will had told her how simple their choices were, over-the-top to take your chances running scared, with bullets flying, death hanging impatiently, waiting to end every heartbeat or they could face the certainty of a friend's bullet at dawn.

They had been 'stood to' one morning, guns in hand with their mothers held tightly in trembling hearts as they waited for the order 'Over-the-top'. The demonic scream of the whistle signalled their advance. Death attended every heartbeat, racing to curb every footstep. Red-hot-lead seared through trembling flesh, puncturing distant hearts, ripping apart-unwed families and fathers from their newly born sons. No longer waiting in the wings, death feasted on young men who lay crippled, screaming, crying for their mothers, their brothers and their Gods who had all forsaken them. And hanging from the wire they danced their final dance.

Both Will's had stood together that morning and before they had covered fifty paces Will B had been shot and wounded in his leg. Falling to the ground, Gwennie's Will lay over him trying to protect him, bandaging his wounds. Out of over two hundred men who 'stood to' from their company that morning only thirty-two had made it back to the trenches. Having waited all day, in a shell hole, quivering in no-man's land, Will dragged his best friend back to their lines, under the cover of darkness. He had left his rifle and kit where they had both fallen, unable to carry them while pulling Will B along the ground.

Their comrades had helped to drag Will B back over the edge but as Will prepared to roll back in beside him, a shell exploded close to where he lay. Miraculously he was physically untouched by its flailing hell and he was quickly pulled down into the dazed and confusing nightmare that followed.

Will had fallen to the floor of the trench, shaking and trembling, not really knowing or understanding where he was or what was going on. Their commanding officer, not having seen what had taken place ran up and down the trench, shouting and screaming at him, 'Where was his rifle? Where was his kit?' 'Stop shaking! What are you frightened of boy?" But Will just sat trembling, oblivious to his outrageous commands, firmly entrenched in his own private nightmare.

The officer had lost all reason, a victim of the fighting just like Will. He ordered him to be bound and secured and to wait for dawn, saying he lacked the moral fibre needed to be a true soldier. The men had pleaded and begged with him on Wills' behalf, but their petitions had fallen on his insanely deaf ears and were finally made while staring into the breach of the officer's revolver.

They had kept him with the wounded and Will B was able to be with him through the night. He tried to talk to him, but Will had just sat there shaking and trembling, continuously mumbling to himself. Sometime just before the dawn, still trembling he became slightly more lucid. Not quite understanding where he was or what was happening to him, he spoke the only discernible words of the night, 'Where's Gwennie?'.

"Ooh, damn words haunt me ey do! Ess now! Damn war!" Gwennie said after regaining her composure, but she then broke down again, unable to continue for several minutes, trying desperately to control her feelings, apologising through the splashes of her tears.

The fighting had broken Will B and on his return he had come to tell her of his nightmares. He cried constantly as he related the account of how his best friend and her future husband had saved his life and lost his own, in the madness that was the war. Two others had been shot with him for refusing to be part of the firing squad that eventually killed them all. She said that Will B had suffered more than her, having had to witness the execution of his best friend at dawn for trying to save his wounded friend.

Will B had told her that following the next sortie they found his commanding officer in no-man's-land. He had been shot in the back, with one of his soldiers lying dead next to him. The soldiers hand, had to be ripped from the collar of the officers tunic, having dragged him out of the safety of his trench to where they both lay.

Will B had tried to comfort her, but each time they met, it would bring back the guilt and pain of the awful memories they shared. So his visits became less and less frequent. She told us that whether the years were cruel or kind, it didn't matter, it hadn't helped much anyway and they had both struggled with the awful spectres that their lives had brought to haunt them.

We all sat in silence, tears of our guilty innocence rolling down the girl's cheeks with Hefyn and I struggling to fight back our own feelings. There was nothing we could say or do and we were trapped in the silence with no escape. Old Gwennie set us free. She looked up at me and said,

"Diolch yn fawr!"

"What for?" I asked,

"Oore, you help'd my dog then, 'ou did!" Gwennie spoke quietly as she bent down to pat the Hound from Hell, which was quietly licking Anne's hand. She had been watching, as Hefyn and I had cut her dog free. Gwennie had tried to free the Hound herself, but was unable and had gone home to fetch some scissors and on her return, I had been cutting the dog free.

"Is she dangerous?" Hefyn asked, indicating to the hound lying quietly at Anne's feet. "Udy udy! Ooh, 'es now!" She smiled at us, a deep warm smile,

"Ooh, no not sos' you'd notice then!'Er an' Maggie my only companions! An' we watch over you lot in the woods 'ey!" She bends down and strokes the animal, pulling at the ruff of her neck.

We started to climb up through the rock passage leading to the world above. When out in the light again we promised, in turn, that we would never reveal the secret of her private place, hidden inside the mountain of tears, deep in the Italian Woods and Anne had whispered to her as half kissing Gwennie on the cheek.

"We'll keep your secrets with us, forever!"

That night Anne and I stood talking at the front gates of the bungalow, talking of Old Gwennie and her life without love. We hugged and kissed as though it would be our last, until eventually her father came and dragged Anne, kicking and screaming from my heart. I could have asked her to stay and she would have. There was no pressure on her to go on the holiday, but she knew her mother wanted her with her. Anne was close to her mother and had told me I was the only other person she could talk to in the same way that she spoke to her mother and father.

I thought I understood, but now, I'm not so sure.

CHAPTER TWENTY ONE

Hefyn and Megan were spending more time together and although I saw Hefyn a couple of times during the week they didn't really want me around. I understood and tried to make the most of my time. I filled the week with as much magic as I could, but I was desperate for it to end so I could see Anne.

I had a film of photographs that needed developing and was eager to see the images I had created. I also had a painting in my head, a river running through it, which would not go away until it flowed out onto my paper in colours as pure and clear as Anne's skin and I imagined her hair tumbling from my brush. I would create a painting that would be Anne and the image of her face constantly filled my head.

I caught a lift into Mold with my mother, dropped off the film then went looking for the art shop I knew was somewhere just off The Cross. I searched through the various sheets of watercolour paper and selected one with a rough knot. It would be two days before the photographs came back and although the sketch I had made of Anne was better than the first, I wanted to wait for the photos before doing the drawing for the painting, waiting for more inspiration if that was possible.

I prepared everything. Stretching the watercolour paper onto a thick board, I studied the sketches for every detail, staring at the pure white paper. Slowly Anne's image began to stare back at me, like some vision created by Dali. The blank sheet seemed to come alive in my imagination as I brushed thoughts of Anne deep into its surface.

Every evening at eight o'clock I would walk down to the village, to the telephone box just outside the post office. Getting through to Anne she would phone me back and we'd talk for long hard minute's; about times we were not spending together, of love that stood alone and the moment when we would be together again.

On the Tuesday I collected my things together and walked down to the stream, following it up to the Ruby Pool where I sat down to think. I spread my books and papers around me, having brought some of my favourite poetry books for inspiration. Thumbing through their pages, I underlined words and verses that inspired me and conjured up dreams of Anne in my mind. I would write a letter, a poem in words that would flow through the miles that separated us.

I flicked through the notes I had kept in a little note book, recording words that had special meanings to me; words that conjured up images in my mind. There were also quotes and verses that inspired me. It contained all the things that dreams and magic are made of.

I had never been a good student, slow at reading until quite old, I never read a book from cover to cover until I was about fourteen. That had all changed when a new English teacher came to our school. As you can imagine, my spelling and punctuation were awful but Miss Owen smiled and persevered. She gave encouragement where necessary, looking and searching for the key that would unlock my mind. Then one day we read a poem by Alfred Lord Tennyson, 'The Lady of Shalott;'

I can remember Claire Morgan reading it and I thought how lovely her voice was. She read beautifully, but it wasn't just her voice or the way she read it. It was the words, not just the words, but also their meanings, the way they were placed one next to the other, giving purpose and direction to sentences. Magic fell from her lips, images that conjured stories in my mind, which rhymed somewhere deep in my soul. It seemed to call to a part of me that had lay sleeping all my life. It spoke of tragedy, love and magical times, long since gone. I was captivated, enthralled and when she read the last verse, I was standing at the wharf side looking down into the boat. Her cursed beauty had caught my stare and I read in my mind, following Claire's voice as she read, '…she has a lovely face; God in his mercy lend her Grace, The Lady of shallot.'

I was bitten. I wanted more and searched through the books in the library and the shops in town for greater inspiration. Most of my direction however came from my older sister Carole, who already had an appreciation of these things and I studied some of her books on the Pre-Raphaelites gaining a basic insight into their movement. I remember a few weeks later, on a trip with my art class, visiting the Tate Gallery in London. Wandering through old Masters and modern interpretations, I stumbled aimlessly into a room full of Pre-Raphaelite paintings. 'The Lady of Shalott', the painting by John William Waterhouse hung in the middle of the far wall.

Although surrounded by numerous others, it was the image he had created at which I stared. Her tragic love and the life's blood draining from her as she loosed the chain: It captivated me. The boat and her singing her last song as she floated down the river's dim expanse into Camelot were all unveiled before me. I sat for what must have been hours, transfixed by the painting, feeling all the pain of all her cursed and tragic love. From that day on, poetry and art were my passions. They drove me forward and I was hungry to fill my starving and neglected mind with more.

Not gaining the inspiration I needed, I walked a little further upstream and sat on a large rock straddling the small brook. A small waterfall tumbled over its other end, whose phosphorescence of bubbles danced over a crystal clear pool, shattering its surface. I could hear and feel my love for Anne flowing through me, like the trickle of water that fell at my feet and I submitted my heart to the lines of the paper. My mind raced and my heart skipped through fields of images conjured up by the words I wrote.

Llys Onen,

Rhydymwyn,

Flintshire.

Dear Anne,

We sit here, the stream and I, thinking only of you. With its river flowing, trickling and tumbling inside me it seeps over me to you.

I close my eyes and I can see you on the path through the woods. You look back at me with your eyes smiling. I can't remember my life before I met you and my life would wither and die without you. I barely exist with these long miles between us. But in quiet moments, I hear your laugh in the breeze off the mountain and I can smell the lazy haze of the summer wood as it distils through your hair. At night, I see the stars melting as they race across the universe of your eyes and I hold you close in the arms of my dreams.

I am Dante; separated from his love by the marriage of time between us. You are my Beatrice, my beginning, my end and my eternity. I walk through the woods by the stream, down along the narrow lanes and over mountains and hills. I talk to them and they long – just like me – to see you, to be with you once more and like me they are empty without you.

You are the beating of my heart. You are the morning sunlight that creeps into my room, waking and warming my thoughts at the beginning of the day, and you are the covers I pull over me in the darkness of my lonely nights.

Were the passing of time but steps, I could walk to your side. I am lost in love forever and will love you till time itself can wait no more.

                                              David.

On the Wednesday Mum took me back into town to collect the photographs. I posted the letter on the way and calculated that it would reach Anne by Friday at the latest.

I paid the money and took hold of the envelope containing the photographs. Holding them firmly in my hand, I walked out of the shop, eagerly pulling at the envelope, desperate to see the images it held. Sitting on a bench outside, I gazed at your face looking back at me. I was breathless, having to physically force my chest in and out as if your image of had taken all the involuntary and conditioned reflexes from my body. All my energy was sapped from me by your unexpected presence.

Mums old Agfa had caught everything, the early evening sun casting warm colours on your face, your hair highlighted in its bright light, forming dark mysterious shadows in the nape of your neck with your hair tumbling like a waterfall over your shoulders. The lens hadn't missed a thing, every line; each detail. The wild beauty and the power, I always feel whenever you're around, oozed from the photograph and I felt your presence quietly enter the space between us.

I could already see the washes of paint in my mind. Skin tones bled into pools of clear water that would soak deep into the paper; pale light red, delicately highlighting her nose and cheeks. Dark bold colours contrasted with the white of the paper to emphasise the catch lights in your eyes.

There were photographs of sunsets reflected on the mountain pools and silhouettes of rocks against the brightness of the colours painted across the evening sky. The bridge, the pools and the waterfall, but none could match the image I had created of you and I couldn't take my eyes from it.

As soon as I arrived home, I prepared everything; sharpening pencils, cleaning rubbers, selecting paints and checking that brushes were clean and soft. On my trip to the Tate Gallery, I had bought a Japanese ink brush, long before they ever became fashionable for watercolour painting. It had a large head, capable of holding vast amounts of paint, but it never lost its point and you could paint both large washes and pick out finer detail with it.

I was a good draughtsman and quickly began to work with my pencils. Fine, faint lines captured every movement, every moment and every memory of every feeling, I had, had that summer. With each line, I could see where paint would flow. My pencils outlined every feature and I only scarred the paper where absolutely necessary.

After several intense hours – the type of hours taken over by the ebb and flow of images caught up in the swollen rivers of your mind – it was ready and I could see you breathing life into the pure white surface of the rough and knotted paper.

When I was eventually satisfied I stood back, with the drawing leaning against the wall. I gazed, staring with my eyes flitting from sketch to drawing and drawing to photograph. Occasionally a rubber or pencil would take away clutter or add intimate detail.

I had been minimalist in my drawing and would be the same in the painting, allowing the water to flow and mingle with the colours on the board without unnecessary interference or too much control. The drawing remained in its place for the rest of the day and through the night. I returned to it, again and again, studying it for long periods, reassuring myself of its accuracy.

I rose early the following morning; you were staring back at me from the paper on my board. Gathering my things together, I walked to the stream and followed it to the place where I had written the letter. Filling my water jar from the small waterfall, I wet the paper and commenced the portrait.

Your skin first, wet into wet, light-red mixed with plenty of water caught the colours of the early evening sunlight on your skin, with touches of French Ultra Marine bled into the subtle shadows around your face and neck. My brush dragged and moved colour from one area of the paper to another. Colour seeped deep into the flesh of your nose, your cheeks, your neck and your chin. I used a fine brush to paint your lips, your nostrils and finally your eyes. Deep eyes; the kind of eyes that filled the paper; eyes that held me captive and bid me never look away; eyes that continually smiled back at me.

Darker colours and tones then, for your eyebrows and hair, which seemed to flow and tumble naturally from my brush. Rich tones blended the hair into the nape of your neck, emphasising your soft jawline and chin. The deep, out of focus washes of the background seemed to bring your image to life, making it stand out from the paper in front of me and I looked at you and longed once more to be with you, listening to your whispers in quiet moments.

I returned home and in Taid's shed I found an old frame that looked as though it had been made for my painting and after asking Nain if I could use it, I spent the next day cleaning it and polishing up the glass. Cutting a mount from a piece of coloured paper I placed the painting inside. Carefully replacing the string, eventually I was satisfied and it was finished.

That night, as I phoned Anne, she told me she had received my letter by second post. She said how much she missed me too and thanked me. She started to cry, saying she wished her father had never arranged the holiday. I asked her what was wrong, but she only said she missed me. There was something more, but Anne would only talk about being together again. I told her that I didn't think I could wait until collage and she agreed that we couldn't go without seeing each other just one last time, before the summer came to a close.

I remembered the last tune the Crazy Line had played at the institute. So almost whispering into the phone I said, "Shall we dance? Dance in the moon light?"

She interrupted me. "Let's kiss, All through the night?" She paused and then said, quite curtly,

"NO!" But then with a whisper, she said,

"Not just for the night David, forever!" A torrent of feelings welled up inside me, cascading down stream as she continued,

"No matter what…we must see each other on Sunday, when I get home! We could go to the cavern together;" I interrupted her,

"Are you sure?" I said,

"It's Gwennie's place, we could go to your place on top of the cliff?"

"No, the cavern is a place for lovers!" Her words lit a fire inside me, burning through my body like the autumn stubble.

"Then maybe some night swimming!"

"Night swimming?" I asked.

"Yes" Anne continued, but in a low whisper so no one else could possibly hear.

"In the Ruby Pool! I want to swim naked with you and dream together, under the stars and moonlight, where pearl divers have swam!" My feelings began to run out of control.

"Ar hyd y nos…all through the night!" Anne said quietly,

"Ar hyd y nos!" I whispered.

My mind and body could not cope with the feelings running through them, so I changed the subject, telling Anne I had a present for her and I told her it was something special, and that I would bring it with me on Sunday. She pleaded and begged me to tell her what it was, but I only told her that it contained all my love.

Walking slowly back up the hill to Nain's, I gazed up into the clear night sky and could see the temple of stars above me. I recognised Orion and Orion's Belt, followed by the Big Dipper pointing to the North Star, as Anne and I had done under the moons silver glow that night on the cliff top. At that moment I knew Anne would be looking up into the same sky, at precisely that same time and I cursed the universes that had come between us. The more I looked, the more I could see. Star upon star, galaxy upon galaxy, universes stretching far beyond my imagination. My mind wandered out past the stars, each star a sun in its own right with countless solar systems revolving around them. I wondered how many planets, in how many billions of solar systems there were. Was there someone, like me, staring back across a lifetime of light years?

One thing I did know was that no matter how many universes or galaxies I would have to travel, I would never find a love comparable to that which I had found in Anne. Looking down at the darkness of the ground at my feet, I felt empty and alone without her. Anticipation ran through me. It was the wild anticipation of our seeing each other again that Sunday-evening and of moonlit night swimming, of becoming lovers and those thoughts seemed to keep me alive.

CHAPTER TWENTY TWO

I wrapped up the picture in brown paper, cello-taping the ends, tying string around it and finally wrapping it all in polythene. We had all been sent to our rooms to get ready for school the next day. I already had everything sorted for college, so Andy would tell Nain that I had just popped out with the painting for Anne. 'He won't be long', I knew she'd understand, it wouldn't stop her worrying, but she would understand. Leaving quietly by the front door I made my way through long shadows, up the road and down through the darkness under the trees of Parry lane.

Dad hadn't left for London, but was visiting his mother and sister in town. Mum was busy getting things ready for the kids in the morning, so no one would miss me and I calculated Nain would probably be fast asleep long before my return. I was just hoping Dad didn't look in our room when he came in; he would sometimes sleep on the settee, and I was hoping he didn't that night.

Low cloud was lightly threatening the sky, but I could see brighter colours of the sun from where it lay reflecting into the clouds above the mountains. Dusk fell into the night as I reached the woods. A thin veil of misty rain started to fall as the anticipation of seeing Anne ran through me, momentarily making me shiver. I walked over the bridge near Old Gwennie's; with none of the strange feelings I had felt that summer; just an uneasy guilt. There was no light at her cottage window.

Walking quickly along the path, I passed the old winding house with darkness seeping through the woods, like black ink clouding the water on rough-knot heavy watercolour paper. The ghosts in the mineshaft were resting behind me, fast asleep in peaceful dreams as I stepped, rock to rock, just as I had done all that summer. I passed the Ruby Pool with a faerie wisp of mist clouding its dark surface and a shiver of fine rain wetting the trees above me. Thoughts of wild swimming in the moonlit pool seemed too distant a possibility to light my path. Stepping over the Wooden Dam, my feet seemed to know every rock and pebble of the stone staircase, having walked it countless times that summer.

Thinking of Anne continuously spurred me on. 'She would be home by now', I thought quietly to myself. Climbing the wall by the old beech, I dropped into the field on the other side. Having placed the painting on top of the wall, as I turned to pick it up, there was a sudden thrashing of wings and a cry in the branches above me.

I looked up suddenly to see a giant owl bent forward, screeching and squawking at me. An Eagle Owl. Its wings were spread wide and I jumped at its phantom like figure. It's frightening flurry at being woken, settled, as quickly as it had erupted. Its huge head bobbed from side to side as it settled back on its perch. Its outstretched wings must have measured a little more than my height, with its talons almost as long as my fingers. After the first excitement of our confrontation the huge bird seemed not to pay me any attention. The owl had obviously escaped, but its presence there explained the missing lambs earlier in the year and I stared long and hard into its eyes before continuing to walk up to the farm.

Making my way across the yard one of the dogs barked, rising to its feet, but on seeing me, it settled back down with its companion, in the warm hay of the small shed they slept in. It was just after ten; the house being in complete darkness except for one small light glowing behind the curtains of a downstairs room. Looking around the yard I couldn't see the car anywhere. They should have been home and my mind strayed back to our phone calls, trying to remember what time Anne had said, but I could recall only that she had said.

"You better wait till later…dad does his books sometimes."

I made my way towards the front door. My intention was to throw small stones up at Anne's window and I would have to pass the door to get around to the other side of the house where Anne's bedroom was. Carefully walking over the gravel, past the door, it suddenly opened startling me and I could see the silhouette of Anne's father as he stood in the doorway.

"David, what are you doing here?" He asked and thinking quickly I said,

"I've got a present for Anne" pointing to the parcel under my arm.

"You'd better come in then, they're not home yet!" He said,

"Do your parents know where you are?" He forgot his question the moment it was asked.

"I'm getting worried! They should have been home over an hour ago"

The headlights of a car lit up the doorway and I could hear the sound of its tyres on the cobbles. Anne's father raised his head looking towards the lights.

"Here they are!" He went to continue, but stopped and gasped. I turned around to see a police car pulling up next to us, with the passenger getting out followed by the driver. Taking of his flat cap the passenger walked forward and said,

"Mr Jones?"

"Yes!"

"Nothing to worry about", but he went on to inform us there had been an accident. He had been at the scene and everyone seemed to be all right.

"No need for worry then!" He had said it in a very matter of fact way, instantly calming us as we both breathed a sigh of relief. He continued to tell us that Anne was the only one who had any injury, having banged the back of her head. The accident had opened a cut at the top of her neck. He had personally seen it and had heard her talking and joking with the ambulance crew. There had been 'a bit' of blood, but that was usual with head injuries.

"She's fine!" Questions and answers quickly followed. He told us they were en route to the hospital in an ambulance, the boys travelling in another police car and for us to meet them there.

We pulled up in the Land Rover outside Nain's little bungalow. Anne's father left the motor running, while I went to the front door where Nain was standing as if waiting for me, her long grey hair hanging down over one shoulder. She stood in a long nightdress with a thick nightgown wrapped around her and had obviously just got up out of bed. She would never let herself be seen in public like that, anywhere, but there she stood waiting for me.

I explained quickly and making my apologies, I asked her to tell my parents where I would be. She stopped me as I turned to go, took hold of my head and kissed my hair. Then raising my head, she looked straight into my eyes, her fading eyes drawing me in close, searching deep into mine.

"You'll be all right?" I nodded and turned to go and as I ran back to the Land Rover, I tried to work out whether she was stating a fact or asking the question, but the thought quickly fell from my mind.

The journey to the hospital was full of tense conversation with long moments of silence slipped quietly in between. The painting lay on the seat between us and I gently touched the wrapping and ran my fingers over it as if Anne was at my side. My mind was caught up in supplication, prayer or something, I didn't quite know what, but it danced between pleading and begging with, whatever power fills the universe, for clemency, and my heart called to its majesty.

We pulled up outside the hospital and still clutching the painting tightly under my arm we walked through the entrance. The smell of disinfected corridors and warm, neatly folded-down rooms hit us as we stepped through the door.

A nurse walked out of casualty and after introductions, she led us into a corridor with old wooden seats lined down one side, under large windows. Anne's mother and the boys were sitting there, her head supported by her hands, her cheeks wet with tears. She looked up and ran to Anne's father, throwing her arms around his neck. She cried uncontrollably and they both hugged one another. In her sobs, I could hear her saying,

'I'm sorry, I'm sorry!' over and over again.

"What's wrong, where's Anne?" Her father asked.

The door opened behind them, 'Intensive Care' written above it. A tall thin dark haired man wearing a white smock coat unbuttoned down the front, walked out of the room. He looked just how I would have imagined Hefyn to look ten or fifteen years later and had it not been for the serious look in his tired eyes, my confidence would have grown.

"Mr Jones?" he asked quietly.

"Yes!" Anne's father said in a broken voice.

I stood a little way back from the group, the painting still held firmly under my arm. The conversation was caring, but conducted with great urgency and deliberation. Listening, I could hear individual words, 'urgent', 'essential that', 'bleeding', 'concerns', 'sleep' and 'David'. On hearing my name, my heart skipped a beat, the river inside me flowing faster, falling over rocks and everyone turned to look at me. I could see Anne's father had tears rolling down his cheeks and he called to me,

"David?" He loosed my name as if it were an arrow form a bow and it struck deep into me, piercing my heart; I felt all my strength draining from me. The painting dropped to the floor, I heard the crack of the frame, breaking glass, like sharp shards, breaking at the back of my throat, falling into my heart.

"Yes" I said.

"Anne wants to see you!" His words were softly spoken, with quiet concern.

Anne's parents then turned away, her father supporting her mother as they walked with the doctor into the intensive care room. I picked up the painting and could hear the shards of glass splintering with the movement.

I sat next to Anne's brothers and they told me of how Anne had taken off her seat belt and was kneeling on the front seat to pass them some crisps and sweets. They could remember bright lights and the thump of the crash, but they couldn't remember seeing Anne after that. They talked about the police and the ambulance, blue flashing lights, bells and sirens. Their car had hit a tree, having swerved to avoid an oncoming car, on their side of the road. The other car hadn't stopped. The ambulance men had been at the front of the car with their mother and they could remember hearing Anne's voice, but hadn't been able to see her, the police keeping them back.

The door opened and out walked Anne's parents followed by the doctor. They both had tears on their cheeks and Anne's mother had her head buried into her father's neck. The doctor walked over to where I sat. He looked straight into my eyes. I felt an uncontrollable urge to run and hide, but I couldn't move.

The doctor smiled while he explained that Anne had been asking for me. Telling me of their urgent concern for her and that they suspected she was bleeding inside her head; they needed to put her to sleep so they could treat her, but she had refused to let them, saying she wanted to talk to me.

I stood up and the doctor led me into the room. Anne lay motionless on what looked like an operating table surrounded by machines that were continuously bleeping, pumping and ticking. Nurses and doctors worked quickly, but carefully around her, adjusting monitors and making her comfortable. She had a tube coming from her nose and one into the back of her hand. I could see the leather lace from the crystal held tightly in her hand. Walking slowly forward I stood over her. Her beautiful hair lay matted with thick patches of blood that had stained the white sheets. Looking down into her eyes, one of her pupils was large and black and she stared up into the room like 'some bold seer in a trance.'

"Is that you?" She seemed to struggle.

"I'm here!" I said, again the shards of glass breaking at the back of my throat. Anne was weak and as I looked at her, I could sense the lonely stranger deep inside her, wandering, lonely and lost on some strange path in a distant wood. I took hold of her hand and she slowly turned it over, placing the crystal in mine.

"They won't let me wear it in here, keep it safe for me, David!"

There were greater powers at work in that room than I had ever seen or felt before, and I could not step between, Anne and their unknown forces, vowing that they would never touch her, as I had done with 'The Hound from Hell. No hand of mine would lift her from the darkness that surrounded her, into the safety of the light and from that moment on countless prayers passed from my lips.

A nurse looked up at the doctor who, slowly and quietly, nodded his head. The nurse then stepped forward with a needle and she injected it into the tube that led into the back of Anne's hand. A voice from behind me said softly.

"It's time now!" But leaning forward, I whispered into Anne's ear,

"Don't go, please stay, stay with me; please stay." Fighting against the drugs that were seeping through her veins, she whispered, "Forever!" Mustering all her strength, she went to whisper again, but the drugs were too much and the words fell back inside her.

I felt someone's hands on my shoulder, guiding me towards the door and as I turned away doctors and nurses frantically set to work. The river rushed inside me, sapping all my strength.

'I love you, Anne Jones, from the farm above the Italian Woods' was screaming in my head, but the words remained unspoken. Back in the corridor, everyone looked up at me. Nain was sitting with my father, next to Anne's parents. My father looked awkward, he had never met Anne, my mother only meeting her on two occasions. They did not know, and I thought they would not understand the feelings I had for her.

Nain got up and walked towards me placing one of her hands on my shoulder as she turned and we walked down the corridor away from the others. She whispered quiet words in Welsh, to comfort me. I did not fully understand, but I felt their understanding and their meanings seemed to fill me. Her tenderness had opened the sluice that held back all my feelings and I cried uncontrollably. She understood, she always understood, and the power I felt from her reached out to me, touching me, holding me.

The painting Of Anne lay discarded and broken beneath the seats and her brothers had fallen asleep on the chairs above it with coats draped over them. We waited for what seemed like hours and eventually a doctor slowly opened the door and moved quietly towards us.

"I'm very sorry! Anne passed away a few moments ago. We did everything we could, but the bleeding inside her head was too severe" He lowered his eyes; his head dropping forward, his arms slumped at his sides. A nurse came out of the door behind him and walked along the corridor away from us, tears rolling down her face.

CHAPTER TWENTY THREE

I was drowning under a wave of feelings that crashed over me, forcing me out into deep water. There was a howling storm inside my head and a river raged inside me, tearing at my banks, ripping through me, dragging me off downstream, and I drowned in its depths. I didn't understand. I had only just spoken to her.

Anne's parents were hugging each other and crying. Her mother couldn't take any more and she flopped to the floor. She sat there, crying in the kitchen of a mothers love, all her memories, the year's that she had spent loving and raising her daughter flowed over her as her tears washed them away.

Anne's brothers still lay fast asleep on the chairs; calmly unaware of the devastation that lay in wait for them.

I couldn't take any more and the want to run overcame me. Nain followed a short distance behind. The cool night air seemed to temper some of my feelings, quenching the pain, like red hot steel dipped in the waters of the stream and I took a deep breath trying to hold back the dam that was crumbling inside me. I looked up into the night; the sky was awash with the same mist of rain.

Nain stood close by; waiting silently for me to compose myself and after an eternity of standing, looking into the night I turned to her and asked,

"Why?" The glass broke at the back of my throat again. She moved over to me and wrapped her arms around me.

I still had the crystal in my hand and held it up into the night. My mind drifted as I walked down the path through the woods. I stared down into the 'Ruby Pool', with Anne looking up at me. Holding her arms out, her deep green eyes smiling up at me; she beckoned for me to join her.

I looked around at my grandmother, her fading, but warm eyes seemed to smile as tears gathered and I tried to smile back, but the dam was straining under the pressure. Her quiet understanding overwhelmed me and somehow she felt all my pain; she maybe didn't know fully what I was feeling, but I knew she felt my pain and it cut as deeply into her as it did me.

A tear rolled down my cheek and I could feel it gathering on my chin. Nain held out her hand, catching the tear as it fell, she clenched her fist around it. Opening her hand she placed it over my heart and then pulling me close, she whispered,

"This is where we keep our tears, David Bach!"

We turned towards the hospital, Anne's parents were no longer in the corridor but the boys were still fast asleep. Dad told us that they were in seeing Anne and asked if I wanted to see her as well.

"I don't think I can!" I said quietly, but Nain put her arm around me once more and said softly with the sure knowledge that all her years had brought her,

"It'll be all right, David bach!"

The door opened and Anne's parents emerged. Her father had tears running down his checks and her mother sobbed, crying openly. Dad stepped forward and held the door for us. Nain was standing close to me. I could feel the warmth of her hand filtering through my thin shirt and her arm across the top of my back. I closed my eyes, preparing myself. Breathing slowly in, I longed to open them and look up at

Bet's sweet smile, and to see the classroom door in front of me, but I knew I wouldn't; the nightmare was real.

Nain started to walk forward, but my legs seemed unable to move. Her fingers tightened slightly on my shoulder and my legs found the strength from somewhere. The room was still and quiet; trolleys and machines had been moved to one side. The operating table was silhouetted against a blank, plain wall, which I stared at, unable to look at Anne.

Gently pushing at me, Nain's hand left my shoulder and traced a line down my back and then fell from my broken world. My legs continued to walk towards where Anne lay, but my eyes kept their gaze firmly fixed on the bare wall beyond. Eventually, I looked down into her pale face, Anne's eyes were closed but she looked beautiful and her presence seemed to fill the room. Leaning over her my lips almost touching her ear I whispered quietly to the night.

"I love you Anne Jones" And echoing in my head I could hear the words, 'From the farm above the Italian Woods!'

With my head bowed, I closed my eyes. I could hear my own breathing and the beat of my heart. The room was deep in the hospital, but I became aware of a slow movement of air over my face. I opened my eyes and quickly looked down at Anne. Her lifeless pale skin seemed to be glowing slightly, as if she had caught the moon's milky glow; just as I had imagined the first time I saw her in the startled shafts of morning light in that old musty schoolroom. There was still a faint movement of air across my face and as I breathed slowly in, I could sense the scent of wild garlic and the smell of pines in the summer woods.

Raising my eyes up to the blank bare wall in front of me, I could almost see the swaying of the moss soaked trees and hear the birds hidden in the leaves of their boughs. The sound of the stream trickled into my ears and its cascading waters tumbled through my heart. A myriad of sights and sounds burst onto the wall and the hum of the summerwoods appeared to be all around me. The leaves quivering on the trees cast a patchwork of dancing shadows on the leafy mould of the path through the summerwoods, but as my eyes traced its meandering footfall, I longed to see Anne standing by its stream.

My heart broke, again and again, as my eyes searched the woods, along the path, over the stream and into the shadows beneath its trees; I was frantic, but she was nowhere to be seen.

CHAPTER TWENTY FOUR

Mum and Dad had gone to Mold to fetch flowers for Anne's parents and with my brother's and sister's at school; Nain was left to watch over me.

Standing at the window of Pallor Bach, I watched as towers of rain drifted across the valley, over the trees and woods. With my tears gone an empty numb ache filled the pit of my stomach as I tried to make sense of everything.

The rain continued unabated, the wind whipping it onto the window pane. It seemed to drench everything in its path, beating it into submission. I listened to its storm moaning through the eaves, its torrent spilling from the gutter; its unrelenting tempest tearing into me. Like some malevolent spirit it rattled at the windows, its cantankerous claws pinching between the tiles on the roof. I wanted to be trampled under its stampede, to drown in its flood and to die in her arms.

Turning aside, I made for the back door. I could hear Nain behind me. Stepping out into the rain she called to me.

"David…David bach…oh cariad!" I pushed at the gate and stood on the path of Taid's vegetable garden; how I longed to see him, bent over his fork, racking through the rich dark earth for that last elusive soul.

I stood with my head tilted back; my arms hanging loosely at my sides. What I was waiting for, I didn't know; I had no care. The rain cried into my eyes, with its lonely tears gently falling on my face, soaking into me. Something moved in the rain and I felt the storm of Anne's hair on my skin; I felt her finger tracing the line of my mouth and her lips on mine; I could taste the blood red strawberries and smell musty haylofts.

Nain stood on the back door step; she was patient, waiting for the right moment.

"Come back in cariad!" I looked back at her, sensing her love and concern.

The afternoon emptied into the evening with my younger brothers and sisters asking awkward questions. Those who thought they knew better seemed to give me a wide berth as I struggled through long moments of silence. Mum spoke to me. Anne's father had asked if I would like to call in at the farm, any time; it didn't matter. The thought hit me like a bolt of lightning. I didn't know whether I could face them or how I would feel, but I decided that I would go up early in the morning, maybe even for milking, depending on how I felt.

The chilled night lingered on into morning. The rain had stopped but the woods were still wet. Mist loomed over the dusky waters of the stream as if in some vain attempt to hide its face from me. I heard the squawk of a magpie and a wave of feelings threatened to overwhelm me.

Just below the farm, I paused for a while, beneath the big old beech, with my hand clutched tightly around the crystal in my pocket. Hesitating, I dragged at its string, slowly bringing it up in front of me. Staring beyond its faceted exterior, the glow of Anne's skin seemed to radiate from its depths. The Universe of misty star light penetrated the tumbling waterfall of her wild hair as her image appeared in the midst of its revolving cosmos. Every detail was open to my memory, the line of her mouth, her deep green eyes, her laugh, the way she looked, the way she smelt, the feel of her hair on my skin and her taste on my lips. Everything came flooding back; the fire that burned in the catch light of her eyes and the way her eyes smiled at me. Her eyes caught mine, just as they had done on that first day at school, but as quickly as her image appeared Anne faded back into the light.

Placing the crystal back in my pocket, I looked up at the farmhouse and broke down, knowing, but finding it impossible to believe that Anne wasn't there. It was as though I was walking through some hideous nightmare, and I pleaded and begged with the power of generations that it was all some awful dream, but I knew it wasn't. Anne was gone and I would never see her again. I broke down again and wondered if I would ever make it to the farm that morning. By the time I had composed myself sufficiently, I could hear the cattle on the cobbled yard, walking towards the Shippon and I started to walk slowly up the field.

As I did so a curious feeling gripped me, some presence a power even; feelings I had felt in some small way throughout that summer. It was as though my grandfather was walking at my side. Hesitating slightly, the feeling became stronger. The hairs on the back of my neck racked and tingled and I dare not look behind me. It is difficult to explain; as are many things I saw and felt that summer, but I could feel the power of generations following me up the field as though it were a great army of souls. A whisper of feelings ran through me and I knew, without any doubt, I wasn't alone.

I had been walking forever, but was no closer to the farm. Stopping a little way up the field I could sense the rise and fall of my chest as I slowly breathed away. Eventually I composed myself sufficiently to look behind me, although I knew there would be nothing there.

Looking down into the woods, beneath the darkness of the trees, my eyes could see nothing. Although the greens of the wood were bright in front of me, for some reason they seemed to fade to black and white at the periphery of my vision. My eyes were fixed and I couldn't move as the woods and field seemed to hedge up around me with the colour draining from the trees.

Something was there. I could no longer hear the cattle being herded in for milking and the dogs were unusually silent. I couldn't turn away; no matter how hard I tried. My stare was fixed on the big old beech tree and the woods beyond;

everything else was a drab shade of grey. It was as though I was peering down a corridor whose walls were monotone and colourless. The woods were strange, different somehow. The wall we used to sit on had disappeared, but the big old beech tree remained.

Suddenly the feeling of that other presence became overwhelming as he stepped out from behind the beech tree. He was as real as anything I have ever seen or ever experienced in my life and if I was dreaming, I felt that in my dream, I could see and feel and touch everything thing around me.

I instantly recognised him as he began to walk through the morning mists towards me with a slow smile brightening his eyes. Taid seemed not to have changed at all, although he appeared to be young and walked without a limp. His presence filled me until I thought I would burst with the river of feelings dancing over the rocks of the stream inside me. I longed to run forward, to throw my arms around him, to talk to him, but I knew that if I moved one jot the vision would fail. His eyes were bright, and he continued to smile at me.

Suddenly I was aware of others, between the trees. I looked and, one by one, the ghostly images of people I had once known, stepped out of the woods, and a ghostly throng started to make its way towards me. Within the woods I saw them as ghostly images, but as they stepped from between the trees, they changed as if they were stepping back onto the path of this life.

I looked out over my new heavenly companions and could see more and more ghostly images appearing from between the trees, pressing forward towards me. The more I looked, the more people I could see, as if stretching back through time.

Their faces were all somehow familiar to me; some I knew, others I recognised from old photos, but most were strangers, with only an air of familiarity. The more I looked the more faces I could see. There were miners, farmers, cooks and scullery maids, all of whom had the appearance of just having finished their work. And I knew all of them had come to that place, just to see me.

There were seamstresses with sewing still held in their hands and a blacksmith with a thick leather apron wrapped around him and a large Cats Head Hammer resting on his shoulder. There was even an ancient warrior on horse-back with the blood and dirt of battle staining his face and arms. There were men and women dressed in furs, armed with primitive tools and weapons.

In my vision or whatever it was that surrounded me, I knew they were all simple, humble people, people whose lives you would never have considered amounted to much, but nonetheless there. They were all my generations, all those who had held my life in trust. It was incredible. The more I looked the more faces I could see and somehow dimly recognise; a sea of welcoming faces smiling back at me.

There was an old soldier, who came and stood close to Taid. His eyes were blue within blue and he had a smile that could have melted any heart. Taid continued to walk at their head with the old soldier at his side. He was tall, dressed in his soldier's uniform that somehow had the appearance of being pure and white— although I could see its drab colours marked with the stains of battle. My mind stumbled at his presence; he was almost like a stranger in the midst of my family, and yet I knew him.

Without taking my eyes from this familiar stranger, I realised that everyone there seemed to glow as if their continence were pure, like refined gold caught in the gaze of the sun. They shone more brightly than any summer's sun, but as I looked at them their image didn't glare or hurt.

I recognised the soldier, it was Will. His face seemed to light up with my recognition. He was holding someone's hand, but I couldn't see or make out who it was; lost in the crowd. But as I looked again, I saw her for the first time.

She was wearing a white veiled dress that floated free and she pushed forward, stepping towards me through the mist as her eyes smiled. Her hair flowed loosely, tumbling with the stream, down over her shoulders into the centre of her back. It was no longer matted with blood and I could sense, no pain within her eyes that seemed to shine with a brightness I had not seen before. Her smile reflected all the colours of summerwoods as Anne blazed like a flaming torch at the head of all my generations. I wanted to run to her, to hold her in my arms, to touch her, but I was held fast by some unseen power. All I could do was smile as tears rolled down my face.

My senses were frozen and my heart broken as I realised that I could not go to her. Anne smiled continuously at me and as she stood there, more people pushed forward through the crowd, gently stepping past Will and my grandfather. One by one they pushed forward, stepping up towards me, as if they wanted to see me for some unknown reason, and they came and stood close to Anne. They were all part of Anne's reason for being there. An old man and woman stood on either side of her, placing their hands gently on her shoulders, as more and more strangers tenderly pressed their way forward.

Anne smiled her smile and held me with her eyes looking straight into me, but then she turned to go, quietly walking back through all the generations of her own family, who turned to follow after her. As the solemn procession led her back down to the woods, the silent generations of my own family turned to follow. They all whispered and talked quietly to each other as they walked with an air of excitement rippling through them. When all had passed from my view, only Will and Taid remained. They stayed a few moments longer, as if checking that I was all right, but eventually they too smiled back at me and then turned to go. I stood and watched as they walked silently back down through the mist and disappeared between the trees.

My eyes frantically searched for Anne, but all I could see were the woods and its barren tree line. Something moved and I caught sight of her again as she stepped out from between two trees. She stood in the shadows with her smile holding my stare but eventually she tore herself from me.

CHAPTER TWENTY FIVE

I slowly became aware of my surroundings and found I was still standing underneath the big old beach tree. I was exhausted, but gradually, piece by broken piece, my senses returned. Tears were flowing freely. As my senses woke, I can remember crying out, but no words escaped from my lips. I could hear the cows on the cobbles and as my faculties regained some of their strength, I resumed my onward path. My vision or dream had faded back into the morning mists, but its images still filled my head.

As I reached the top end of the field, I could still feel Anne's presence close behind me, but I calmly fell in behind the last cow and filed into the Shippon with Anne at my side.

The dogs greeted me eagerly, wagging their tails as they looked around wondering where Anne was. Anne's father nodded at me as I looped the chain over the neck of the first cow in the parlour. His eyes were raw and he struggled to compose himself. We both worked quietly. I had been on the farm so often that summer that I knew the whole routine backwards. It felt a little awkward in the silence, but the familiar sounds of the cows chomping on their cake and the scuffle of their hooves on the cobbles seemed to ease my pain. Their quiet milky sounds were silhouetted by the monotonous drone of the pumping and sucking at their udders.

Anne's father continuously struggled to compose himself and I could see that my being there was just as difficult for him as it was for me. With the milking finished he turned to me and in a broken voice he said

"Come then David bach, let's see what's for breakfast!" He placed one arm over my shoulder and we walked out of the Shippon with the last of the cows sauntering back towards the fields, the dogs herding them through the gate.

"Thank you for coming" he continued,

"It's a big thing, David bach!"

While walking across the yard, Anne's father talked to me. His tears flowed openly at times, but he somehow continued. Some of his words were instantly lost in a confusion of feelings, but most of what he said, I remember, although I cannot write it all. Anne's parents had read my letter to her and he told me of the feelings he knew she possessed for me. He went on to explain that she had always been happy as a child, but would often seem dreamy, off in some quiet place, hidden away deep inside herself. He described it as 'a little distant'. It was nothing they had been overly concerned about. She was never moody and he told me that they could not remember the last time she had lost her temper, if ever, but they had always worked hard to reach out to her; desperate to be near her.

"When you returned David bach…she seemed to come alive somehow." He began to cry uncontrollably. I found it strange, almost eerie, Anne's father talking about Anne, and more tangentially me, in that way. His words cut into me, tearing at my heart, but he was caring in the way he spoke. He understood the effect of his words on me, but I knew he sensed their meaning important enough to warrant his saying them.

I looked up at him, as he stood in the doorway under the porch and marvelled at his control amid his overwhelming feelings of grief. I knew, like me, he had been ripped apart, but in his devastation he cared enough to think of others and their feelings, or my feelings to be more precise. It would be many years before I would comprehend those things that exist in the space between a father and his daughter and standing here today, I still marvel at the way he spoke to me.

He went to open the door, but stalled and looked straight at me, holding my stare. "My wife isn't handling this well" He stumbled with his words and had said them in a subdued almost frustrated voice, as though he had been working towards something all his life and had just failed to achieve his goal. At first, I misunderstood his meaning, thinking he was stating the obvious, but he paused again, almost as though he was searching for some divine inspiration to assist him in moving forward. He alone knew the devastation that waited beyond the door.

"She blames herself for Anne's death you know" He said it quietly as he groped in the darkness that gathered around him. The arrow of his words struck deep into my heart and the river inside me started to rage downstream. I grieved to myself at the awful thought that had just been conjured in my mind. I could not comprehend or even begin to imagine what Anne's mother must have been feeling and I felt a strange feeling of guilt rising inside me. It was almost as if my presence in her life had somehow made me equally culpable.

Something quickened my mind and I could see Anne's mother standing in the hospital, when she threw her arms around his neck saying, 'I'm sorry, I'm sorry', over and over again. I knew then what she had been pleading for. She had been begging in vain for forgiveness from Anne's father, the children, God, or anyone who would listen. It was some vain attempt to gain relief from the pain her nightmares would forever bring to her.

A single tear dropped onto my cheek from the well that had built in my eyes. The door opened and we walked into the guilt and dust that had gathered to suffocate Anne's mother in the kitchen of all her dreams. Looking across at her, I struggled to compose myself. She was standing in front of the cooking range, trying desperately to maintain a hold on her life. Anne's brothers both sat at the table, dumb; trapped in some way by their mother's guilt. I saw them both jump slightly at my presence. They wanted to rush to me, to talk, to ask questions, but they looked up at their mother sobbing at the sink, clearing the tears from her eyes with the tea cloth and in the confusion of their mother's nightmare, they sat back in silence.

Breakfast was quiet, Anne's mother barely coping and crying openly at times. One of Anne's brothers, who had remained quiet throughout breakfast, spoke and broke the silence. He found his way through the numb and perplexing confusion that surrounded him to ask me,

"Do you love Anne?"

I was amazed at how calm I felt when he had asked it, but I could make no reply. Only an awkward smile edged onto my face as the spoken word of my love screamed inside my head.

Anne's father got up and left the kitchen. He returned a few moments later with the parcel containing the painting of Anne under his arm.

"You left this at the hospital!" he said calmly, and he held it out to me,

"Maybe you'd like to open it?" I didn't, I couldn't, and as he handed me the parcel, I heard the broken glass inside and their shards splintered in my heart.

I sat at the table struggling to cope, as Anne's father brought me a box to put the broken glass in. Opening the old polythene sheet I untied the string and started to fumble at the brown paper while horrifying and senseless pictures flashed through my mind. I carefully picked the broken glass from the frame as Anne stared out at me from the paper. It had been less than two days and already I had to be reminded of how beautiful she was.

Clearing away the last pieces of glass, I could see they had cut slightly into the coloured mount, but miraculously it had not touched Anne. I turned it around and held it up on the table towards where her parents stood. Anne's father's hands rested on her mother's shoulders with her mother slightly more composed, but it didn't last long. Tears welled in her eyes as she looked at the painting and she brought the back of her hand up to her mouth, turning her head away, unable to control her feelings. She started to cry uncontrollably.

"It's…!" Anne's Father stumbled and his words fell back inside him. He didn't have to say anything. With the tears welling in his eyes, I could feel the dam in my own heart, breaking, and I struggled to keep it all together.

"The painting is Anne's, please keep it for her!" I said quickly and then, thanking them for breakfast, I opened the door making my escape, unable to cope with the searing heat and pain I left behind.

CHAPTER TWENTY SIX

The morning air and familiar surroundings of the woods, helped to calm me as I looked around for some sign of those generations who had visited me only moments earlier, but I could only hear the sounds of the birds in the trees and the tumble of the stream's water over its rocks. Walking below High-banks I thought of how, only just over a week earlier, Anne had laughed calling me an idiot as I stumbled unceremoniously, falling from its heights, trying to be clever. Her ghost and the spectre of our love followed me as I walked downstream, with its rivers crashing over me. I walked past pools where we had caught trout and I carefully stepped, rock to rock, over the pool where I had painted the portrait and written the letter.

On passing the Ruby Pool, I could hear our splashes of laughter, echoing through the woods of time. Anne's face became clearly imprinted on my mind as I stood and looked into the deep. I held the crystal tightly in my hand; the temptation to return it from whence it came was great, but together with a photograph, it was the only physical reminder I had of her.

The sun attempted to creep through the leaves of the trees and a single song thrush sang its mournful melodies from the branches behind me. So many broken memories were wrapped up in its song and they hit me like a tidal wave. I struggled with senseless images as I tried in vain to rein in my feelings.

My memories drifted and I could see Anne walking out of the bushes, holding her clothes in front of her, dropping them to the floor to reveal her swimming costume. I remembered the look on her face, her smile, her laugh and the way the pool, and I, had both invited her to dive in.

I can remember little of what followed that morning, I cannot remember the path through the woods beyond the Ruby Pool; my last memory of my homeward journey was of standing, looking into the depths of the Ruby Pool with a song thrush singing in the trees above me.

My mother phoned Anne's parents. The funeral had been set for the following Friday and I would not have to go to college until the Monday. I kept myself to myself as much as I could. It's difficult in a large family and people felt awkward around me. I hadn't visited Anne's parents again, and decided to visit them the day before the funeral.

Nain was the only person who seemed to understand and I leant on her quiet understanding. Walking, often in the shadows of despair, I was only occasionally able to lift myself with Anne's memory as she whispered in quiet moments to me, but the pupils of her deep green eyes were lifeless, large and black as they stared back at me, in my haunted sleep. The morning's sun creeping into my room warmed and lightened me and I felt Anne's presence in its soothing rays, but then the nightmares would begin again.

Walking the rocky staircase, I passed the Ruby Pool, and my steps became heavy. I could hear the splashes of ghosts, but I turned from their memories. Hypnotised, my mind was blank as if some giant key had been turned deep inside me, locking my conscience.

I seemed to come too, standing in darkness. A confusion of thoughts ran through my head, not really understanding where I was or how I had got there. My senses gradually woke, but the darkness that surrounded me seemed to overwhelm my thoughts. Was I dead? The thought sparked in my head. I was sure I was standing, so I discounted the thought as quickly as it had sparked inside me. I panicked slightly, unable to see anything in front of me. A flicker of light played around me and I realised I was holding a candle. My mind groped at the darkness in front of me and I realised I was standing in the edge of the grotto, high above the underground lake.

In the darkness my senses struggled to fully comprehend how or why. There was an eerie presence that surrounded me; as if a host of demons stood behind me wait for my final, dive into the deep. Their thought inside my head, needled and pushed me relentlessly towards the edge. My legs trembled and I submitted myself to the searing pain that instantly returned to my heart.

I couldn't take any more, and looking down into the flickering darkness below, with some ghostly throng urging me on; I paused and thought of Anne. I could clearly see her frightened face, just as I had done when I held out my hand to lift her out of that same darkness, pulling her into the light; the day we first met Old Gwennie.

Slowly, I took the crystal out of my pocket and held it out in front of me. Every apparition turned away; covering their faces; hiding themselves from the crystal's glow as it reflected in the flickering candlelight. I could see Anne's face clearly in my mind. She was walking towards me; her eyes smiling as she held out her arms, and I desperately wanted to step towards her.

"David Bach!" The voice came from somewhere behind me, dragging me from the vision, I had fabricated in my mind. It was a young vibrant voice; Anne's voice. I turned in eager anticipation with my eyes desperately searching the shadows from where I had heard her call, but Old Gwennie's dim grey eyes, stared back at me.

"Ooh, bin waiting I hav', Ess now! Knew you'd come, I did!"

"I can't go on!" I bleated.

"It's too much!" Tears filled my eyes. She held out her arms and walking over she hugged me, whispering into my ear.

"Ooh, what's to do with us then? Shall we step up and be with those we love ess now? Too much, it is, then! Ess now, but 'ou can do it, David bach...see then. Not easy is it, but 'ou can do it then!" I knew that she understood, more than anyone else; Old Gwennie understood.

She had heard about Anne from one of her few friends in the village and had waited for me in the cave each day, figuring that I would be drawn there just as she had been. She explained her own pain after hearing about the death of Will. She had hidden herself away, keeping her secrets deep inside. They were feelings that had festered, making her, as she said, 'Bad Company'.

Old Gwennie told me how she had watched us all from the shadows of the trees when I swam into the deep, bringing the crystal out of the pool, watching as I gave it to Anne. Hidden in the trees, she had witnessed our love. It had brought back memories of Will and the love they shared.

"Ooh, inspired me you did, ess now!" Her words were quiet,

"Ooh, Don't end it this way David bach, be with Anne again you will, soon enough...Ess now, soon enough 'ou will!" She stared deep into my eyes.

"I'm not sure I believe..." I half stuttered, but she interrupted me,

"Ooh cariad...believe not...'ou must know! No belief there is, when you know! See Anne and be with 'er again, you will!" She was firm, telling me that the knowledge she had that her and Will would be together once more was the only thing that had kept her alive.

She asked me to search my feelings and that if I did, I would know the truth of what she was saying. I didn't have to search very far, Anne had already visited me. The memories of all my generations walking up the field and the vision of Anne and all her generations came flooding back to me. I told Gwennie about it; I described all my generations and then I described how her Will had been with them. Gwennie threw her arms around me; hugging me as she whispered in my ear.

"Bin given much 'ou hav, bin given much David bach! I will be with my Will soon enough! Not long for this life am I, Ess now, but 'ou must be strong!"

We walked through the woods together, the potion of Gwennie's words soothing into my mind and heart. We parted near her cottage and I felt calmer as the sun warmed into me and with the sun came deeper feelings and as I walked up Parry's Lane I knew I wasn't alone.

That evening I sat up late into the night, reading poems and verse, quotes, trying to cast some light into my darkened world. I tentatively contemplated what the morning would bring. Thinking of a poem I'd read by Christina Rossetti, I frantically searched through my books for her words; for their power to light my way. I found a poem, 'Song' but it wasn't the one. In desperation, I thumbed further and eventually found what I was looking for. 'Remember'.

I folded back the page and sat crying, quietly to myself, as I imagined Anne reading the words to me. 'You tell me of our future that you planned, only remember me, you understand.' She read it, over and over to me. Again and again her words whispering in my ear as my pen struggled to write and I fell asleep to the sound of Anne's voice rehearsing the poem in my ears.

CHAPTER TWENTY SEVEN

It had been raining forever as the car pulled up outside the church. I got out and waited under the shelter of its Lychgate. The funeral-barque drifted 'down the rivers dim expanse,' winding slowly along its streams and paths towards me. A black shuttered hearse came into view at the far end of the small lane and the slow procession began. One foot after the other, stepping, rock to rock, the day pressed relentlessly on, crushing every last feeling from me as the rain washed them all away.

Anne's mother's heart had been ripped from her and the devastation showed as she was dragged through the bitter gall of her torment. Demons still taunted her and Anne's father struggled to cope. Every time I thought she was beginning to compose herself, something would stoke the fires of Hell and her torment would begin again.

The Church was cold and damp. We slowly followed the coffin down its dim expanse, but I couldn't imagine Anne lying inside it, I could not even conceive of the imagining. It cut its way silently through the waters that had gathered inside the little church. I looked and looked again, desperately wanting to run forward and carve 'around its prow', deep into its dark wood; 'Anne Jones, from the farm above The Italian Woods.

'Knight and burger, Lord and Dame', all thronged the wooden galleries, some sobbing, some crying openly and others slowly walked, stunned, having cried a lifetime of tears.

The painting of Anne looked back at me from the front of the Church. Its broken glass replaced and the frame polished like new. My eyes fixed on her beauty with her eyes smiling back at me.

The vicar droned on, 'Who is this and what is here'. His words were at best inadequate and tore at my sensibilities. He tried to comfort with kind thoughts and scripture, but their empty sounds only echoed in my head. He didn't know and could not understand; could never have understood the love, the pain and the anger that others, and I, were feeling. He had never looked into Anne's eyes and watched the stars and universe reflected in their mirror. He had never spoken to her in quiet moments, with Anne whispering back, filling the spaces between them like the water of the stream, lapping between its rocks.

They lowered her gently into the ground, the vicar again spoke empty words and the people 'crossed themselves in fear', praying inadequate prayers that had been repeated over hundreds of graves without ever once changing or referring to the life that lay beneath them.

I stood there, the sky raining into me. People slowly turned to leave, touching, crying and reaching out with kind understanding; trying desperately to mend broken hearts that had no wish to be mended.

Standing at the side of the grave I looked into the darkness below. The squawk of a magpie emptied into the rain. I looked up and standing under the Yew trees at the far corner of the graveyard was Old Gwennie with the Hound from Hell sitting quietly at her side. Maggie was perched on her shoulder. She understood and would always understand, somewhere inside the pain of a life without love, she knew.

With little surprise, Nain walked across to her and they spoke quietly as the Hound from Hell (I never knew the dog's name.) nuzzled at my grandmother's coat, and Nain stroked the dogs head as if they were old friends. Nain then gave Old Gwennie a hug and they seemed to bury themselves in each other.

I stood waiting until only Anne and her family remained. Mum and Dad waited at the gate, but Nain came and stood behind me with Old Gwennie moving out from under the Yew Trees. Taking out the poem I had written down the night before, I 'mused a little space' and started to read Christina Rossetti's poem, Rermember. The rain hid my tears, washing them into the ink that cried from the paper as the glass broke at the back of my throat, falling into my heart.

"Remember me when I am gone away……..!",

I struggled to cope with the words and the poem filled every part of me. The dam inside me burst and I looked over at Anne's mother's bloodstained tears washing over her as she stood in the ruins of her life.

"I remember you, Anne Jones, from the farm above the Italian Woods!" The words were screaming inside my head, but standing alone, I only whispered them to the moment.

I held out the paper, which was drained of all its tears and letting it go, I watched as it drifted down into the darkness of the river below. I took the crystal from around my neck and pressing it gently against my lips, I held it up once more, looking into Anne's eyes and then I sent it back into the deep.

Nain placed one hand on my shoulder and crying silently, we turned to go. My parents were waiting for me at the gate. I promised them that I would be home shortly, saying I wanted to walk by the river for a while. They were hesitant, but relented.

The rain had slowed to a drizzle, which fell softly on my face, trickling through me before disappearing into the river. A desperate feeling entered my head; I wanted to, no, I needed to hold the crystal up in front of me. I needed to see Anne's eyes once more and I bitterly regretted sending it back into the deep. I broke down, falling to my knees, severely crippled with treacherous feelings tearing me apart.

"David Bach!" The voice came from behind me.

"Ooh, what you looking for 'ere then? Maybe this, ess now?" I turned to see Gwennie standing on the path behind me with Maggie on her shoulder, the crystal hanging from Maggie's beak. Taking it from her half blind bird, Gwennie held it out towards me.

"Ooh, Maggie wouldn't leave it there! Not a place for memories is it!" Her voice was soft and gentle as she handed the crystal to me, then she turned to go with Maggie squawking her goodbyes. The hound from hell sauntered over to me, nuzzling at me where I knelt on the ground. I looked at the crystal, quickly checking it and then looked up at Gwennie.

"Thank you!" I called after her and she stopped at my words.

"Thank you for everything!" I bowed my head as she turned to face me and I slowly raised my eyes to meet hers. The pain of the years lay softly between us as I looked into her fading eyes.

"Ooh, all right it is then now!" She said, as her memories broke out to trickle down her face.

"Nain Hughes it was then…good friend she was, ess now! Only person who understood. Understood she did, when my Will died, ess indeed!" Gwennie sighed, a deep sigh in trying to hold back the years.

"Ooh, stood by me she did, when others failed me…she had someone too…someone who didn't return…you understand now?" She bowed her head.

"She was stronger than me!"

Old Gwennie turned for the last time and walked off through the trees and the rain. She seemed to struggle slightly, but paused to regain her strength. Coughing, she wretched and then spat a glob of spittle out, but I paid little attention to her with the crystal in my hand once more. I held it up and felt the flow of the stream inside me as Anne smiled back and walked towards me along the path through the woods.

CHAPTER TWENTY EIGHT

When you went away, I wondered how I would ever cope, but heartbeat followed heartbeat as footstep followed footstep and I stepped rock to rock following the stream of my life. I wandered for a long time on the scorched ground of autumn fields, feeling the burnt black earth where the fire had seared through me. The cold winter rain thawed into me, seeping through the charred dirt; trickling into a stream already swollen with tears. I ploughed-in the autumn fields and felt the cold of winter as it froze the stream inside me. Wandering through dark dreams, I hid from their passing ghosts, which haunted my waking thoughts. With spring following winter, fresh signs of life sprouted in me, bringing new beginnings, with the new season.

Megan, overnight had become quiet and withdrawn. Hefyn had tried desperately to raise her spirits, but she just pushed him away and they slowly drifted apart. He had asked me to try to talk to her, but being alone together was a catalyst that broke glass into both our hearts.

My father's work had moved once more and we were preparing to move back to England. Dad had got an important promotion to the Midlands Road Construction Unit and we were told that as a family we would be much better off. In some ways I welcomed the change. There were too many memories in Rhydymwyn, too many ghosts, but your memory has always followed me.

It was strange, moving back to the same area we'd lived in the year before, but it was good to see old friends. People still tiptoed around me, probably sensing the emptiness I felt every waking moment. I busied myself at college, choosing to drown myself in paintings, which you seemed to paint with me, and poetry you continuously read to me. I fell asleep at night, turning to your heartbeat and I felt your presence in the early morning sun that crept into my room. Somehow, feeling you close, raised me from my grief. You seemed to walk with me and in quiet moments I could still hear your laugh and eventually I was able to smile again.

There was a girl at college from my old school; Claire. I think I mentioned her to you. She was the one who had read 'The Lady of Shalott' in class; the first time I ever heard it. We had been friends before. I had even taken her to the pictures back then. When I returned, she seemed to understand. She was patient and kind, but she would never be more than a friend and she understood that. The summer was fast approaching. I had achieved some good grades and the tutors were complimentary about my work. It wasn't quite what they were looking for, but good nonetheless. (It was all modern art in those days and I was still painting what I could see.)

We were due to go back to North Wales for a couple of weeks in the summer. I looked forward to it with restless anticipation. I had not been a big writer; the letter I wrote to you was one of only a few I have ever written. So it was with some surprise I received a letter, addressed to me, from Nain. It had been contained in a letter she had sent Mum, and as Mum handed it to me, I could see the quiet concern in her face. I was almost ready for college and she gently smiled, saying.

'If you don't feel like college David, take the day off!"

Nain's letter was delicately written, softly spoken, in quiet, gentle, caring words, but nothing could stop the pain of the message it bore,

"It is with great regret that I must be the one to tell you, Old Gwennie passed away early yesterday morning!"

I lay the letter on my bed unable to continue reading, its words cutting deep into me. Standing up, I walked across the room and looked out of the window, gazing at the people walking below. The wailing and screaming in my head had returned.

"No, Please no?" The river was raging; pushing relentlessly at the dam inside me. Closing my eyes, thoughts ran swiftly through me. I imagined Anne and Old Gwennie walking along the path through the wood with Will at their side. Gwennie had once poured balm on my broken heart and the thought of her with Will and Anne was a potion that I drank, quickly feeling its potions working deep inside me.

Calming and composing myself, I returned to the letter. Anne's father had found Gwennie near the wall under the big old beech tree. She had collapsed and was moaning, clutching her arms to her chest, but her dog had stood over her growling at him, protecting its master, not letting anyone near.

An ambulance was called and the police had to attend with the dog still on guard, growling and biting out at anyone trying to touch or get close Gwennie with Maggie squawking from the branches above. One of the policemen took hold of the shotgun and tried to take aim, but seeing his inept way with the weapon, Anne's father took his place. Old Gwennie died before they could get her to hospital and Anne's father buried the dog beneath the tree.

The funeral was quiet, with only a hand full of people gathered around her grave. I stood with Nain, Hefyn and Megan standing the other side of me. Megan was eventually managing to smile through her tears, but still seemed somehow lost. Anne's father stood on the other side of the grave and I smiled awkwardly across at him. He told me later, his wife couldn't have coped. As the coffin was lowered into the ground, Maggie squawked from the old Yew trees in the corner of the graveyard.

I stood at the head of the grave and when the vicar had left I opened my jacket and took out the old frame that contained the picture of Will and then holding it out, I dropped it into the deep. I heard its old wooden frame crack as it hit the coffin and the glass shattered across its boards. Dipping into my trouser pocket, I pulled out the string of pearls and threw them onto the shattered glass.

A spade lay on the pile of earth to one side of the grave. It didn't seem right for a stranger; someone who misunderstood her, should bury her. So Hefyn and I took turns to shovel the earth into the grave as Maggie frantically squawked, flying from grave stone to grave stone, eventually flying off towards the woods.

We never got to Rhydymwyn that summer; Nain was taken ill. She had been a diabetic for as long as I could remember, injecting herself with insulin every morning and evening. But with fading eyes her self-administration had failed too.

The necessities of living dictated that we drag her away from the shadow of the mountain she had lived on all her life. The separation was too much. I can remember Nain sitting in her chair, being confused in her new surroundings in the middle room of our big old town house in Rugby. She asked me to 'pop up the fields to fetch 'Mabe' and then asked me who I was. I tried to explain, but she didn't understand; couldn't remember. With the power of generations failing her, and following some long visits to the hospital that winter; Nain died.

We took her back home to bury her on her mountain. Early on the morning of her funeral it started to snow and by eleven a.m. there was over a foot of snow on the ground. A veil of pure white covered the mountain and village where she had lived since a child. The hill was too steep for the funeral cars so we all walked down to the church Nain had attended every Sunday evening. I can remember trying to sing the hymn 'Abide With Me', but the glass at the back of my throat prevented me from opening my mouth. But the words, like the solemn toll of the church bell rang in my mind.

Andy and I helped to carry the coffin from the Church. I watched as it was lowered into the grave. I desperately wanted to hear a blessing over it. One of power and majesty, life and love; the type of love my grandmother had shown us all our lives, but instead, only empty words echoed from the ground. Where were the words that spoke of The Power of Generations, and a lifetime of sacrifice, love and care? I raised my eyes to the sky and looking up through the veil of pure white snow falling on my face, I could feel her power deep inside me.

CHAPTER TWENTY NINE

The day has crept endlessly by, edged with an air of quiet anticipation, as I wait patiently for the night. I went for a walk first thing: nothing special, just down the way, over the fields to the Old Ford. I like it there; so would you; sitting by the water, watching and listening; the stream trickling through me as life seeps endlessly by.

It gave me time to think of those things that have come and gone since you went away. As I have said, I knew Claire from before; she was a good friend. I was young and bright and although quiet at times, I refused to let life pass me by. People would say; 'You're quiet!' or 'You don't smile much!', but the guilt I felt, living without you, slowly faded with time.

Listening and waiting, Claire seemed to understand; although I assured her that we could never be more than just friends. A year passed and we had grown to be more than friends, although I didn't realise it at the time. My life seemed to drift aimlessly on, but Claire helped me to put some order to it. One day I realised I had fallen in love with her. It wasn't the same as with you, but it was love nonetheless; something secure and certain.

She has been good to me over the years with the patience of a mountain. As I have indicated, I was young and seemed more than capable of gathering the pieces of my heart together, slowly building a new life for myself, although you were never far from my mind. Claire and I built a good life together and we were happy, I thought. We have three children; Jack, Cerys and Rhian…oh and a beautiful little granddaughter who is the light of my life. But over the years the ghosts of that summer have increasingly haunted me. Claire left a few months ago, telling me how much she loved me.

"I just can't compete with ghosts!" She said, crying as she left.

There's no one else and she's still good to me, despite everything. I know she's waiting, but I need to piece it all together before I can go home. The thing is I'm not sure I can. You are always there. I still live with glass in my heart and I sit here thinking of you.

The morning sun was hot and after the first chill of the day, it smothered the already parched and ripened fields with its dry inferno dragging me from my memories. I still love the summer, but I miss the summerwoods, with its dancing-shadows and the tune of wild waters.

Walking back, I stopped to listen to a song thrush as its shrill voice repeated its song over and over again. I walked on. It ceased its singing, flying off down the hedgerow. Perching itself in the uppermost branches of a young ash, it opened its song sheet at just the right page and commenced singing its shrill summer-songs again. The memories its song brought to me were devastating; I think I frightened a lady walking her dog. I try to look back with happy sad thoughts – if you understand my meaning? I know you do! – But sometimes the pain of that summer is too much.

    Cerys phoned me when I got home. She had been trying for some time, but had not got through while I was out; checking in on me as usual, making sure everything was still alright for the morning.

"Why don't you get a mobile Dad?" She grumbled, not for the first time.

"It would make things so much easier! All ready for the morning?"

"Yes!" I said quietly. She does fuss. I don't like doing business with machines. 'A mobile phone!' The very thought fills me with dread; another way for people to interrupt my life's slow and quiet ways. Well, I suppose my work gets a little hectic at times, forcing me to carry a pager, but my life outside of work is pretty quiet.

"Are you sure you won't let me bring my boots? I'd love to walk with you Dad! Jack's free…I don't like you climbing the big mountains on your own…Let me come, please!"

"I'll be fine!" I told her and she paused a moment to think. I know she understands.

"Weather looks a bit grim overnight, but it may brighten up for you…I'll pick you up at five or soon after! Are you sure I can't walk with you?"

"No, not tomorrow Cerys!"

"Okay, just thought I'd ask! Jack told me to…you know what he's like…I think he's a bit jealous we're not all doing Crib-Goch together; we must all go up again soon, before the weather comes in too much…See you in the morning Dad!"

I said goodbye and waited; cutting the phone off with a touch of my finger. I stood there, thinking of nothing in particular as the monotonous tone of the hung-up phone hummed in my ear. Eventually the robotic lady on the other end started to give me my instructions, and I put the receiver down and smiled to myself. Cerys seemed a bit chirpier than she had been; her hormones must be settling slightly.

The morning dragged slowly on as the afternoon called to me again and I went out on my bike. Can you believe I'm still building bikes from old racers that other people discard? I love tinkering with them.

Before I left the house, I caught a fleeting glimpse of myself when passing by the mirror in the hall. I'm still not the type to bother much with the stories its fading reflections tell, so I don't know why I paused, but I stopped to take a better look. With my cycling helmet in my hand I smiled, not wanting to put the helmet on. Cerys bought it for me; grumbling that it would be safer and so I reluctantly wear it, giving in to her wishes once more.

Looking back at my aging face, I stood daydreaming, waiting for the world to pass me by. You would no longer recognise the stranger who waits for you here, but his heart is still young and true. I wear my hair shorter than I used to, but it's still quite long and suitably unkempt, although this morning it had fallen neatly into place after washing it: It looked pretty good and I think it would have pleased you. It's still thick and wavy. My blue-green eyes are gradually fading. I'm greying a little, but not so much as you'd notice without close inspection. I am reluctant to get my hair cut, but Cerys nags me till I do; old habits die hard. I carry a little weight, but nothing that wearing a shirt outside my jeans can't hide. I try to keep myself fit, walking, running occasionally, and cycling.

I slowly put the helmet on and locking the door behind me, I got on the bike after making one or two minor adjustments to the brakes and things; you know me and brakes! I cycled out to Bradgate, its lovely there, you'd like it. No mountains, but there's hills and a stream that flows between them. In places, cascades tumble over rocks with some trout.

The afternoon was hot and close and I soon built up a sweat. Some of the hills are quite steep, but they're nothing compared with the hills of our youth. Cycling back you could almost feel the pressure building; it was close; very close. Dark billowing clouds towering in front of me; hair tingling stuff and I only just got home before the storm broke.

I stood in the front porch and watched the forks of lightning while listening to the thunder bouncing from cloud to cloud. At one point it came overhead. The electricity went off for a few seconds, after one huge fork of lightning hit the ground somewhere in the village.

I closed my eyes and searched back in time for those memories we share; memories that still haunt me. As I said, when things get too much, I pack my rucksack, call up the kids and we all climb to the mountains. But tomorrow is different: tomorrow is our day, when we will once more be together.

The rain is falling outside as I sit here with a pen in my hand, surrounded and submerged in my memories and these years later, I quietly think of you. The passing ghosts in the rain tap gently at my window, they whisper your poems as they patter through the leaves of the trees outside and their streams trickle through me. I quickly write down their words, amid the silence and tears as I wander back through my dreams and the years. Tomorrow we will climb to our mountain and the spectre of our love will walk with me, but I will step out rock-to-rock alone, to test my love once more. I know you will wait for me there, but I am determined as climbing out onto the edge of life, to finally be with you.

CHAPTER THIRTY

The faint scent of the pines and smell of wild garlic growing thick on the banks of the stream, drift out between the branches of the trees to greet me. In the first grey light of the morning they intoxicate my mind. Morning mists loom between the trees; laying a deep thick veil over the flow and ripple of the quietly waking waters.

The woods are still and quiet; our summer together has just begun. I look up through the trees towards where you lie, unseen in your bed, soft and cosy with your hair spread lightly over a white lace pillow. My feet are eager to walk the short distance through the woods separating us, along and up the rocky staircase of the stream to worship at your side, but I pause for a moment to take in the wonder of it all. Closing my eyes I can hardly believe I am here once more.

I listen. Nothing, not one sound stirs; the gentle hum of the summerwoods is still slumbering and only the trickle of the stream at my feet can be heard, running over the rocks of time into deep dark pools. I stare down into the dusky waters as they flow from under the bridge and I can see the shadows of young trout darting clearly through the waters of my mind.

The large rock in the centre of the stream is barely visible; its damp surface veiled from my view, hidden under the morning mists. My young legs push out from the bank and I jump down onto the rock, but as I land my feet slip slightly. Regaining my balance I gradually start to breathe again, as the years that have come between us, savage through me.

Autumn leaves begin to fall. Landing on the surface of the water they float off downstream into the mists. Frantically looking up, I wonder where the summer has gone and mourn its passing-ghosts as my eyes search the dying colours in the leaves of the trees above me. My head drops in despair to where listless trout float, gulping and dying, beneath the surface of the stream's poisoned waters.

Grief sears through me as I carefully step, rock-to-rock, under the bridge; emerging into the dim light of the bitterly cold, bare winter woods on the other side. My breath blows great clouds in front of me and as I place my foot onto the last rock before stepping out onto the bank, I slip.

Reaching out in desperation and blind panic, I catch hold of the railings on the bridge. The frozen metal immediately welds itself to my hand. Quickly jumping to the bank and dragging at the railings, I pull my hand free. The pain of flesh ripping from it cuts deep into me. Dropping to my knees, holding my hand out by the wrist, I look at the white patches of skin hanging from it, loosely lying over my dark-red naked flesh; flesh still frozen as it floats free from the railings, falling into the poisoned waters below.

Looking up I can see Gwennie's cottage, floating eerily in the morning mists. A light sparks in my nightmare as a door opens in my mind, and Gwennie the witch steps out into my fear. The nemesis of all my fears slowly turns towards me as I kneel, writhing in pain on the bank of the stream. Long straggly grey hair hangs like rats-tails, covering Gwennie's face. Her crooked fingers with the dried and cracked mud of her dead flesh, part the lank curtains of hair and with eyes burning like coals, her stare vipers across the woods towards me. Striking out at me, she bites her deadly poisons into my heart.

Mortally wounded, I raise myself up and stumbling forward, her potions scalding through me, she looses 'hell's hound', followed by her demons and they bound eagerly over the poisoned waters towards me. Startled and frightened, I run deeper into the woods, which seem to gather in around me, hedging up my way.

The open mantrap of the old mineshaft, parts its ancient coverings of wooden beams, in eager anticipation of my fall, but struggling against the demonic forces that bid for my possession, I quickly run deeper into the woods, recklessly searching for you. The broken bodies of dead lead-miners crawl from their eternal grave, dragging themselves across the desecrated ground, with flesh-forsaken arms clawing out towards me.

Every shadow I pass seems to raise itself slowly up from the dusts of hell, forming some fiendish spectre or ghoul, which joins the chase and fray of demons who endlessly pursue me. They tear at me, holding me back: pulling at my hair; ripping at my flesh; wailing and howling. My head is full with their cries and I desperately search the path for some sign, any sign of your presence.

My eyes suddenly catch a fleeting glimpse of you, deeper in the woods and I stumble, ever more slowly towards you. With your back to me I call out, but the suffocating tendrils of the chasing demons smother my words and not a sound escapes my lips. Severely crippled and with grief searing through me, I fall onto the wounded earth of my darkly wooded night, where the hosts of hell drag me relentlessly back to the frantic edge of the bottomless pit.

My pain is stained and covered with the blood of the love I feel for you, but you continue to walk away, oblivious to the chase and bay of the satanic hordes that bite and drag me into that miserable gulf. I can see your long dark hair as it tumbles past your shoulders, down the centre of your back. A pure white veiled dress flows loosely over you, showing the shape and curve of your young body beneath it.

Gwennie's ghost floats over the haunted ground towards me, moving closer and closer. Her arms gape open, and her gnarled and crooked fingers claw at the air; dragging me towards her. The burning coals of her eyes seem to penetrate my very soul, piercing and searing through my heart.

  Struggling, I desperately fight against the hound of perdition that has me pinned in the dirt, and as the hosts of hell savour the feast below their damned and twisted minds, I break free and run to where I last saw you, your image still fixed in my mind, spurs me on. Turning a corner, my eyes once more rest upon the perfect symmetry of your exquisite reflection, but the hordes of perdition recklessly pursue me in one last wanton effort, to keep me from the salvation of your arms.

I slow, drawing near to you, with every apparition cowering from the unexpected sight of your beauty, they cover their faces in dreadful anticipation and I pause, calming myself as I reach out. You turn to me, but to my horror I am starring into the fire of Old Gwennie's evil eyes; her mouth is black with the dead dark flesh of her funeral barque and its thick blood spews out, running down the front of your bridal veil in a molten sea, writhing with worms and maggots. I wake up, screaming and feel to see if you are resting at my side, but my heart breaks as empty tears fall towards the darkness of the dawn.

CHAPTER THIRTY ONE

Wanting to lose the madness, I make this journey each year, visiting those places that bring back the deepest memories of you. But today is different. I cannot continue this way and something must give. My choices are simple, but the feelings tied up in them have clouded my mind.

As the car pulls to a halt, Cerys begs me once more to let her walk the mountain with me, but I just shake my head and smile.

"I'll be fine!" I say quietly,

"I'll see you later in the car-park on the other side."

"Don't go up Crib-Goch on your own!" she says sternly, looking me straight in the eye. Expecting to see some kind of compliance, she is disappointed and sighs in despair. With a rucksack of memories on my back, I walk into the car park at Pen-y-Pass. Watching Cerys' car drive off into the distance towards Llanberris, and I am alone with my memories at last.

Cerys is good to me and has given me a lovely granddaughter. Without question, on August Bank Holiday every year, she brings me to our mountain, watching as I walk off alone, up its steep slopes. I start on the footpath at the far end of the car park, stepping, rock-to-rock, as I have done all my life; along its streams, up mountain trails and through its woods.

I think back to the morning, with Cerys waiting patiently as I walk the lanes, past cottages and farms that drag the memories from deep inside. I climbed the now overgrown stream, where young fish once leapt and swam in the pools of my mind.

Many things in the village have changed; some you would approve of, but others, even I don't recognise anymore. The wild strawberries still grow thick on the banks up towards the Common, on the Twm-path by Dros-yr-Afon. I stopped there to pick some, the best are past now, but their taste is still on my lips.

Stepping down onto the rock in the centre of the stream, I walked under the bridge past Old Gwennie's, which is now tumbled down with the ravages of time. The smell of the woods still intoxicate my mind; the wild garlic, the sap dripping from the firs, but the scent of the past is too much for me and I can only bear to walk its paths on this one day, every year.

Cerys stood, looking at me, with tears filling my eyes as I stared into the depths of the 'Ruby Pool,' remembering each moment as it flowed into my mind and its waters trickled over me, to you.

We drove in silence towards Snowdon, pausing briefly at Bettws-y-Coed and then ever on. Cerys broke the silence, asking to walk with me, telling me that I shouldn't climb the big mountains alone, but somehow she knows and understands, the footsteps of the ghosts that follow me and each year she makes the pilgrimage with me to greet them once more.

My legs are not as quick on the path as they used to be and an ache in my heart will not let me increase my pace. The day is perfect as I walk the path we once walked; hardly a cloud in the sky and I can see the brushstrokes, splashing watercolour over mountain-streams, seeping reflections into the lakes and laying broad washes over the mountains, until eventually, I can see you, with your paint-brush in your hand and I can feel your presence walking close beside me.

The day continues as we tread the rocky path together, scrambling up the steep slopes, climbing to Crib-Goch. I traverse the thin knife-edge of rock at the top; calmly walking, sometimes scrambling, climbing the great edifices of rock that block the way; with you, watching my every movement, just as I did yours, all those years ago.

Continuing the journey along my jagged path, I scramble along what remains of Crib-Goch. The thrill and rush of standing at such height traversing the thin knife-edge of rock, no longer holds any fear for me. My only care is being with you and I calmly walk the path as though destiny will meet me, with every step I make.

Cerys is waiting for me at the top and she walks out to greet me. Perhaps she has sensed a different atmosphere to the day or some strange whim in the awkward determination of her 'old man', but she's caught the train from Llanberis, just to see me once again and wish me well at the top. Her tender love and concern deeply moves me.

I would usually avoid the crowds of people who gather at the top, day-trippers, with their sun hats and sandals; it doesn't seem right somehow. They sometimes venture onto the trail, which is fine until the mountain gets steep or throws up some severe weather, as it has a want, most of the time, even in the summer. But today, instead of walking quietly by, I have a pleasant distraction.

Cerys and I sit awhile, talking quietly, eating sandwiches and sharing precious moments together, but as I look into her eyes, I can see you staring back at me. I don't know how or why these things work or what price the cruel twist of fate paid influence, but Cerys is the spitting image of you, and each time I look at her, I see you, staring back at me. You haunt my waking thoughts and stalk the rest I seek in my dreams, but there is no rest, no silent night, not here, not now.

Eventually I rise to continue my journey towards you. Cerys walks with me to the pinnacle of rock that marks the beginning of my pathway down. We talk as we walk, long hard words and she extracts a promise from me that I will meet her in the car park at the bottom of the mountain and she will not let me go until I swear it to her. I swear it, but as we part, I can see tears swelling in her eyes. Cerys smiles through the haze as I falter at her tears. I look straight into her, nod my head and turn to go.

Treading carefully over the edge, I pick my way down the steep slopes at the top of the Watkins Path, traversing the scree and climbing down the big steps in the side of the mountain. Cerys stands at the top, watching anxiously. I remember when she was young; feeling those same anxious feelings, as she bounded off up the mountain paths with me walking behind her, jumping nervously with every step she took. I smile; secure and safe as I sense the power of her prayers in every step I make, but I do not walk the mountain alone; you and the 'power of generations' walks with me.

Part way along the path, I come to the long scree slope, which is still precariously strewn down the mountainside towards its treacherous cliffs. I remember the heartache they caused and the rush of rocks beneath our feet as our legs stumbled quickly out of control, but my mind steadies itself and I climb over my thoughts, to you.

Reaching the bottom of the steep slopes, I look back to where I can just make out the figure of Cerys at the top. She waves, standing part way down the path and then turns to go, with her prayers for the day over.

The afternoon is hot and the path leads forever on, with you walking ever closer. Down past the old quarry and on towards Cwm-y-llan. The Mountain River sings its songs as it lights my memories. The spill of water into pure clear mountain pools, brings it all back.

My heart grows heavy on reaching the waterfalls and I stop at the bottom unable to move. The pool where we once swam calls out, beckoning for me to move closer and I watch my memories splashing as they swim through the haze of a mid-summer afternoon.

I tentatively step onto the narrow plank of rock, high above the stream; out onto the edge of my life where you wait patiently for me. The cracked blue woad of battle dries in my heart. My body begins to tremble as I sense you close and near, and the Last Celtic stirs within me as I stumble blindly through his lost and love-forsaken world. I grieve to myself, 'this life is a time to get things right', but sometimes life itself takes what is right from us, leaving us groping in the darkness of the void that remains. Thinking only of you, I remember: I remember everything and the memory of that summer comes flooding into me; an ocean of memories crash over me, pounding and braking my empty heart and I lay exhausted, washed up on the deserted shores of my life with the driftwood of my memories strewn around me.

All my senses are stirred and I can see and feel our long lost summer, hearing every sound as though I were there; the old schoolroom, the woods, the stream, the mountains, with us swimming in cool lazy pools. Could it be? Could I really be there again? Can wanting something so much lead you back through time to reorder a life already lived? Closing my eyes, I breathe everything carefully in, not wanting to disturb the reality. I feel Bet's hand resting on my shoulder as it warms through me and I wait for her to push me into the classroom where you wait patiently for me, but slowly opening my eyes, my heart breaks. I cry out loud

"No please no!"

I sit on the bridge drained of all feeling and old age ravages through me. It is some time before I regain my composure. Still sitting on the bridge, above the mountain stream, I plough through memories, turning them over and over again, searching; trying to make sense of what happened that summer. It is unbelievable now, almost inconceivable as I look back, thinking of you all those years ago, when life was young and so wildly beautiful. I am at the end of my mountain pilgrimage, the ghosts of my travelling companions have all but left, and I sit alone with you, waiting, one step away and I look down, contemplating that step.

My mind steadies itself and you whisper to me, taking my hand. Standing I turn to walk over to our pool, but as I move, I freeze. Looking up towards the cascading waters, my eyes catch sight of your ghost, splashing and playing in the pool and I relive everything; I see your smile, your laugh, your wild beauty and the vision of your tumbling hair.

Standing on the bridge, I struggle to hold on. With every step I make, you pour into me and the spectre of our love urges me on, dragging me back through years that hold me bound. Stumbling in my grief, I walk to the water that washes the years away. I feel your hand in mine and we sit once more, the fall of the water cascading around us as we slip into the deep. I open my eyes and looking through the clear mountain stream I can see you. I catch the spark in the catch light of your eyes as you stare back at me. I can feel your lips on mine as we kiss with the crystal flashing around your neck as I lift you from the deep, pulling you close my lips touching your belly.

Mum's old Agfa now, the faded pictures of time; every line of your face, the movement of your lips, your hair tumbling over your shoulders into the centre of your back. The shutter opens itself to you, recording all in one quickly fleeting moment as I stare at my faded dreams. I can see the watercolour of the evening sky seeping through the damp paper. Colours of the sun's light draining and reflecting in the pool beneath the bridge. I remember my hands working the pencil trying to catch each detail, every last memory of you; my eyes resting on you, in you, around you. I wanted more, more than life could give.

I mourn for the poems I have written that you have never read; watercolours painted that you have never seen. You sit on the rock where you once sat, my eyes eagerly searching, staring at you, my Pre-Raphaelite. I long to be with you and that longing is more than any other feeling I have ever felt.

You take my hand and standing, I calmly follow you back to the bridge. I look down into the stream's waters, as it flows, endlessly cascading and crashing over the edge of the world, tumbling into the eternities below. Standing alone, I hear you calling. Looking out over the prison of my world; your endless beauty surrounds me, fills me, as you call again and again.

The night has fallen fast around me and I can barely see the stream below the bridge. With my toes on the edge of the huge slab of rock, I stand with the breeze on my face as you call me home. I raise my arms up with all my soul pushing me to lean forward, but the clank of iron as someone opens the gate bars the thought momentarily.

"You alright Dad?"

I turn and see you staring back at me through my daughter's eyes as she waits patiently on my reply. Her eyes are searching, but not intrusive and her quiet understanding drags me from the edge. It takes me a moment to rein in my memories as I turn to her and home. But as I reluctantly climb back to the path the words scream in my head.

"I love you Anne Jones…from the farm above the Italian Woods.

Cerys's mobile disturbs the silence. It's her mother, Claire. There's a brief conversation and then she hands her phone to me.

"Mum wants you!" I know her words are deliberate

I hesitate, but it's lost in the darkness of the night as I reluctantly take the mobile from her.

"You ready?" Claire's voice is quiet, almost subdued.

"Ready for what?" I say, barely able to comprehend my own thoughts.

"You ready to come home?" A rush of feelings warms into me, but she doesn't give me time to gather my thoughts.

"Would you like me to wait at home for you?" She asks, leaving the question hanging in the breeze off the mountain.

"I think I'd like that more than anything else in the world!"

EPILOGUE

It starts to rain on the way home. It seems to calm me somehow. Maybe it's because I still feel you in its trickle of water, but it got me thinking about the day and all that has come and gone. I woke up this morning from a dream of you, begging for a new dawn to rise and my thoughts are of you, no longer swimming in the pools of my life. You were the dew on early morning leaves lost in the rain as it drips from the trees. You are the unrelenting water that flows through me and my memories are still snagged on the barbed wire of life, tossed to and fro in the breeze, unable and unwilling to free themselves from you. Sifting through what remains, I see clearly many of the things that happened that summer, but there are still blurred, out-of-focus images, surrounding intimate detail, lost somewhere in time.

That summer was a time of wonder and magic; a time when the children in us played and loved with all the strange and exciting feelings of the adults in us pressing wilfully forward. There comes a time in all our lives, when the child we once were, and adults we are to be, live side by side, neither quite understanding the other; not knowing the other's needs or the path they must tread. It was at that uncertain junction we met. It was a time when I saw clearly the person I was to be, the path I was to walk and you standing on it, with your deep green eyes smiling back at me. But the indefatigable march of time dictates our years and the adult inside me left the child behind, ignoring its pleas. I have learned through bitter experience that if we neglect the child inside us, leaving them to stand alone, a part of us dies.

I always imagine, in that summer, we felt the love we once possessed in that other world, that other time, that other place and that in the blindness of wild adolescence, we thought we were falling in love for the very first time. Hand in hand we walked where the echoes of our past sounded in the dreams of our future and we began to live the dream, our dream, a beautiful poem that rhymed somewhere deep inside us. We created a secret place in the space that grew between us. In my life that space became a refuge; a shield even. The child within me hid itself away, dreaming only of your return, but you left me to walk the path alone.

Some people never step out onto the edge of life, choosing instead to swim in quiet backwaters. Maybe they are afraid of the strong currents that swirl and rage around them, but our love was forged in that stream. So I continue to make my pilgrimage; and each year I walk the jagged path we both walked over the mountains, scrambling down to the mountain pool, where we once swam and played. Stepping rock-to-rock, I climb out onto the edge of life, with your memory at my side. Perched precariously on the bridge, I know, one day, the temptation will be too great and ultimately I will fall.

But it cannot continue this way; this wasn't part of our dream and where dreams end and reality begins, I don't know anymore. The love we occupied is as real to me today as the ghosts of those who helped me following the end of our summer together. They shared their love with me just as they now share their lives with you, but there is one who still remains and I have hurt her.

When you left, Claire was the one who checked for those faint signs of life within me. Cutting at the bent and twisted metal, she dragged me from the wreckage of my life and slowly pieced it back together, creating a space where the child within me found a place to play once more. It was her quiet understanding that saved me.

I love her, but more tangentially, she loves me. It is not the same as those things we shared, but it is a beautiful love story nonetheless. You will always be there, but now I must go.

Some men search all their lives and never find a love to soothe that burning in their heart. I found you and when you went away, Claire picked up the pieces and helped me back to the path. I love you, I always will; I know you understand. So until we meet again, I must leave you and beg her to forgive me.

Printed in Great Britain
by Amazon

I think you know how hesitant I was, stumbling into that old classroom, all those years ago, but in the uncertain light of that musty old room, I saw you with your long dark hair cascading down, your deep green eyes smiling up at me and with that look you give; a look that will forever draw me in. In the last week of school, I fell in love with you.

With good friends, the Italian Woods became our playground as we enjoyed the carefree summer days of our youth. The children in us imagined witches and wolves in the shadows beneath the trees, but stepping beyond childish fears we explored; climbing the mountains, walking through the woods, wild swimming in 'Ruby Pools' and staying out all through, quietly-waking, slowly-revealing, moonlit nights. When alone, we endlessly kissed; pushing at the boundaries of our growing young love. I know some will scoff at what they think, is possible in love at such an age, but our love was never in doubt.

Above the Italian Woods is a quiet story, for the most part; it is our story. It chronicles the profoundly beautiful love that grew between us, a love that still binds us tightly together, but like the stream through the woods, it tumbles over rocks and boulders, eventually cascading towards the horror that brought the summer to an end. Forgive me, but I have written these few words, not only to chronicle our love, but also in an attempt to exorcise the ghosts that still haunt the summer of our dreams.